TELLING THE SEA

On the secret beach the tid~~e~~ ~~was higher~~ than Nona had seen it before. She'd come to tell the sea her troubles, as she always did. The white waves flashed their encouragement—'Tell us, tell us,' they urged. But the awful numbness was still there. No words came out. She couldn't even cry.

'Wait, wait . . .' the sea called, as she struggled to her feet. Her boot struck something in the dark. She stooped, and touched the hard cover of a book . . .

Soon Nona's troubles are entwined with those of Owen, whose journal she has found. Together, they defy their families, sharing their secret longings and fears. But finally—alone—Nona faces the trap the beguiling sea has set for her.

PAULINE FISK's gripping new novel, set on the rocky coast of west Wales, is a story of winter darkness and new spring life, every bit as exciting as her fantasy novel *Midnight Blue* which won the Smarties Book Prize—the most prestigious British award for children's books—in 1990. Pauline lives in Shropshire, England, with her husband and five children.

Specially recommended for readers of eleven and over

TELLING THE SEA

Pauline Fisk

A LION PAPERBACK
Oxford · Batavia · Sydney

Published by
Lion Publishing plc
Sandy Lane West, Oxford, England
ISBN 0 7459 2246 5
Lion Publishing
1705 Hubbard Avenue, Batavia, Illinois 60510, USA
ISBN 0 7459 2246 5

First edition 1992
First paperback edition 1993
10 9 8 7 6 5 4 3 2 1

Author's acknowledgments
Especial thanks to Walt and Gabriella, who kept the common alive
for me when I was away, brought me the rabbit (I shall never
forget it) and said some of the things that set me 'singing' this
particular song...

A catalogue record for this book is available
from the British Library

Printed in Great Britain
by Cox & Wyman, Reading

Contents

PART ONE

'We'll Be Safe Down Here...'

1

'I'm scared,' Mum said.

Nona looked down the road. There was no sign of Uncle Brady's new, metallic, lime-green car coming back before it should have done. The pavement was empty. Curtains were twitching, but they didn't matter.

'It's all right, Mum,' she said. 'All clear.'

Mum locked the front door, posted the note she'd written through the letter box, crouching to peer through it down the long hall for the last time.

'Goodbye!' she whispered.

'Let's go,' said Nona.

Down in the furniture van, the others waited, packed tight behind the driver's seat. Mum climbed in. Nona scrambled next to her.

'No turning back!' Mum said, with a wobbly smile. She switched on the engine. Drove off without a backward glance.

The day they ran away was Nona's birthday. What a birthday! Big deal! It was nearly a week before Mum found where she'd packed the birthday cake, and when she did it was all squashed and the damp had got at it and the colours had run. You could still see the pink *Thirteen*, but the embarrassing *Our Teenage Girl* had been flooded, thankfully, with the yellow piping round the side.

Well at least Mum remembered, Nona thought later—at

least she tried. You couldn't expect much, could you, when you were running away, and your mother had never driven a furniture van before, and all she'd got to help her was a ragbag collection of useless children, the oldest of whom was only just thirteen.

It was a dreadful journey too. Mum drove them down the motorway for three hours without a stop. She'd never driven on a motorway before, and she did it dementedly, foot down, in the fast lane all the way. And when they came off, she still wouldn't stop. She drove them for another two hours of what she called 'blasted Welsh tracks'. She shouldn't have moaned about them really. It had been her idea to move them all to this place she'd found, by the sea.

Nona, by her side and holding the map and *still* not knowing exactly where they were going, could understand Mum wanting to run away. She wouldn't have stayed if she'd been in Mum's shoes. But what she couldn't understand, as the road became windier and the landscape more desolate, was why they hadn't moved somewhere *sensible*.

'I'd have picked a place where there are all-night supermarkets,' she muttered to herself as the van rolled down yet another mountain, 'and fish and chip shops, and buses running up and down the road, and a library and a cinema and a choice of shops. Somewhere lively, after that stuffy avenue where you never saw anybody except behind net curtains.

'What's that?' said Mum, and Nona felt guilty. Mum was trying so hard. Probably she thought the sea air was what her pale, thin brood needed more than night life and exhaust fumes.

'I can understand the sea,' Nona said, trying to be cheerful. 'It'll be nice, the sea will. And I can understand Wales—with a name like Bronwen I can see why you'd feel at home. But why not Rhyl or Barry Island, where Susie from school says they've got round-the-year fairgrounds? Why not some place where we can have fun?'

9

Mum looked pale, distraught. She was small. Thin like the rest of them. She had a mass of untidy, dark hair and a pointy face underneath it all that seemed to get pointier the more worried she became. It was stiletto sharp now.

'We don't want *fun*,' she said. 'It's peace and quiet we're moving for. I've had enough of fun.'

She spat the word 'fun' out, and Nona didn't understand. Thinking back down the years, she couldn't remember a time when Mum had ever had what she would have called fun.

'But why down here?' she persisted. 'We surely didn't need to go so *very* far away from everything.'

'You wait and see,' Mum said. 'It's the best place in the world. I came to it when I was a girl, for holidays, you know. I couldn't believe it, when I read the advertisement! Still rented out, after all this time! It's a *safe* place, Nona. Somewhere I went with my own mum and dad. A place where everything was *all right.*'

Nona thought about that, all the time they bumped and swore along the winding Welsh roads. This place had *better* be all right.

'I'm going to be sick,' Sharon complained from the back of the van. It was surprising, knowing her, that she hadn't found anything to moan about before.

'We're nearly there,' Mum called. 'Can't it wait?'

'No..!' wailed Sharon.

Mum drew into a farm gate, and rushed round with a paper bag. When she opened the doors, not only Sharon but the standard lamp and carved oak bookshelf fell out. Sharon wasn't sick, but she made a lot of nasty noises all the same. It wasn't until she'd stopped and Nona had stuffed the furniture back into the van, that they looked around them at the view.

Beyond the field and a rim of trees, the ocean gleamed. The trees were bright with the changing colours of late September and with the sun, and the water was blue. Nona had somehow expected the Welsh sea to be grey, like the hills, and the rain Susie had talked about. Upon the blue sea, a small, white triangle of a boat cut a fluttering path.

'Come on,' said Mum. The rest of them—bouncing Bryn and dreamy Poppy with the vacant look in her eyes and little Cody always doing what the big ones did—were struggling to get out, and the furniture all over the van was swaying from side to side. 'Let's get going before *everything* falls out. It won't be long now. Only another quarter of an hour.'

She was right. To the minute. They'd just driven into a stone-built village heralded as JERICO. Nona was checking her watch because at ten past three she had been born and she just wanted to think about it, about Mum all those years ago to the exact moment, holding her first baby, bright with optimism and joy, with Nona's dad—whoever he had been—right by her side.

'This is it,' said Mum, right, significantly, on the dot of ten past three. 'This is the village. Look at it, just how it used to be! I remember the garage over there. And the shop, and the launderette. I used to wonder, every year, if it would change, and it's *still* the same. We turn . . . here.'

The sign said TO CWMGWYNTOG BEACH. A homemade board had been hung underneath to advertise MERMAID INN, PUB FOOD, and to point an arrow down the road. Mum went where it pointed. They drove past terraced houses and a chapel, with a stone barn at its side, and school buildings. Where the road bent, they passed fancy cottages with smooth stone walls with bits of shells set along the top of them for decoration.

'You can tell they're holiday places,' Mum said, 'even though their gardens aren't littered with dinghies and shrimping nets any more. They look too tidy. Do you know what I mean?'

'Bet our place won't be like that,' complained Sharon, who'd climbed over to the front and squeezed Nona up tight

11

against the door. 'Bet it's anything but tidy. It'll be some old dump, you wait and see.'

The road plunged down, round a corner and between trees through which they saw snatches of beach, and the flash of white which they soon discovered was the Mermaid Inn. A wall of rock came down to the road on one side of them, and on the other a sheer drop overlooked a wild common of bushes and reeds, set back behind the beach. The road narrowed. A lone walker in a black coat and hat had to step onto the very edge to let them by. A rabbit rushed in front of the van, regardless of the drop, and disappeared down it. Branches of trees began to brush their windows. Mum slowed the van to a limping crawl.

'Did you see that hat?' Sharon said, when they'd gone by. 'He looked like a gun-slinger in a cowboy film. Did you see that rabbit fall . . .?'

'Shut up, Sharon, or we'll be over the edge ourselves!'

'Shut up yourself, Nona. You're always telling me what to do!'

'Shut up, the pair of you. I'm trying to drive this thing!'

Nona watched the man receding in the wing mirror. Then the road opened out in front of them. There were no more trees. They looked down upon a bright beach. Their journey ended in a car park which extended to a sea wall. Beyond the wall sloped an expanse of grey sand, and beyond that rose a craggy headland, with a cliff path snaking up it.

Mum turned the van behind the sea wall. She sighed with relief, as though they had arrived somewhere. Nona looked at the car park, which was empty. She looked at the toilet block, and the pub with its swinging mermaid sign and tiny garden with tables and chairs, just above the beach.

'But where's the house?'

Mum indicated back along the common, away from the sea. A thin, winding track extended past the walls of the public toilets, inland to a tree-covered escarpment, with a tall, white cottage in front of it.

'That's it,' said Mum. 'What do you think?'

They didn't need to get out of the van to see the way the wind was blowing straight up from the beach, across the car park, along the track to batter finally on that white cottage's front door. Rubbish bounced and danced into the bushes on either side of the track. They were sloped, these bushes, away from the beach. Gnarled in the direction that the wind, obviously, always blew.

'It'll be a bit bleak in winter,' Sharon said, unenthusiastically.

'How else do you think we could afford it?' Mum said, not put off at all. 'Nobody else wanted it, so we got it cheap. The landlord's glad to have someone in to keep it warm. It'll be a bit, well, damp at first. But it's worth it to escape. We've taken it until the summer season starts next year. It'll give us a chance to find our feet.'

She turned the furniture van onto the track. 'I can't tell you how many times I've walked up and down here with my shrimping net and bucket and spade! They were such happy, sunny days ...'

'When it rains,' Nona supposed, 'the ruts'll fill up and we'll need wellington boots to get in and out.' None of them had wellington boots. She worked out the cost of six pairs of them and thought, 'It's not going to be as cheap as all that, living down here.'

While she worked out, too, how many miles it was back up the hill to the shops, and thought that they'd have to do it all on foot because they didn't have their own car, Mum drew up outside the cottage alongside what, she said, was the remains of a boathouse wall. She switched off the engine and sat, staring.

'It hasn't changed a bit,' she said. 'We'll be safe down here. Uncle Brady will never find us. We'll be all right.'

13

2

It must have changed a bit. It couldn't always have been so ramshackle. Mum was doing what she always did, Nona thought as she climbed down from the van onto the stony patch of ground which marked the end of the track. She was seeing things the way she wanted them to be. She wasn't seeing the white-wash flaking off the walls and the big, grey stones peering through. She wasn't seeing that the roof was only made of corrugated tin.

Nona gazed up at the tin roof. Yellow moss grew on it. She looked at the windows, which were like black, cold eyes. Dull eyes, because they hadn't been cleaned in ages. Eyes choked with cataracts of spiders' webs. Her gaze travelled down the front path, through an iron gate set in a wall which was topped with an unkempt hedge.

The wall ran in front of another cottage too, which she hadn't seen from the car park. It was a squatter dwelling with the steep bank of trees rising straight up behind it towards the village. A stream tumbled down between the trees. It ran in front of both the cottages and on into the common.

Nona stepped over the stone slab that bridged this stream, and opened the iron gate. On the wall next to it a piece of slate bore the cottage's name: NYTH-Y-DRYW. In front of the slate somebody had placed an odd collection of bits and pieces: stones and shells, a broken bit of crab's claw, an abandoned mud-and-twig nest.

Mum came up behind. 'Oh Nona, isn't it lovely?' she

said, and her eyes turned, with satisfaction, from the unkempt hedge, through the gate, to the ramshackle garden
and the crumbling paintwork on the front door.

Nona wasn't so sure, but 'Mmm . . .' she said. 'Yes. Let's
get inside, shall we? Let's take a proper look.'

Her voice put on the cheeriness that she felt the
occasion, and Mum, demanded. In the back of the furniture
van, the rest of them were hammering to be let out. Mum
gave Nona the front door key and turned back for them.
Nona hurried up the path, anxious somehow to get inside
and see the place for herself, before the others joined her. She
stuck the key in the lock, pushed open the front door and
entered a small hall.

It was just about big enough for three of them to stand
in it without touching. Big enough for the wellington boots
that they were going to have to buy, but not much more.
Two doors led off it: one—which Nona opened and then
shut again—to the left, into a bedroom; the other to the
right, which led her into a dark living-room with no view
outside its window, beyond the front hedge.

The tiled floor of this room had once, obviously, been
covered with paint which had since peeled, leaving a grubby,
two-tone mosaic effect. A small area of this mosaic was
hidden by a plastic, woven mat and around this mat were
arrayed eight or nine large armchairs with nylon covers,
packed so tightly it was hard to get between them. Beyond
the chairs, beneath a mantelshelf and a huge mirror in a gilt
frame, a dusty, black wood-burning stove sat in a pool of ash
and twigs and soot.

'Ugh! What a sight! What a mess! Look at those awful
chairs . . .' Sharon had followed Nona in. She stared with the
expression of one who either still felt sick, or else was
extremely unhappy. Poor Sharon! She was always pouting.
With her lovely hair she'd be so pretty, if it wasn't for those
lips. Even when she was happy, her mouth drooped and her
lower lip stuck out.

'It's horrid, isn't it?' Nona said. She looked from Sharon by her side, to Sharon in the mirror, framed by the living-room door and the other door behind it.

'What's through there?' said Sharon, nodding into the mirror too.

'It's a bedroom,' Nona said. 'It looks very damp. I hope the ones upstairs will be better.'

'If we stuck all the furniture we didn't like in there, you know, used it as a spare room, there'd be space in here for ours.'

'I expect that's what Mum's planning.'

'I don't think Mum's planning anything.' Sharon tossed back her shiny hair. 'I think she just woke up this morning and thought, 'Oh, let's live somewhere else! Let's go to the seaside! What fun!' and she threw everything into a van and here we are.'

Nona dropped her eyes. She didn't know much, but she knew how desperate Mum was beneath that cheerfulness of hers. 'You're being unfair. You know you are,' she said, looking at her thin, inadequate town shoes upon the peeling floor.

Sharon shrugged. 'I'm going to be sick,' she said. 'I knew I would.' She staggered over the armchairs into what, mercifully, was the kitchen beyond. Nona heard her heaving into the sink. 'Now the house has been baptised,' she thought.

'What do you think?' Mum said. 'Do you like it?'

She replaced Sharon in the mirror, a dark figure, only just a bit bigger than Nona. 'We might almost be sisters,' she said. 'Let's have the light on. I can't remember it being so dark in here.' She stabbed at a switch. A truly awful blue plastic shade lit up, right in front of their eyes.

'That'll have to go,' Sharon said, as she wobbled weakly out of the kitchen and collapsed, unsettling a cloud of dust, in the nearest armchair.

'No it won't,' said Mum. 'It'll be all right when we've washed it down. I left our light shades for Uncle Brady. I thought we ought to leave him *some* things.'

Both girls stared at her. The light shades were new. She'd only bought them the other week and they were such pretty things.

'I've left the china cabinet as well,' Mum went on, '... paintings. You know, things we don't need. I thought I ought to leave some things behind. After all...' Cody toddled into the room with Uncle Brady's face in miniature beneath his mass of curly hair, 'I've taken Cody, haven't I?'

Nona swallowed hard and contemplated the homecoming, after his Saturday out with his new car and the lads, of Cody's dad. He was going to be most displeased to find the useful half of the furniture, Mum, and most especially his beloved Cody, gone. She didn't want to think about that— Uncle Brady being displeased.

'Let's start cleaning,' she said brightly. 'Where's the water heater? Poppy can take the little ones to the beach. Sharon, you're feeling better now...'

Sharon, from the depth of her chair, moaned. Cody whimpered something about funny smells and climbed up on her lap and put his small hand into her big one. It was odd really, because she wasn't much good with anyone else, but he always seemed to make for her and always, as now, cheered her up. She put her arms round him, held his soft face close to hers while Mum disappeared up the stairs— which came down into the corner of the room—on a hunt for the water heater.

'Here it is,' she called from above. 'I'll switch it on.'

They heard floorboards creak as she moved first to the corner of the room, and then towards the window. 'Oh, this takes me back!' they heard her exclaim. 'I used to sit up here for *hours*, looking at this view. I used to lie in bed at night and...'

'We ought to empty the van,' Nona shouted. 'You've

17

got to get it to that garage by seven o'clock, and it's gone four now. We haven't got much time.'

'You're right.' Mum reappeared. 'It's a good job that one of us knows what we're doing. Oh, Nona, you're always so sensible. Where would I be without you?'

Sharon sniffed at this, but Nona ignored her. Mum came clattering down the stairs and she followed her outside. Poppy was standing beyond the stream, a world-weary, thumb-sucking eight-year-old who'd moved house one too many times. She eyed both the cottages with the greatest suspicion and no apparent enthusiasm to get any closer to them.

Bryn, on the other hand, emerged from behind the boathouse wall, clutching his telescope and bow and arrow set. His shirt was dirty and hanging out. His trousers were falling down. He looked at home already. He was wearing his usual, irritating grin. 'There's nothing in there,' he said. 'It's not even good enough to make a den.'

'We've got to empty the van,' Mum said, catching him before he darted off again. 'You and Poppy will have to help. At least it's not raining. We'll pile the stuff out here until we've cleaned inside and can move it in.'

'Which one's my room?' Bryn stared up at the windows.

'We'll talk about it later,' Mum said. 'We've got to hurry now. Don't you go off again.' She disappeared round the back of the van, holding onto him tightly, and calling for Poppy to stop staring and come and give her a hand as well.

Poppy didn't even take her thumb out of her mouth. 'Who's that up there?' she said, and she nodded up the rocky bank behind next-door's cottage.

'Up where?' said Nona.

'There,' said Poppy.

Nona followed her gaze. In front of what looked like a shed or something, she saw a figure shift, move towards the trees as if it knew that it was being watched. She saw a flash of blue and—what was it—binoculars?

'It's been watching us ever since we got here,' Poppy complained. 'I don't like it, Nona. Who *is* it?'

'Well, I don't know,' said Nona lightly, although she didn't like it either. 'Just some nosey parker trying to get a better view ... Don't say anything to Mum. You know what she can be like about other people. We don't want to spoil her day.'

The wind had dropped and the sun was getting lower in the sky. It was a shock, after summer, to see the days drawing in. As Nona carried the first pile of stuff out of the van, she noticed that the windows had become bright and golden. At first she thought the lights had been switched on. Then she realized what it was.

'I wonder if that's all we'll get,' she said. 'An hour of sun at teatime, and probably even less when winter sets in. I wonder if that's why it smells so musty and cold. I wonder if it's always dark in there and we'll have to keep the lights on all the time.'

'I don't remember it being dark at all,' Mum said again, in that faraway voice that she reserved for talking about her perfect childhood. 'All I can remember is sunshine. Sunshine while we trailed up and down the track. Sunshine on the beach. The sun shining on the house while we sat out in the evening and watched it setting into the sea. I can't ever remember it raining. Do you know that?'

Nona believed her. She stood with her arms full of the clothes that Mum had hauled out of Uncle Brady's wardrobes and thrown hurriedly into the van. She looked briefly up at the trees, where there was no sign of a watcher now, then away to where Mum pointed; to the glistening bit of sea with the cliffs coming down on either side of it. If Mum had forgotten what Uncle Brady had said he'd do if she ever left him, ever took his Cody away, she wouldn't find it hard to forget a smattering of childhood rain...

'Water's hot,' called Sharon, who'd been sent to see.

'Good,' called back Mum. 'We've got almost everything out of the van. Let's get that place *clean*.'

'One thing you have to say for Mum,' Nona thought, 'is that she knows how to get things nice. She might be small, but when she puts her mind to it she can certainly scrub.'

They left all their belongings on the ground beside the van, sent Poppy down to the beach with Bryn and Cody, and began to clean. Sharon washed the living-room walls, and the speckly, flaking floor. She cleared away a summer's worth of magazines and put terrible thousand-piece jigsaws away in a cupboard in the downstairs bedroom that they all, mutually, decided to abandon.

Nona beat the mattresses and vacuum cleaned the carpets and brushed down the cobwebs around the windows. Mum did the kitchen. She unpacked the vegetable rack and switched on the fridge and filled it with food. She washed the stove and bleached the stone sink and scrubbed the muck off the floor and even found polish for the kitchen table. She packed away all the existing pots and pans, so that the cupboards were ready for her own ones.

She kept the china though, which she washed, because she'd left their own for Uncle Brady.

'I'll put it away,' Nona said anxiously. 'It's nearly half past six. Come on, Mum. You've got to go ...!'

As she spoke, there was a knock on the front door.

'That'll be Poppy,' Mum said, for who else could it be? 'Oh dear, and I haven't even thought about what we'll eat. Sharon, go and let her in,' she called. 'Nona, will you make the tea while I get ready?'

She got to her feet, brushed dust off her skirt, ran her fingers through her untidy hair. 'I never thought they'd be gone so long, but then the beach is like that, isn't it ...?'

Beyond the living-room, Nona heard voices, first Sharon's, then another which she didn't recognize. She went to see. Sharon stood in the little hall, staring into the hostile eyes of a woman with huge legs which looked like pink sausages in thick skins, and a face that looked as though it had spent a lifetime filling itself with cake. The woman's hair was blond and permed. She wore a blue, nylon overall. She was the watcher from the wood. Nona realized straight away. She turned from Sharon as Nona appeared. Gestured with pink hands which smelt of bleach.

'This girl here doesn't seem to understand,' she said, in a sing-song, unfamiliar accent that made Nona feel a million miles from home. 'I'm Miss Parry from next door, see. You've got your furniture all over my bit, and if you don't do something before my brother Billy comes to take me to his house after tea, I don't know what he'll do. I go to a lot of trouble, keeping my bit nice, I do, and Billy gets awful funny if people upset me, see. He's a big boy now and he likes to look after me. We don't want trouble, do we? He'll set his dogs on you. Awful fierce, his dogs are.'

3

Mum found herself bundled into the furniture van, with Nona's bicycle slung in as well to bring her home, and a warning that its lights were wonky so she'd better try to get back before dark.

'Come on. Hurry up . . .' Nona danced from foot to foot, extraordinarily impatient to get rid of her. 'We don't want to have to pay extra on that van . . .'

Nona was sensible about money things, that's what it was. Mum smiled as she allowed herself to be sent off. In the wing mirror she could already see Nona organizing the rest of them, like busy ants, to move the furniture.

'You're a pain in the neck, Nona!' she heard Sharon complain. 'Why can't we do it without you bossing us?'

It was a good question. 'What on earth are they in such a hurry for?' Mum thought, wondering if she should rescue Sharon. Those two always argued if she left them on their own. In the mirror again, her eyes caught the side of next-door's cottage where their visitor lived, the friendly lady who, Nona said, had called to ask them if they were settling in. By now Mum was half way down the track. She could see, ahead of her, a low, red sun. She smiled, contentedly—decided to let the children sort out their own problems. A gull, above the beach, wheeled and yelled and, unexpectedly, it made her want to cry.

'I feel free at last,' she said, out loud. 'I *am* free!'

She turned the van out of the car park and onto the road.

Drove up beneath the overhanging cliff and round the corner with its holiday cottages and through the village.

Up at the main road, she waited for the traffic to clear, then turned right, towards the harbour town. The sky was alight now, the clouds unreal and wonderful, like the set of a technicolour Hollywood movie. She thought of the last of the sun shining on the cottage windows, thought of herself trailing up from the beach, the little girl she used to be, the little girl she felt so sorry to have left behind all those years ago.

'I've found her again,' she said to herself. 'I'm so happy. It's going to be just the way it always was ...'

Nona sat on her own in the living-room. All the others were in bed, exhausted from the rigours of the journey, fallen asleep without even finishing the crummy tea she'd slung together for them. Even Sharon, to Nona's relief, had stomped off in tears long before her proper time. She was cross because Mum had said that Nona could sleep alone— which meant she'd have to share with Poppy—and cross too because Nona wouldn't help her haul her bed upstairs.

'I won't sleep on one of those damp old mattresses,' she'd cried. 'They smell of other people, they do!'

'Oh, shut up,' Nona had replied, quite out of sympathy. 'I'll help you get your bed up tomorrow, when Mum's back. But I'm too tired tonight and that's all there is to it.'

'I don't want to share with Poppy,' Sharon wailed. 'She snores, but you wouldn't care. I hate you. I think you're horrible!'

She'd gone then, slamming doors behind her. 'Good riddance,' thought Nona, who'd had enough of Sharon and her endless moaning and her big mouth which had wanted to tell Mum what that woman next door had *really* said.

'She knows as well as I do that it would have spoiled Mum's day,' muttered Nona, trying not to listen to Sharon crying theatrically above her. She stared cold-eyed at the black iron of the stove, wondering if there was dry wood on the common behind the house. When she couldn't bear the sound of Sharon any more, she went outside to see.

A path led round the house. You could just pick it out between the brambles. It led past the back door, along the edge of the escarpment, and into the wooded end of the common. The boundary of the garden had long since gone. Nona found a bit of fence lying on the ground, but apart from that there was no sign where the garden ended and the rest of the common began.

She picked her way between the trees. It was nearly dark. A short way on and she could hardly see the house any more. She noticed a dead tree, stripped of its bark. Keeping it within her sights she pressed on, downwards into a clearing where the grass beneath her feet squelched like sodden blotting-paper.

Ahead of her, against a distant ring of trees, she spied a collection of old, ramshackle sheds and an abandoned, forlorn caravan which was covered in moss. Looking back, she couldn't see her landmark tree any more and, afraid of getting lost, she squelched back, resolving to explore further another day. She came upon the dead tree unexpectedly. Its bare trunk was almost white, absolutely ghostly in the darkness. She hurried past it. With some relief, she could see the kitchen light ahead now. She looked around for dry wood, finding herself back on the path, with broken branches strewn everywhere. She stooped to fill her arms. And then she heard the engine on the track.

She'd forgotten about Miss Parry and her Billy, as if the lie she'd told Mum were true and there was no nasty brother who kept fearsome dogs. How could she have thought that? She stood in the shadow of the house. Headlights illuminated the pile of furniture now safely in their front garden. They turned and lit what Miss Parry had called her 'bit'.

A horn honked and Miss Parry's front door clicked open and then shut. Down the path she came, carefully on those

24

legs of hers. Billy came to meet her. He took her bag, led her to the pick-up truck and opened the door for her. The black dogs in the back thrashed, and a young boy's voice yelled at them. Nona saw the boy's outline as he helped to haul Miss Parry in. She heard them speak, all three of them in Welsh which, of course, she didn't understand. She saw them look towards the pile of furniture. She flattened herself against the wall. But they didn't see her. Billy climbed into the driver's seat and drove them away.

Nona emerged. She stared at the red tail lights fading down the track. She hoped Mum didn't pass them on the bicycle. Hoped, if she did, that they wouldn't speak to her. She wanted Mum to be happy today.

She dragged the wood indoors. Inside she drew the curtains—ghastly things, they'd have to put up their own tomorrow—and set about lighting the wood-burning stove. It had a metal handle which pulled the door down. She made a little teepee of twigs with a twist of newspaper and a match at the centre of it and, when the twigs had caught, she set the larger bits of wood carefully on top of them.

Soon the whole lot was blazing. The smell of it drove away the mustiness that their scrubbing had failed to removed. Nona went back outside and found a box of books which she arranged on the shelves on either side of the mantelpiece. Then she turned out the blue light and sat thinking to herself. The room looked nice by firelight. It was getting warmer too. Her mind drifted from one thing to another. Every time it came to something she didn't like— Uncle Brady, Miss Parry, where they would go when the summer season began—she steered it away.

It came to rest, briefly, upon the Welsh language. Mum had said, as if it would be no problem at all, 'You'll learn Welsh in school, of course, though they do teach in English too. It must be great to be bilingual. You'll pick it up. They say it's easy at your age.' She began to think about the school. What would the pupils be like? Would they be

25

welcoming? Would there be a friend like Susie Lennox who'd promised she'd write every week? They'd changed schools so many times now. They were always making new friends, always losing them.

A rattle on the window woke her from her dreaming. Mum's voice called,

'Nona, open up. I'm back. It's me.'

Nona rushed to open the front door and Mum came in. 'Those wretched lights! I've just walked all the way from town,' she said. 'Oh Nona, and it's your birthday too... Have this old wren's nest I found at the gate. It's pretty, isn't it? I used to feed the wrens. They'd come out of the ivy especially. I did it every year. I'll get you a proper present next time we go to town. I don't suppose you found your cake...'

They had birthday cocoa instead, made with the last of a tin of evaporated milk. Mum lit a candle and put it on the mantelpiece. 'Doesn't it look nice?' she said. 'I'm glad to be back again. The garage was right the other side of town, beyond the harbour. I knew it would be. I nearly didn't get there in time...'

Nona's head began to droop.

'Go to bed,' Mum said. 'You look exhausted.'

'But we haven't brought in all the furniture,' Nona replied, 'What if it rains?'

'It won't rain,' Mum said. 'The sky's lovely and clear.'

Nona dragged herself to the front door just to be sure, and Mum was right. The sky *was* clear. The wind had dropped completely too. In the quietness she noticed the unfamiliar sound of waves. A strange sensation—the way you feel before a storm or a treat—came over her, and when Mum called, 'Come in. Shut the door, it's getting cold in here,' she was glad to shut the sea out, glad to rinse her cocoa mug, pick up her wren's nest, and go to bed.

'I'll be up soon, too,' Mum said. 'I just want to potter for a bit. Maybe it was the walk. I'm feeling restless. I don't think I could sleep yet.'

Nona, up in bed, heard Mum moving around. It was a happy sound. She was taking down those living-room curtains, putting up her own ones. Rearranging the books. Stirring another cocoa. Humming. Nona was glad they hadn't told her what Miss Parry had said. She was probably really a nice neighbour when you got to know her, and her brother Billy probably didn't come down all that often, and the dogs probably weren't anything like as bad as they looked.

Mum came upstairs. Nona heard her next door. The walls were paper thin. She could hear her undressing. Hear the clothes dropping to the floor. She would be standing in front of the dressing-table mirror now, brushing the tangles out of her hair, looking at her bruises as she looked at them every night, especially that cruel cigarette burn that she'd said had been the final straw. She'd be thinking that she was safe now, that he couldn't get her now, that the bruises could fade, the burn eventually would go away.

'I don't really mind the house being damp and the shops being miles away and the kids at school speaking Welsh,' Nona thought. 'Not if Mum's happy, and not if it means we never see Uncle Brady again. I'm glad she didn't leave him the curtains...'

And she fell asleep.

4

They'd never done much on Sundays at Uncle Brady's. Just crept around while he and Mum had what he called 'their one chance in the week for a bit of peace and quiet,' up in the bedroom with the door firmly shut. Just watched the telly or gone back to bed themselves while the weekend's washing-up grew, seemingly of its own accord, in the sink.

This Sunday, though, their first full day at Nyth-y-dryw, even Sharon was up first thing. There were arguments to be had about whose bedroom should have the standard lamp and where the oak bookshelf should go. There was a common to explore ('You can go round the back and up through the trees, but don't go off the track into the marshy bit'), toys to unpack, carpets to lay down. There was the beach to see ... Nona hung back with Mum when the rest of them went down to it with sandwiches for lunch. She made the excuse that she, like Mum, had things to do. But that wasn't the reason really.

'You should have gone with them,' Mum said.

'What, with all these jobs to do?'

The trouble was that all she knew of the sea was promenades and piers and hot dog stalls. She was frightened, wasn't she, of those wild, lonely, beating waves that she'd heard last night outside the front door?

'You can go down after tea,' Mum said, not realizing. 'We'll have done the jobs by then, and you'll enjoy it better on your own...'

After tea, the little ones showed no sign of going to bed and Nona said she couldn't possibly go out.

'Oh yes you can...' Mum looked at Nona's weary face. 'You've done your bit. You deserve your break. Sharon'll help me, won't you, Sharon?'

Nona doubted that Sharon would, and it was school tomorrow and they all needed an early night. She lingered.

'Oh, go on,' Sharon said ungraciously. 'We can manage without you sometimes, you know.'

It was a lovely evening. Despite everything, Nona found herself relieved to get out of the house. She picked her way between the ruts of the track. As she came into the car park she saw that lights were on already in the pub, and the sign which said that bar meals were cooking had been lit up. Beyond the pub its garden stood empty. Beyond the garden, up from the other side of the sea wall, came a first whiff of salt and seaweed.

Just as Nona was passing the pub, its door flew open. It was a thick, heavy thing that she could well imagine holding its own against whatever weather poured in from the sea. The man who opened it was thick and heavy too, with a bald, brown head, and bare arms in which he held a writhing animal. He threw the creature down and Nona saw that it was only a cat. She watched it, ginger and shaggy, streaking over the sea wall and bounding like a wild thing onto the shiny sand.

'How's the Wren's Nest then?' the man called to Nona.

'What?' said Nona, thinking of Mum's present on the table by her bed.

'Nyth-y-dryw—Wren's Nest,' the man explained. 'That's what that house of yours is called. How are you settling in?'

'Oh, we're fine,' Nona replied, reminding herself that it wasn't the stuffy suburbs here, where nobody asked what you were doing, or even noticed that you were new. 'Mum's got all the heaters working and we've broken up some wood for the stove. We've unpacked our things. We're managing very well, thanks.'

'You'll have a battle on your hands,' the man said, shaking his head. 'It's so damp down there. See the way the track dips..?' He pointed. 'When the mists come in, Wren's Nest's always the last place to clear. How are you getting on with the Great Herself?'

'The Great Herself?'

'You must have met Her Next Door...' The man grinned, knowingly.

'Oh, Miss Parry...!' Nona smiled too. She couldn't help but tell him. Mum always said their business was their own, but it just spilled out until, 'it's all right now...' she tailed off at the end, hoping Mum wouldn't find out what she'd done.

'You'll have to watch her,' the man warned, unimpressed. 'Territorial, that's what she is, and that brother up in the village too. In the years since they moved here, they've been nothing but trouble. That patch outside the cottages is yours. Don't you let them tell you otherwise. Get in touch with Emlyn Hughes if she comes round again. Drives the 'Taurus Meats' van. Keeps an eye on the place in his spare time. Landlord's agent. Drinks down here. He'll put her straight.'

'Oh, yes. Thank you,' Nona said awkwardly.

'I'm Ralph,' the man said. 'If you want anything—phone, cup of sugar—I'm your man. I came down from the big city too. Years ago that was, and I'm still not what you'd call a local. But I'd never go back...'

Ralph's neighbourly introduction was interrupted by the arrival of a customer from out of—as far as Nona could see—nowhere. She hadn't walked down the road from the village, or stepped out of a car, or come up from the beach. She was just, suddenly, there.

Nona stared at her in surprise. She was quite a sight. Her

hips and shoulders were wide apart and there was lots of her in between. She wore a loose-fitting, black, flapping garment that hung off her like a tablecloth on a clothes line. Her legs beneath this garment were surprisingly thin, like the little legs of a blackbird. She wore yellow tights. Her ankles wobbled above patent high-heeled shoes that struggled through the sand that had blown up from the beach. Her mouth was exaggerated with bright pink lipstick, her eyes with stark black lines. When she got close enough, Nona saw that she wore so much mascara that her eyelashes stuck out like bristles on an old toothbrush. Beneath them a whole network of fine, tired lines crawled down the sides of her face.

She could have pictured her in the sort of nightclubs Uncle Brady had dragged Mum into for fun nights out. She was not what she would have expected in a place like this.

' 'Evening Griselda,' Ralph said, standing aside to let her in.

'Get me an orange juice,' she croaked as she and her jewellery clanked past him. 'Don't just stand there talking. You're supposed to be in charge round here. Have you any pills? I've got a sore throat.'

'I'm not surprised,' Ralph said, 'living like you do.'

With a roll of his eyes and a farewell nod towards Nona, he followed her in and shut the door. Nona wondered what he had meant about 'living like you do'. She dug a hand into the pocket of her cardigan and walked up to the sea wall. The ginger cat was down at the shoreline, keeping back from the waves. Sparrows were picking at the seaweed. The cat was watching them, while pretending to look the other way. The low sun shone on the water.

She was glad to be on her own again. She got onto the sea wall and followed it along to the end: watched the gentle waves shushing up the sand and hissing down it; watched the cat catch its sparrow; smelt the salt breeze. She jumped down onto the soft sand and it slithered into her useless city shoes. She took them off. Took her socks off too. It was going to be all right, this lonely ocean. She could tell that now. Stooping, she picked up a stick that had been stripped of its bark by the tide. Then she put on her shoes again and headed for the cliff path.

She climbed over the stile and past the sign that warned about the edge and about adders. She could see the cliffs across the bay now, sliding slabs of brown and grey with tenuous clumps of vegetation growing out of them. At their top stretched ploughed fields, and beyond them the blue silhouette of a mountain.

Her path took her up through a tangle of undergrowth. She looked down it, to the foot of the cliff and the sea. She wondered what secret coves lay down there, and round the headland; bays that could only be reached by boat or when, like now, the tide was low . . .

Her thoughts were interrupted by rustling bracken. She stepped back quickly, remembering the sign about the adders. But all she saw was a bright tail rising through it. Ralph's marauding cat!

'Wherever have you come from?'

The cat stretched itself, as if delighted by her surprise. It blinked its green eyes, unleashed its talons and then pulled them in again. As if to answer her question, it turned around and padded back the way it had come. Nona made out a steep track, down through the bracken.

Perhaps a secret beach?

She couldn't resist picking her way down to find out. The cat had disappeared now. Nona was glad she'd brought that stick with her, for she was a blade of grass and a whisker's width from the edge. The track bent sharply, bridged a tiny stream. She saw the cat again. Then she saw where she was heading.

She had been right. It was a small, secluded beach. A chequered, black-and-white pebble beach that cupped a bit of ocean in its hand. Nona slithered down between shoulders of rock. The cat leapt on ahead of her. The last bit was the steepest and crumbliest and worst, but she found three wooden plank steps at the bottom where she otherwise would have given up. She jumped off the last of them onto pebbles that weren't black-and-white close up, but brown as bracken, pink as roses, smoky as bottle glass, creamy as sand.

In front of her lay the discarded flotsam of the last tide, and a pile of driftwood, and masses of tiny yellow shells. She looked down at the water, which seemed to have a golden skin, seemed so *alive* that she lingered by the steps, nervous again. But the waves lap-lapped so gently that she felt a fool for her hesitation. She'd never found a secret place like this before. That's what it was.

Absent-mindedly, she plucked a flower which grew out of a rock. Daisies still, this late in the year! She poked it into her hair. Then, somehow reassured, she edged down the beach towards the water. The pebbles ran down in front of her feet. She selected a dry, smooth patch of them and sat down. She fixed her eyes on the clear water. There was something hypnotic, wasn't there, about its slow inching up towards her...

'Well, we've left Uncle Brady,' she heard herself say, as if the ocean were a person who could understand. 'We've had three dads between us all, and *none* of them have worked out. I hope Mum means it when she says she'll never fall in love again. I can't stand the moving. All the dashing about. I've been to six schools now. I'm thirteen years old and I liked the last one and now I've got to start again. I can't bear the effort of making new friends. And of learning Welsh. It just doesn't seem worth the trouble when you think that in six months' time we'll be off again...'

The waves lapped against the pebbles. It was ridiculous, of course, but Nona felt as if they understood. As if their little ripples said, 'Yes... Yes...'

'*I'll* never fall in love,' she went on. 'Look where it gets you. Those bruises of Mum's, I mean, and how she can't look people in the eye. She used to be so friendly, once upon a time. I hope it's going to be like that again. I hope . . .'

But what else she hoped was never said. A small landslide of stones came running down the beach and hit her in the back. She spun around, surprised. The beach was empty. Her gaze went up to the bottom, protruding step. Something shifted underneath it and she forgot everything she'd been going to say. For it wasn't the cat that skulked under there—he'd padded off over the low rocks—and whatever it was let out a sigh, and moved again.

Nona scrambled to her feet, heart pounding, stick clutched tightly in her hand. If only it could have been the cat! It was too terrible to think that a *person* had heard what she had to say!

'Come out,' she cried, as more pebbles trickled down. 'Don't think that I'm afraid of you. I'm not afraid of anything!'

There was a pause. And then a youth crawled out. His hair was almost black and his eyes and skin were brown and he was thin and tall. Straightening up, she saw he wore, incongruously, a smart dark suit, white shirt, black tie. Even though his shoes and socks were off and his trousers were spoiled with a damp, sandy tidemark round the bottom of them and his jacket was crumpled, he looked too smart to be on a beach. Looked out of place.

In the split second before she screamed, Nona thought of smuggler's gangs, gun-running, the mafia, the IRA. Could he be a junior member of some ORGANIZATION?

'Don't . . . !' the boy said, 'Please . . . !'

And Nona screamed . . .

34

5

The youth didn't pounce at her. He didn't crouch ready for attack or put his hand inside his jacket to reach for his gun. He just betrayed that he'd heard every word she'd said by blushing brightly and shuffling his bare feet upon the stones.

'I'm really sorry. I really am,' he said. 'I didn't *mean* to startle you. I didn't mean to listen in. I'd just been piling up the driftwood for a fire, and you came along and I didn't want you to see me, so I ... hid...'

Nona's eyes blazed. Her cheeks burned brightly too. It didn't matter that he wasn't a hardened criminal after all, or a juvenile member of the IRA. He'd heard everything she'd said. Things she never usually talked about. Things about her family, her life, her feelings, even—oh embarrassment—about falling in love ...

'You pig! You eavesdropping beast! You slimy, nosy toad!'

She threw her stick at him and he leapt out of its way. She advanced on him and he backed off, hands before his face. Astonished, both at her fury and its effect on him, she would have stopped herself, but she couldn't. She didn't need to pick up her stick to beat him back. She had her anger and back he went.

It all happened very quickly. One minute, she was towering over him on the very edge of the shore, and the next he was over, sinking seemingly, in the sea.

She stared at him in horror. She hadn't touched him, had

she? His head broke the surface of the water, his eyes bulging, his mouth spurting like a whale. His arms floundered and she rushed in to help, shocked to discover how quickly the beach shelved down. But he pushed her aside, struggled to find a foothold, squelched out onto the pebbles and stood dripping and glaring soddenly into her eyes.

'You pushed me in!'

'I never did!'

'You pushed me with your hands!'

'I did...?'

'Of course you did. I didn't jump in and ruin my best Sunday suit for fun!'

'You shouldn't be wearing your best clothes on the beach! If you get them in a mess you can't blame me!'

For a moment, she thought he was going to hit her. But instead he took took off his jacket and wrung it out. He was turning blue. His white shirt stuck to his chest. His arms were shaking underneath his sleeves.

'I'm sorry,' Nona said, hardly noticing that she was dripping with sea water too.

If he'd left it there, it would have been all right. But, 'Oh yes?' he said. 'I'm not surprised you've been to all those schools. I'm not surprised you can't make friends. I'm not surprised you couldn't keep your dad.'

'YOU BEAST!'

Nona lunged for the jacket, with the single intention of throwing it back into the water. But the boy was ready for her this time. He stepped aside and it was she now, who went straight in. She felt the shock of the steep slope again, heard the boy's revengeful laugh. As she came up to the surface she saw him squelching fast as he could over the low rocks—the way the cat had gone—which she guessed must lead round to the big beach.

'Nobody comes here except me!' he shouted back at her. 'If you hadn't trespassed on my beach, I wouldn't have heard your silly secrets...'

And he was gone.

She rolled over in the water. To her surprise, she wasn't frightened. Nor was she floundering, like the boy had done. She knew her eyes weren't bulging. She didn't look ridiculous. The boy had gone now and she should be climbing out but instead she spread-eagled her arms and legs and almost contentedly let the water bob her up and down. It was nice to lose your temper, let yourself go, do the things you always felt, inside, that you wanted to.

As she came in to land and struggled to her feet again, the cold finally got to her. She thought of the boy's blue lips and his arms that had shaken as hers were now beginning to do. She stared at her fingers, out of which the blood had drained.

'Did I really push him in?'

All the fight ebbed out of her, for tomorrow she was going to find this boy living up in the village, maybe even attending her new school. Tomorrow he'd tell everyone how she had behaved, and the whole village would know that the new girl at Nyth-y-dryw was completely mad.

'Wretched, blimming boy...!'

All she wanted now was to get back to the cottage and change her clothes, but she couldn't go yet in case the boy was still around. Biding her time, she clattered up the pebbles to the wooden steps. Idly curious, she bent down to see where the boy had hidden, underneath them.

It went back further than she'd expected. She poked with her stick, but didn't reach the back of it. Her mind went straight to gun-running and smuggling again. This would be just the sort of place for things like that. Secret beach, just like in Enid Blyton, secret cave. Wondering at her foolhardiness, she crawled in. The whole coldness of the cliff seemed to cling to her, just as her wet clothes did. She was about to turn around and come out again when she found...

Sliding out into daylight, she left the book upon the pebbles. Went back for the other things. There was a sleeping bag, wrapped up in a groundsheet, a knapsack full of packets of powdered mashed potatoes, a torch and some matches in a polythene bag. She opened the book on the first page.

ABOLUTLY PRIVATE was misspelt and untidily written and she shivered, with delight as well as cold. She'd got him now! He'd never dare to tell her secrets because she'd know his too! She turned the page, and began scanning scribbled writing.

'Made up Aunty's stupid model kit. Dull and easy, she thinks I'm still a little kid... Went with Father for a walk... we had meat pie for tea...'

It went on and on like this. The most boring stuff Nona'd read in her whole life. She tried again, somewhere in the middle. But there was nothing she'd have bothered to label ABOLUTLY PRIVATE. Not even a name and address.

Disappointed, she shut the book. What was the point? She could hardly turn the pages anyhow; her whole body was almost rigid with the cold. She'd have to come back and have a proper go another day.

She put the things back where she'd found them; decided that the boy must be well and truly gone now. Shivering, she turned and followed his path over the black rocks. She slid through pools, among anemones and tiny crabs and shrimps, over slimy weed, between edges worn knife-sharp by the sea until, just as she expected, she reached the big beach. Then she plodded up the wet sand, towards the sea wall. The cat ran up to her.

'Do you know what he's up to?' she said. 'Do you know what all that mashed potato is for?'

The cat shook its huge, ginger body and ran away. She tried running too. It was getting late and dark. She was going to be in real trouble when she got home. With stiff, unwieldy legs, she struggled over the wall, past the Mermaid Inn, back towards Nyth-y-dryw.

It was on the way along the track, that she heard the

crooning. The unexpectedness of it slowed her down. Her heart beat faster. Was it the wet boy, dying in the bushes of the cold? It was a low, moaning noise. Like the wind, except that there was no wind tonight. It changed key. As the track bowed slightly, she saw a light in the bushes on the common. The moaning turned into a tune. A tune...!

Nona stepped off the track and crept towards the bushes. The light came from inside a tent. There was a camper on the common! She saw a washing line, strung between a red-berried rowan tree and a drooping willow. Saw a pile of flat stones, with the remains of a fire sheltering behind it.

Creeping closer, Nona saw a fur coat hanging from a tent pole. A fur coat! Then she saw a silhouette moving about inside the tent. It settled down and the tune settled with it. It was the autumn hymn that every schoolchild knew. 'We Plough the Fields and Scatter.' The harvest hymn. She stood transfixed.

The hymn died back into a low croon. Then it stopped altogether. Nona heard the unmusical sound of a throat being cleared. 'Blasted tonsils!' she heard a hoarse voice complain. It was that woman with the jewellery and the high-heeled shoes. The big woman. Griselda. The voice struck up again with 'Land of Hope and Glory,' but it wasn't up to it, and it stopped.

Back on the track, Nona contemplated what a place this was turning out to be, with its mad campers, cats as big as dogs, spying—maybe even dying—boys, weird Miss Parry next door. What a place, with its ocean that was as real as a person you could tell your secrets to, and where she—mad as the rest of them—tried to drown people for no good cause, found secret hoards of mashed potatoes, read other people's diaries and came home, blue, worse than numb, shaking all over.

'Why ever did Mum think we'd be safe down here?!'

6

The ginger cat joined them in the car park—where Sharon lingered to stroke it—and followed them all the way to school. Sharon had never been to big school before. She trailed nervously behind the rest of them, encouraging the cat which Nona had tried, unsuccessfully, to drive away.

It wasn't a very good morning for Nona, who had to cajole a reluctant Poppy too, and call an already dirty Bryn out of one tree after another all the way up the road. By the time that he and Poppy had been deposited at the Junior School, Nona and Sharon were late and the cat still wouldn't let them go. It shook its wretched, orange tail and appealed with its huge green eyes for more attention.

'It's because you've made a fuss of it,' Nona said, crossly.

'You're the only one who's making a fuss,' Sharon retorted. 'It knows where it is. It'll go home on its own.'

'Oh yes?' Nona took a few steps along the path that joined the schools. The cat followed them. 'It's our first day and we're late,' she said miserably. 'Look, everyone's gone in!'

But she was wrong. A girl came running along the road, with a big bag slung over her shoulder. She turned onto the path, skidding past them both, and round the cat. A thick, gold plait bounced down her back. She twisted her head. Slowed down. 'You're the new girls from Nyth-y-dryw?'

'That's right.'

'Don't mind King Offa. He's always up in the village.

40

He'll go back when he's ready. Come on. I'll show you where to go.'

She led them into school and up to the office. 'You'll be in Mrs Thomas's class with me,' she said to Nona, while the Secretary checked them in. 'She told us on Friday, and then Mother and I saw your van go by—we don't get strangers down here in the winter, see. We knew you had to be Wren's Nest.'

She led Nona through a labyrinth of corridors, while Sharon was taken off another way. The school was one of the old, blue-stone variety that had obviously outgrown its original intention many years before. Endless annexes were tacked onto the main building. By the time they'd reached the prefabricated hut that was Mrs Thomas's classroom, Nona was completely lost.

'You're lucky to start in Mrs Thomas's,' her guide said. 'Everybody wants to be in her class. She's not like Mr Williams or Miss Brian. They're really horrible. Here we are. We've got the furthest classroom from the main building. It's great, it is. We're really on our own. My name's Beca...'

Registration was just finishing. Mrs Thomas welcomed Nona and said that, as she wasn't usually, she'd let Beca Lark off for being late. A bell rang, and the class began scattering for first lessons. 'Beca, you stay with Nona while she copies out her timetable,' Mrs Thomas said. 'Then you can take her to—what is it?—Welsh?'

School wasn't as bad as Nona had expected, though it seemed to go on for ever, in the way that new things do. During the Welsh lesson Nona didn't understand a thing, and there was plenty of Welsh spoken out in the playground. But Beca stuck by her side, translating for her. And English, much to her relief, was spoken too. During break, she looked nervously for the boy from the beach. She didn't see him anywhere. She saw Sharon, in her element, being admired for her lovely hair. But the boy, she began to hope, didn't seem to

41

go to this school after all.

The day ended in the prefabricated hut where it had begun. It was literature, with Mrs Thomas, who read one of Shakespeare's sonnets and sent them home to write one of their own.

'You're going to *write* this year,' she exhaled enthusiastically. 'Stories, diaries, lists, lies, fantasies. I don't care what. Words are the key to understanding who you are...'

'I don't know that I want to understand who I am!' thought Nona, whose limited experience in self-knowledge and expression had ended with pushing people into the sea. Yet, even so, she found herself falling under the spell of Mrs Thomas's soft, Welsh, incanting voice, white face, shock of nut-brown hair, glowing enthusiasm for the words in front of her. She resolved, never having done such a thing before, to return, next day, with a completed sonnet.

'See what I mean?' Beca said, as they packed their bags together after the bell had rung. 'She's great, isn't she?'

When Nona and Beca got out of school, Mum was waiting with a bag of shopping which she'd bought from somewhere called *Bella Pugh's* up on the main road. Sharon had already taken charge of Cody in his pushchair. They collected Poppy and Bryn and walked down all together. Beca went into her house, opposite Sion Baptist Chapel and next door to the Junior School. Nona and her family walked on.

'Has the day gone all right?' said Mum.

'Yes,' said Sharon, shaking her silky hair.

'Mmm,' said Poppy, thumb in mouth.

'Brilliant,' said Bryn. 'Miss said if our Poppy doesn't stop sucking her thumb, her teeth will go all crooked.'

'What have you done with your day, Mum?' Nona asked, for Mum looked tired.

Mum sighed, and pulled a face. 'I've been finding out about Social Security,' she said. 'It's been exhausting; I've

42

spent the whole day queueing. I had to go to so many different places, and Cody kept running everywhere...'

'We're going to have to be careful with our money, aren't we?' Nona said, anxiously.

'I'll get a job, once we're settled in,' Mum said. 'It'll be all right...'

They reached the beach, climbed onto the sea wall. The tide was out. Bryn threw a stone, but it didn't reach anywhere near the water. Plopped instead into the wet sand. The wind was up. It blew their hair every way and there were white edges to the waves as they fell, one on top of the other, onto the beach.

'Mrs Thomas says it's *awful* I've not done Shakespeare before,' said Nona, her mind drifting back to school. 'She says I'll have a lot of catching up to do.'

Ralph came along the wall to them. 'Afternoon,' he said. 'All right, are we?'

'Oh, yes, fine,' Mum answered, in a voice that didn't invite company.

'I meant to tell you yesterday,' he said, not at all put off, 'you won't get telly down at Nyth-y-dryw. Something to do with that cliff behind your house. Any time there's anything you want, come down to us. The telly's in the bar, but you don't have to wait for opening hours.'

The television being one of the non-essentials that Mum had left for Uncle Brady, the children's faces brightened. But, 'We're looking forward to life without television,' Mum said firmly. 'Thank you all the same.'

There was a cacophony of, 'But what about...' 'You know my special programme's...' 'Mum, you're being totally unfair...' Even Nona, who realized that it wasn't the television that Mum wanted to keep at bay so much as friendly, curious neighbours, couldn't resist protesting too.

'The telly's the real world, Mum. You know, the outside world we've left behind. We don't want to forget what it's like out there.'

'Oh yes we do,' said Mum, determinedly. 'We're going to read and listen to the radio, and play board games...'

'The radio and board games!'

Ralph grinned. 'Good idea,' he said. 'But the offer's there. Any time you want it.' And off he went.

'We used to listen to the radio when I was a girl,' Mum addressed the row of rebellious faces. 'It's just a matter of getting used to things.' She jumped off the sea wall, turning away from the beach. 'I'm going back to make tea,' she said, as if there was nothing left to discuss. 'Come on.'

As they passed the willow bushes, a queenly figure in headscarf and fur coat was getting her windswept washing off a line. The rest of them stared at her, but Nona stared only at her tent, which in the light of day she now saw had been erected upon a wood-and-stone platform, to keep it dry.

Sharon called 'hello', but the woman didn't answer. She called, 'Your towel's blown away. It's over there.' Then, when they'd passed she whispered loudly, 'Who on earth's she?'

'Her name's Griselda,' Nona said. 'I think she lives down here.' 'What d'you mean, *lives* down here?' said Sharon, who didn't like Nona knowing more than her. 'Why does she live down here?'

'I don't know everything!' said Nona.

'Surprise, surprise!'

Nona ignored Sharon. She handed Mum a note which she dug out of her pocket. 'There's a harvest barbecue and sports day at the beach on Saturday,' she said, to change the subject. 'Read what it says. There'll be races and a band and a fancy dress competition and lots of food. They hold it down here every year, after all the summer visitors have gone. Mrs Thomas says it might seem late, but they always have the best day of the year. They're asking for cakes. We'll make some, won't we? We can go, can't we?'

'*You* can,' Mum said, wincing slightly. 'I wouldn't fancy it...'

'Why ever not, Mum...?'

44

The noise of an engine interrupted them. Mum pulled them onto an animal track, which cut between the reeds of the common. The pick-up truck appeared. Nona, who'd almost, *almost* forgotten about Miss Parry and her Billy, watched it rush past them as if blown, like everything else, by the wind. Miss Parry sat up at the front, with shopping bags on her lap. Billy drove. A small, ginger-haired boy clutching a school bag sat between the two of them.

'I want to be on my own,' Mum explained emphatically.

By the time they got back to the cottage, Miss Parry must have gone inside, for the truck was turning. It waited to let them by. The driver nodded. He looked quite human. Perhaps he wasn't so bad after all. At least he hadn't got his dogs with him. The small boy stared at them, in curiosity. As they drove away, he turned to stare at them some more.

7

Saturday, when it came, dawned with a clear sky and not a breath of wind. Nona had looked forward to it all week, not just because of the harvest barbecue, but because a first week in a new school seemed so endless. She was exhausted with trailing up and down to Jerico, getting to know new teachers, pupils, classrooms, exhausted with collecting and delivering Bryn and Poppy every day, even with the attentions of that cat who was always waiting either to take them or to bring them home. She wanted to lie in bed and sleep, sleep, sleep...

'Nona...!' Poppy stood, half-asleep, half-crying, in the bedroom doorway. 'I dreamt about our old house. I want to go home...'

Nona grunted. Poppy stumbled across the floor. Nona held out a sleepy arm and Poppy crawled into bed with her, forced her small hand into Nona's big one.

'I don't like it here. It's so dark and the sun shone in the old house all the time.'

'But Uncle Brady's in the old house,' Nona murmured. 'You wouldn't want to go back to him...?'

'I hate Uncle Brady,' Poppy said, 'but I like his house. I'm fed up with moving.'

'Let's try and sleep some more,' Nona said. 'It's very early. If you shut your eyes, you'll dream of something nice...'

'Will I dream of the barbecue?' Poppy said.

46

'Yes...' Nona snuggled back down the bed. 'You'll dream of the barbecue.'

When Nona woke again, Cody and Poppy were playing with building-bricks on the floor. She went downstairs to make a pot of tea. When it had brewed, she poured a cup for Mum and carried it upstairs.

The covers had slid off Mum's bed. She lay with her arms thrown out and her dark hair in a tangle all over the pillow. Her bruises were beginning to fade. Even the awful burn was getting better, despite Mum's distrust of ordinary antiseptic cream. On the bedside table were the medicines she was prepared to use; her marigold headache pills, her rosemary ones for nerves. Behind them stood a framed photograph of the dead grandparents that Nona had never known—Mum's parents, who'd brought her down here all those years ago.

Nona moved the picture, to make room for the cup of tea. Mum looked happy now, even in her sleep. She never would have slept like that in the old house, with her arms apart as if she was safe.

'Mum,' she shook her gently. 'Mum. A cup of tea...'

Mum smiled and turned over and fumbled for her bed-covers. 'Oh, yes, thank you, Nona...'

Nona heard the postman's van outside. She heard Sharon snoring in the room next door. She heard Bryn bouncing on his bed and Cody sliding down the stairs.

'No need to get up yet. I'll make breakfast.'

Susie Lennox's letter was full of old school news. But to Nona, even after a week, the old school seemed so far away and Susie Lennox like a dream from another world.

'We really miss you,' Susie wrote. 'It doesn't seem the same now you've gone...'

Sharon protested as Nona hauled her out of bed, with the awful threat of reheated porridge if she didn't get up now, and coconut cakes that still hadn't been made for the barbecue.

'Mrs Thomas knows all about Mum's coconut cakes,' Nona said. 'We've got to do them. We can't let her down.'

'But they're *Mum's* speciality. We won't get them right,' Sharon said indignantly.

'You're so lazy,' Nona complained. 'All you ever do is moan.'

'I'll do it,' Poppy said. 'I'll do it with Bryn. We know the way to make them. We've watched Mum loads of times . . .'

Mum emerged in the middle of the morning to find white pyramids of coconut mixture, with cherries on the top of each of them, laid out upon fresh greaseproof paper in a tin. The sink was full of washing-up and the stove was covered with hard blobs of coconut mix, which Bryn was striving to remove with a knife, along with great chunks of enamel. Poppy was scraping out a pan. She had coconut in her hair and on the end of her nose.

Mum sank onto a chair. 'You should have woken me up,' she said. 'You spoil me, Nona. Put the kettle on. I'm *dying* for another of your cups of tea. Don't throw away those crumbs, Bryn. We'll save them for the birds.'

Nona filled the kettle with water. Mum pulled Poppy to her and wiped the coconut out of her hair.

'Everybody else's mum is going to the barbecue,' Nona said, closing the cake tin lid. 'I wish you'd come.'

'You'll meet Miss,' Bryn said. 'She's great, she is. Much better than old Jonesy at the last school.'

'Please,' said Poppy. Even Sharon said please.

'People will wonder why you weren't there,' Nona said. 'It'll only make them curious, and you don't want that.'

Mum laughed, and ran her fingers through her hair. 'You do go on about a thing! I knew you wouldn't let me off that easily. All right. I'll come . . .'

48

Miss Parry's cake tin flashed in the sunlight down the other end of the track. Nona, relieved that they hadn't all come out at the same time, watched her reach the crowd up at the car park. By the time they'd got up to the crowd themselves, she was lost over the sea wall where strains of band music floated up from the beach.

The door of the Mermaid Inn was open and the garden was full of drinkers, some at tables, some sitting on the grass, faces up to the sun. Mum surveyed this throng reluctantly. She looked as if she'd just as soon go back, but Nona gripped her arm and Bryn cried, 'There's Miss! There she is! Oh, come on, Mum!'

He dragged Mum, with Poppy in tow, off to a young woman who drooped beneath the weight of all the other six-year-olds who wanted their mums to meet her. Nona and Sharon were left, with Cody in his pushchair, on the edge of a crowd where everyone, obviously, knew everyone else.

'I'll be blowed if I'm going to push my way through that lot,' Sharon said. 'You go on. I'll just sit here and enjoy the sun. I'm not that bothered about the beach, anyway.'

Nona took the coconut cakes onto the sand, where long tables had been set up. A golden-haired lady, with plaits pinned on top of her head and a plain frock buttoned right up to her neck, was laying out all the best offerings that the village women had provided. There were fruity bara-briths and lemon cakes and buns and fancy sandwiches and chocolate fingers. There were hard toffees and home-made turkish delight and little squares of walnut fudge. There were flat little Welsh cakes, with currants inside them and sugar sprinkled on the top. There were home-made doughnuts and home-made bread.

'Those look *lovely*,' the lady said. 'They're so *white*. My coconut pyramids always brown up in the oven. You'll have to tell me how you get them like that.'

Beca Lark bobbed up, from underneath the table. 'It's Nona!' she declared. 'Mother, this is Nona, who I told you

49

about from school. You know, from Nyth-y-dryw...'

'Nona who wrote the sonnet everyone liked so much. Ah yes...' the lady with the golden braids put out her hand. Uncertainly, because she wasn't used to stuffy manners and shaking hands, Nona took it. 'How do you do,' the lady said, and Nona couldn't think of anything to say. She stared, mute, at Mrs Lark's crisp, white apron. Mum would rather be seen dead than with an apron on in a public place.'

'The band's just finishing. The races will be starting soon. Are you coming?' Beca rescued her.

'What? Where?'

Beca led her down to where the fancy dress was finishing. The band were packing up their instruments and the race course was being pegged out. Beyond the finishing post, silver waves broke upon the shore. Gulls cried. A fat old lady paddled. A man struggled with his hat.

'I've never seen the point of racing,' Nona said.

Beca grinned at her. 'That's because you've never done it on the sand.' She kicked off her shoes, dug her toes into it. 'Have a go with me, it's fun!'

Nona shook her head and backed away.

'Suit yourself.' Beca laughed at her. 'You don't know what you're missing. Wish me luck, won't you? They're going to start.'

An assortment of dwarves, Walt Disney characters and apparent members of the Royal Family—all from the fancy dress—were lining up with ordinary folk, ready to start.

'Good luck,' said Nona.

'Cheer for me!'

Nona got onto the sea wall, for a better view. She walked along it, behind the barbecues where silver fish and chicken legs baked, until she reached the end, where the cliff path began. There she sat down in the sunshine, and marvelled that it could be so warm in October.

'I'll write to Susie about this,' she thought. 'Mrs Thomas said she wanted us to write a letter. I'll tell her that the fish smelt *succulent.* I'll tell her that the beach was *glazed with sunlight*... The races began. Beca won everything she entered. You could see her gold head shining above everybody else. How she ran! Nona saw Miss Parry with her Billy, shouting as the juniors came in. She saw Mum and Poppy, reunited with Sharon and Cody, shouting too as Bryn pounded up the beach. She saw Mum jump up and down, ruffle Bryn's hair as he came over with his third place certificate. Even Miss Parry was smiling. Perhaps she was all right after all. And there was Mrs Thomas, Mrs Thomas of the English class, lining up for the women's sprint.

'I'll tell Susie that Mrs Thomas was glazed with sunlight,' Nona thought. She turned her head and looked along the wall. A youth was picking his way along, and her smile froze. He was tall and thin. Dark haired. Brown-skinned. Bundle poking out under his denim jacket. Jeans and T-shirt where last week he'd worn a posh, black, oh dear, very wet suit...

Nona got up hurriedly. He hadn't seen her yet. She'd almost convinced herself that the embarrassing events on the secret beach had never been and now here he was, large as life and bearing down upon her...

'Oh...!'

She slipped on the wall, stumbled over a big stone in the hurry to get away. The youth caught her just in time before she went over the edge. He pulled her up again. She scowled, ungratefully.

'It's bumpy along here. You have to be careful.'

'I'm quite all right.'

'Your knee's bleeding.'

'It's all right.'

'Look, about the other day...'

But she couldn't talk about it, what she'd done and what he'd heard her say. Her face reddened, just as his had done when he'd crawled out from under the step. Her chin went up. She felt her face hardening into a mask.

'I must have really frightened you,' he was saying now.

51

'I've thought about it all week long and . . .'

She jumped down onto the soft sand. The fall hurt her sore knee, but she didn't care.

'Hey . . . !' he said. 'I'm talking to you!'

But she was gone. He too flushed, but she never saw. Clutching his bundle tighter, he made towards the cliff path. 'All right, forget it!' he said, but she never heard. She ran to the other side of the barbecue where the food was ready now and a speech was being made to thank the various village committees, the school, the clubs and pubs for all their efforts.

A man in a long coat was making the speech. A light breeze caught the hair that blew out underneath his hat. She'd seen him before, hadn't she? Of course! On that first day. He'd stood aside when they'd driven down the hill, and Sharon had said . . .

The man embarked now upon a blessing of the food. Nona realised that Sharon had got it wrong, about him being a gun-slinger. He was the minister of Sion Baptist Chapel, wasn't he? She stared in fascination. He was so tall. She'd always thought of ministers, when she thought of them at all, as short and fat and red and bald . . .

When he'd finished, she found a paper serviette and wiped her bleeding knee. Someone thrust a plate into her hand, with a piece of fish on it and some rice salad and a roll. She walked down to where a pillow fight was starting on a slippery pole.

On the sand in front of it—unaware of the cheers as one contestant after another came off the pole—Poppy and another little girl were doing a clapping song. They faced each other and clapped each other's hands and sang:

> My boyfriend gave me apples,
> My boyfriend gave me pears.
> My boyfriend gave me kisses
> And threw me down the stairs . . .

When Nona turned, Mum was watching them too, Mum

with her face lapping up the sun and her bruises almost faded away.

'It's just a song,' Mum said. 'They don't know what they're saying. It doesn't mean anything to them. Lucky, aren't they?'

Before Nona could respond, golden-haired Mrs Lark appeared. 'You're Nona's mum? We *loved* your coconut pyramids. How are you settling in? You must come up one day to see us...'

Just before dark, Nona returned to the beach. She wanted to be on her own, to watch the tide smoothing the sand so that you'd never know there had been a barbecue. Voices from inside the pub roared as the day's drinking built up to fever pitch, but the garden was quiet and clear. Ralph was out, stacking up glasses. He waved to her. It was nice to have someone wave to you as you went by.

The beach, which she'd expected to find empty, was not. A man was pulling a red cart along it, picking up the rubbish that had been left behind. He wore a long scarf which trailed in the wet when he bent down. Behind him, King Offa charged the full length of the sand in daring pursuit of an army of dogs who all, obviously, knew that there were tasty pickings after barbecues.

Nona turned away. She'd thought of climbing over to the little beach, exploring beneath the step to see what that boy had added to his hoard. But it was nearly dark now, so she made for home instead. The lights had been switched on in the pub and—as she passed the willows—inside the tent as well.

The lights were on in Nyth-y-dryw too. When she got back, Mum and Sharon were clearing away Bryn and Cody's mountain of discarded clothing. Mum's voice was sharp.

'I knew it was a mistake, going to that barbecue,' she said, as soon as Nona came through the door. 'These things snowball. You do one. You get invited to another. That Mrs

53

Lark's just been down. She wants you to go up for tea on Monday after school. She said, again, that I must go up too. She's never going to rest until I do, you can tell with people like her. Oh Nona, I want to be civil. You know that, don't you? But I don't want—you know—questions asked. I don't want *tea parties.*'

She disappeared with the dirty clothing. 'It's not just Mrs Lark,' Sharon explained. 'Miss Parry's been round too. Nice as pie, she was. She's invited us to tea tomorrow afternoon.'

8

'A headache she's got, has she? Well, never mind. Come into my parlour the rest of you, and sit down. Not that I'm used to children, specially *unsupervised* mind, but we'll make do. Don't touch anything, will you? It's all precious, see.'

Nona, her head full of Mum's warnings not to talk about *private things*, led the family into Miss Parry's front parlour where a small electric fire, set on a tiled hearth, threw out a thin bar's worth of warmth.

Looking around her, she took in a mantelpiece full of neatly arranged photographs in gleaming frames, a dresser packed with china, and a window ledge upon which stood—reminding her of that first day up among the trees—a gleaming, brass-and-leather pair of binoculars. Behind them, plastic blinds hung at the windows, their dusted slats tilted, Nona noticed, just right for seeing next door's garden.

'Careful!' exclaimed Miss Parry. Nona turned and Cody was on the verge of colliding with a Grandfather clock. 'In all the years we've had him, Grandpa's never missed so much as a tick,' warned Miss Parry.

Nona, with Cody firmly in hand, looked past the clock's stiff, gilt face, to see what Bryn was up to. She wished Mum had let the little ones stay at home. She guided them into the centre of the room, where Miss Parry waited for them, smelling of polish and disinfectant.

'Mum's really sorry she can't come,' she said again. It

wasn't true, and Miss Parry knew it. You could see that from her face.

'I made a chocolate cake specially,' she said, removing her blue housecoat, and patting smooth her skirt. 'You'll have to take a slice back for her. Can't have her missing out. You just sit there and don't move. I'll bring in tea.'

They sat on the settee in a row. Cody curled himself into a tight ball at the end. Nona sat next to him, trying not to disarrange the cushions. Sharon, next to her, spread out her lovely hair and hoped that Miss Parry would think she looked nice and not notice the spot in the middle of her dress. Poppy sucked her thumb, and her eyes—as always when she didn't like what was going on around her—glazed over in a day-dream. It wasn't till they were on their way home again that she came round. She didn't hear a word that anyone said.

Bryn, for his part, wriggled miserably. He wanted to explore. Stairs led up, out of the corner of the parlour. A steely glare from Nona kept him in his place.

'Can you help me?'

Miss Parry staggered into the room with the largest tray, full of cups and saucers, teapot, milk jug, sugar bowl with lumps of sugar in it and tongs.

'Chocolate cake's on the kitchen table . . .'

When Nona returned, Miss Parry was handing Cody— Cody!—a cup made of the finest china, edged like the ones on the dresser with a thin line of gold, and decorated with the silliest, curliest little handle that even a *toddler* couldn't get his tiny fingers through. The tea in the cup was steaming, hot and gingery brown.

'Oh, I'll take that!'

Nona rushed forward and rescued the cup. She took the plate of chocolate cake that Miss Parry offered next, and attempted to get it into Cody's mouth without a mess. She was not successful. It was a very sticky cake, just the sort that any self-respecting toddler would try to get his fists into. Miss

56

Parry finished handing round the drinks—why had she chosen to give them such *difficult* cups?—and the sticky cake. There were no knives or forks, nothing with which to wipe their hands. Soon they were all in much the same mess. Miss Parry watched them, smiling. She dropped two neat lumps of sugar into her own cup. Patted her hair, crossed her pink legs.

'Where do you come from then?' she said. 'Bronwen Davies, that's your mam's name isn't it? A good Welsh name, but you don't look proper Welsh to me ...'

Nona, caught off guard, looked up, surprised. She hadn't expected it. At least, not yet. Not like that.

'Oh, Mum's Welsh all right ...' She gulped down her cup of strong, hot brew, and spoke quickly, thinking it out as she went along. 'We've lived away, but she says we've come home now ... Who ... who's that nice man in that photograph? What a *lovely* frame!'

Miss Parry smiled over Nona's clumsy attempt to change the subject.

'That was my older brother,' she said, hardly glancing at it. 'He always used to come down for his tea, but he's passed away now. Poor soul, he was devoted to me, he was. I never set down a bit of cake but what I think of him, or a mackerel sandwich. London was it, where you came from?'

As if on cue, Bryn dropped his cup of tea. Nona could have hugged him. 'It's all right,' she said, as Miss Parry rushed into the kitchen for a hot cloth. 'You haven't broken anything. It's only a bit of tea.'

'Can I use your cloth?' asked Sharon miserably, when Miss Parry had finished swabbing down the carpet. 'I've got chocolate in my hair.'

'You should carry a handkerchief,' Miss Parry said sharply. 'Cloth's been on the carpet. It'll have germs.'

Sharon fingered her hair helplessly. 'My Cledwyn never goes out without a handkerchief,' Miss Parry went on, nodding up at the photograph of the ginger-haired boy they'd seen in the back of the pick-up truck, and again, racing at the beach barbecue. 'Things like that show how you're brought up. I expect your mam forgot to give you one, with her headache and all.'

She removed the cloth to the kitchen. 'Cledwyn's Billy's boy,' she said, when she returned. *That's* Billy. Such a handsome lad, don't you think? It was taken on his wedding day. She wasn't good enough for him, but we don't talk about it any more. I won't have *her* picture up there. Good job she left. None of us miss her.'

Sharon licked her sticky hair. Miss Parry poured herself a fresh cup of tea. Sat back in the armchair. Helped herself to more lumps of sugar.

'He's still a fine figure of a man,' she went on, 'even if he has lost some of his hair. And he does a grand job with Cledwyn on his own. When he's working he brings him down to me. My little love, Cledwyn is. He calls me mam. Billy says I'm more of a mam to him than *she* ever was. Family means a lot to us down here. We can't abide these modern city ways where women go off without their men. Where did you say you came from, London?'

'That's right,' said Sharon. It just slipped out.

'Ah, not proper Welsh at all,' said Miss Parry with satisfaction. 'I thought not. Where's your dad then?'

But even Sharon couldn't be tricked twice. She looked to Nona for help.

'Coming later, is he?' Miss Parry said, leaning forward on those legs, as if she scented victory. 'Down here we think a dad's real important, like.'

'Our dad's dead,' Nona burst out, desperately.

'Why, how sad!' exclaimed Miss Parry. 'You poor little things! Long ago, was it? How did he die?'

Nona opened her mouth to say that it was so long ago that she couldn't remember exactly, but she realised, just in time, that Cody was only eighteen months old.

'A . . .a year ago,' she lied. 'It was terrible. We don't like talking about it.'

'Of course not,' Miss Parry said at once. 'That's how Billy and Cledwyn would feel if it happened to me. In fact, my Billy says he'd *kill* himself if I died. I tell him not to be so silly. But you can understand it, can't you, when you've got a sister who's as good to him as me? He has a shotgun, Billy has. He could do it too... Do you like ducks' eggs? Billy brings them down, and I can't eat them all. Perhaps you could take some back for your mam... I wonder how her headache's getting on...'

'You all look exhausted, and you've only been next door,' Mum said, when they returned home. 'How did it go?'

'It was fine,' Nona said, daring Sharon—any of them— to say how it had really been.

'Good,' said Mum. 'Did Bryn behave himself?'

'Yes.'

'Did Poppy suck her thumb all the time?'

''Fraid so.'

'Did Miss Parry ask, you know, anything *private*...?'

'Don't be silly, Mum. She wasn't like that. Honestly.'

'I know I'm being silly. But I dream some nights that Uncle Brady finds us, even down here, where I know he won't. I'm glad you had a nice time. What's it like inside? Is it the same as in here?'

'Not a bit,' said Nona, with some feeling. 'It's smaller, and dark because of the way she tilts her blinds. Everything's clean and smelly, you know, like doctors' surgeries and public toilets.'

'She's got an old dresser,' Sharon chipped in. 'Lots of china, hundreds of photographs in frames and a grandfather clock that *booms*...'

'You're sticky,' Mum said to her. 'Cody looks terrible, and what have you got in your hair?'

'I thought I'd licked it off,' Sharon said, embarrassed. 'It's chocolate cake. She sent some for you too. And these ducks' eggs.'

'That's kind.' Mum took the offerings. 'I'm glad it wasn't so bad. Perhaps I'm worrying about nothing. People are bound to want to be neighbourly, aren't they...?'

School, next day, came as light relief with Mrs Thomas embarking on Great Welsh Poets and a whole afternoon spent in the art room, drawing bits and pieces of bark and leaves.

Sharon, Nona and Beca spilled out together at the end of it all.

They walked down to Beca's gate, where Nona, who'd been invited to tea, said, 'Tell Mum I'll be back by seven.'

Sharon pouted. Nobody yet had invited her to tea. 'Mum said we'll get a take-away from Ralph's tonight,' she taunted. 'Sausages in batter and beans and chips.'

'Well, poor me! I'm missing my favourite tea...' Nona pulled a face and wondered why it was that she could find endless patience for the others, but none for Sharon. She followed Beca up her path without a backward glance.

The house was bigger than the others on the road. Beca led her round to the back door. They stepped over a pile of shoes and wellington boots into a kitchen twice the size of Nyth-y-dryw's, with faded curtains and furniture that was worn. The kitchen was dominated by a stove upon which saucepans bubbled. In front of it stood an old table, covered with apple peelings, flour, a rolling pin, and a collection of pans. Mrs Lark, with rolled-up sleeves, looked up from making an apple pie. Behind her, the walls were filled with cookery books and kitchen utensils, which hung on rows of hooks, and framed prints of chubby angels and Victorian family scenes.

'How long will tea be?' Beca asked. 'Do we have time to get our homework done?'

Mrs Lark wiped a strand of gold hair out of her eye. 'Oh, yes,' she said. 'You've got an hour. Take some biscuits with you, if you like...' she reached for the biscuit jar, '...and a glass of milk.'

When they came down again, the table had been wiped and cleaned and was laid for tea: knives, forks, table mats, a bowl of fruit. At the far end of it, a man sat reading a book which he held in huge hands that you could have imagined crushing the book between them. You'd expect hands like that on a gun-slinger, Nona thought, remembering again what Sharon had said. He was the tall man with the funny hat and black coat—the minister of the Sion Baptists.

'Father, this is Nona,' Beca said.

The man raised his eyes, and Nona should have realized. They were just like Beca's, even though he didn't have her golden hair.

'How do you do?' he said. 'I'm Mr Lark. It's very nice to meet you. How are you settling in at Nyth-y-dryw?'

'We're fine,' Nona said, in a stilted voice that didn't sound like her. 'We're all fine. Poppy's taking the longest to settle in, but she always does. Everyone's being very kind.'

'Oh, good.' He closed the book, and put it aside with a shadow of a sigh, as if he didn't really want to stop reading. 'Come and sit down. I think we're ready to start. That's right. Next to Beca—over there.'

Nona shrank into her seat where she was bidden, between Beca and her mother. Mr Lark sat alone, at the other end of the table.

'Where's Owen?' he said.

Beca's mother set down a casserole full of brown dumplings. 'He's out till later. Don't you remember? I said it'd be a nice, quiet day to ask Nona round. He's doing his homework at Aidan Hughes's house.'

'Ah,' Mr Lark frowned. 'Perhaps you did say. I wanted to do some Greek with him tonight, but never mind.'

'I'm sorry.' Mrs Lark handed Beca the vegetables. 'You should have told me.'

'I sometimes think that brother of yours has a sixth sense about things he doesn't want to do!' Mr Lark said, taking the pot from Beca and passing it on to Nona when he'd finished

61

with it. 'Let's seek the Lord together.'

For a minute, Nona didn't know what he was on about. But Beca bowed her head, so she did too, and then Mr Lark prayed over the food and she filed *'omnipotent bounty'* away in her mind to go down into the new word book Mrs Thomas had given her. By the time she dared to open her eyes again, Mr Lark was already eating. Nona could tell that, although he tried to be civil about it, he was impatient to get the meal over.

She picked up her own knife and fork. Beca and her mother were eating too, their golden, plaited heads bobbing over their plates. Their knives and forks flashed. Round faces, pink, blooming cheeks—such a contrast to dark, thin Father. They were like the fresh, shiny apples in the bowl. Like the fleshy, round Victorian angels framed upon the wall.

'How's Miss Parry?' Beca's mother asked, lifting her head and looking across at Nona.

'Miss Parry . . .?' Nona hesitated, just as she'd done when Ralph had asked her the same thing.

'It can't be easy, with a Parry next door,' Mrs Lark went on. 'I just wondered how you're managing.'

Nona hated the way she hid her real feelings. But she couldn't help it. 'Oh, we had tea with her yesterday,' she heard herself saying, cheerful as anything. 'She made us a chocolate cake. She was very nice.'

'You sometimes have to watch the Parrys, when they're being nice,' Mrs Lark warned. 'Pardon me for mentioning it. I don't mean any trouble. But I just thought I ought to say.'

Mr Lark shifted uncomfortably at the other end of the table. 'Now then, Mary,' he said, mildly. 'Speak no evil . . .'

'Oh, I wouldn't speak *evil*.' She blushed. 'It's just that I wouldn't want to live next door to either of them, you see, and not know. Forewarned's forearmed, they say, and I thought . . .'

'Thinking's one thing. Saying's another.'

'Yes, dear. I'm sure you're right . . .'

Mum used to answer like that, Nona thought. Uncle Brady would have hit her if she hadn't. Nona looked at Mrs Lark's bowed head and wondered if all men bullied their womenfolk, one way or another. She was glad Mum had decided she'd said 'Yes, dear' one too many times...

Mr Lark scraped his plate clean. He sighed, pleased with himself, picked up his book and rose to his feet.

'You're not going yet...' Beca's mother protested. 'I've made an apple pie.'

'Got to see Mrs Evans from up the Vron,' he said. 'She's in hospital again. Hadn't you heard?' He fished his long black coat off the back of the chair, pocketing his book which would have to wait for later. Mrs Lark looked disappointed, as if she'd especially wanted him to stay and eat her apple pie. But as soon as he'd gone, the mood lightened, changed. Beca began to tell her mother about the day. Mrs Lark brought the pie from the oven. It was the best one Nona had ever eaten and she said so. Mrs Lark looked pleased. Beca told her about spending two hours drawing boring bits of disintegrating tree. Mrs Lark told Nona how they'd moved here themselves, only a few years ago, and how easily they had settled into village life.

'Jerico's a kindly place,' she said. 'I'm sure you'll settle too. It's a funny place. Like the end of the world, the furthest people can get away. There are lots of newcomers down here, and we've all been made very welcome. I'm sure you'll find it friendly. Everybody does.'

Nona thought of Ralph, who'd left the city and said he'd never go back. She wondered what Griselda had got away from, remembered Beca, chattering in Welsh, out on the playground. 'Did you speak Welsh before you came here?'

'Oh no,' said Beca. 'I learnt it all down here. It doesn't take long to pick it up.'

'Beca's good at languages,' Mrs Lark said, proudly. 'But you'll learn it too. It's easy when everyone around you is talking it.'

After tea—'Don't bother with the washing up,' said Mrs Lark, 'we'll do it later'—Nona said that it was time to go. She repacked her school bag, put on her coat.

'You must come again,' Mrs Lark said, guiding her round the boots and shoes, to the back door.

'Thank you. I will.'

'So nice Beca's made a new friend. Don't forget to tell your mum to come up for that cup of tea. It must be lonely down at Nyth-y-dryw. Tell her, won't you?'

Nona turned back to wave. Beca had already gone in, but Mrs Lark stood there still. She was the one, thought Nona, who was lonely.

'I hope I haven't worried you, about the Parrys,' she called. 'I didn't mean to speak out of turn. They'll be all right. I'm sure they will.'

It was the summerhouse that got them into trouble with the Parrys. That and poor old Bryn's arrow and his wretched grin.

It sounded rather grand, *summerhouse*, but it was really no more than the wooden shack that Nona had glimpsed up among the trees on their first day. A path wound up to it from the back of Nyth-y-dryw. Mum said it used to be quite a thing when she was a girl, to go up there and sit on the verandah in the old deckchairs and take tea. There was a fine view of the whole of Cwmgwyntog Common and the track and beach. Beyond the roofs of the cottages you could see the pub and the ferry coming in from Ireland. See the light flashing at night from round beyond the Head. See the road snaking down from Jerico, and the cliff path winding up the headland.

It was on the third Saturday that they explored the summerhouse properly. Up until then, there'd been so much else to do and anyhow, according to Mum who'd been to see, the place was locked. But on that Saturday morning, burning to try out his telescope from a better vantage point, Bryn wriggled in through a loose fanlight and, once inside, forced the lock. Having taken possession, he invited the rest of them to join him.

Poppy went up first, with her worn and patchy teddy bear and a box of newly-collected shells. Nona followed her with a tray of cups and juice. Sharon was dragged up by

Cody, making it loudly plain that she was only doing this for him. Two weeks at big school, and she thought the things the rest of them did were beneath her now. She stood well away from Poppy and Bryn and especially Nona, looking down at Miss Parry's washing blowing on her line, and the front hedge shaking in the breeze. She sighed, bored.

Cody, anything but bored, stripped off his sweater and fluffy trousers. It was sheltered from the wind between the summerhouse and the rim of bracken at the end of the verandah. The trapped sun warmed his skin. His stomach bulged beneath his little T-shirt as he strained to see what Sharon and Nona were looking at. Sharon couldn't help but rub the soft bulge affectionately. He laughed at her, and lifted his head to let Nona ruffle his curly hair. He made his trousers into a nest for Poppy's teddy bear. She abandoned the shell garden she'd been making, and picked up his toy kettle and said she'd go down to get water for teddy's tea.

When she had gone, Bryn decided to start shooting. He put aside his telescope and reached for his bow and arrow set. His plastic bow, and arrows with rubber suckers on the end. Red and blue and yellow. Nice and bright . . .

It would have been all right if he'd just *shot* the wretched arrows. But he had to make a sloppy mud solution with the last of his juice. He had to stick a dollop of the stuff on the rubber sucker before he fired it off.

He climbed onto the summerhouse table, to get a better shot. He aimed for the bit of ruined boathouse wall, a nice, big target that wasn't bobbing in the wind. And three things happened. Miss Parry, clad in her blue nylon overall, came out to see if the wind had dried her white sheets yet; Poppy slithered off the path into the front garden; and Bryn let his arrow fly.

'It's poison-tipped,' he said. 'Miss read to us about Indians yesterday. You do it that way to kill the natives.'

The arrow arched through the air, down towards Miss Parry's washing. It hit a clean sheet, failed to stick, and slid down it to the ground leaving a long, mud-coloured streak behind.

Miss Parry looked up. Bryn, on the table, was anything but hidden with his nice, bright bow in his hand. Everybody gasped, horrified. Even from the distance of the summer-house, it was plain to see that Miss Parry's lips were *tight*. And then Bryn grinned. He did it nervously, of course. Bryn's grinning wasn't always the happy thing that people thought it was. But Miss Parry wasn't to know that. He grinned and grinned, as if it was the greatest joke in the world.

'Bryn, stop it,' Nona whispered at him.

He grinned some more.

'Get off that table!'

His face *split* with grinning. Nona pulled him down. Underneath them, Miss Parry gestured over the wall at Poppy.

'That's your fault,' said Nona. 'Poppy shouldn't get the blame. Go down and say you're sorry straight away.'

Bryn didn't move.

'Go on!' said Nona staring down at Miss Parry and Poppy, with their heads together.

Still he didn't move, and she couldn't really blame him. Miss Parry glanced up as Poppy spoke. There was a nasty look in her eye. More than nasty! She said something to Poppy, and then she turned her back on them all, whipped her washing off the line and stormed into her cottage, shutting the door behind her, very loudly.

It felt, somehow, as though the party was over. 'I think we'd better pack up,' said Nona, anxiously . . .

When they got down to the garden, Poppy was waiting for them. She grabbed her teddy bear tight.

'What did she say?' they all asked, crowding round.

'She said that if we weren't poor, tragical children whose dad had died, she'd tell our mum on us,' said Poppy, looking thoroughly confused. 'She said, dead dad or not, she'd tell next time. I didn't know what she was on about. I said our dads hadn't died and she just said, "Dads?" and I said, "Yes," and she said, "Where are your Dads?" I told her I didn't know, about our dads I mean... Nona, what was she on about?'

'Oh Poppy!' Nona stared at her in exasperation. 'Didn't you hear what I told her the other day?'

But before Poppy could answer, Miss Parry's front door opened again, and she sailed forth. She'd taken off her overall, tidied up her hair. She came over her bridge, fast as she could on those legs of hers, then along the wall, across their bridge and up the path. 'I want a word with your mam,' she said. 'If she isn't in bed with a headache, that is!'

'Miss Parry, we're sorry about the washing...' Nona began, but Miss Parry thrust her aside; actually, physically, put out her pink hands and pushed. Then she stomped straight into the house as if she owned it, and they all rushed after her.

Mum was at the kitchen sink, shaking potatoes out of the bag, to see if there were enough for lunch.

'About that summerhouse,' Miss Parry stormed, before she even had time to register surprise at seeing her there. 'It's mine. It goes with my cottage. I'll thank you to keep out and I'd like to know...' she looked round furiously at the little group huddled in the doorway, '...how this lot got in. I've got the key, see, the only key, hanging on my back door.'

'The summerhouse?' Mum said, feebly and astonished. 'Yours?' She dried her hands and turned, clutching the tea towel, from the sink. 'But I used to come down here years ago, for holidays, you know. The summerhouse comes with this cottage...'

'Can't speak for then,' Miss Parry shouted. 'It's mine now and there's only one way these hooligans of yours got in, and that's by breaking down the door. My Billy will have to tot up the damage. You'll have to pay the bill, no two ways about it.'

'But the path ...' Mum said, as if in a dream. 'It comes down into our garden ...'

'So, you want a fight!'

'A fight?' Mum looked confused. 'Of course I don't. But ...'

'I'm putting this in the hands of my solicitor,' raged Miss Parry. 'I'm phoning Billy, right away. You're lucky I'm not calling the police.'

And she was gone. She ploughed between Nona and Sharon, before Mum, any of them, could think what next to say. She slammed the living-room door behind her. Then the front door.

Nona turned to Mum, whose face was ashen. She knew hers was too. 'What'll we do?' Mum said, and Nona didn't know. But, 'It's all right, Mum. We'll think of something,' she said as Mum, distractedly, crossed the living-room floor and sank down by the empty wood-burning stove, staring into the ashes of the night before and twisting the tea towel. She knew now what Ralph meant when he said the Parrys were *territorial*, knew what Mrs Lark had warned about.

Mum leaned her head against the cold, black stove. 'I can't stand being shouted at,' she said in a bleak voice with a threat of tears in it.

Sharon picked up Cody, pulled at Bryn, gestured at Poppy. 'Come on,' she said, just like that, without being asked. 'We'll go and play upstairs.'

'I always used to sit right here, when I was a girl,' Mum sighed, when she and Nona were on their own. 'I used to lean with my back against its warmth. It was a good warmth. I was a good girl. Perhaps I deserved my good, safe life. I've made such a mess of things since then. Perhaps I deserve all this. Perhaps it's my punishment.'

'It's no use talking like that, Mum,' Nona said. 'You've done your best. It's not your fault if things go wrong.'

'Do you really think that?'

'Of course I do!'

'Oh, Nona, Nona. I wish I could have given you a childhood like mine. There was none of this moving around. None of this being one sort of family, and then another. Things always stayed the same. We were always, you know, *safe*.'

'Don't go on, Mum,' Nona said, awkward as she always was in the face of Mum's memories. 'Everything's all right. We're happy with what we've got, really we are.'

'Oh my Nona, where would I be without you?' Mum said. 'What a good girl you are.' She took Nona's hands and held them tight. Tears trickled down her cheeks.

'What we need's some lunch,' said Sharon, unexpectedly, from the staircase. 'We'll all feel better when we've had something to eat.'

'You must go down to the pub,' Mum said, releasing Nona's hands and wiping her eyes. 'Get us another take-away. I'm sure none of us can think about cooking now, and there weren't enough potatoes anyhow and poor old Nona did miss her sausages and chips the other day ... ' She smiled weakly at the memory. 'All of you go. Have you seen my heachache pills ... ?'

It was the first time Nona had been into the Mermaid Inn, and it wasn't what she had expected. They walked into what, apart from the small bar at the end, looked like an ordinary sitting-room. Chairs were set around a long table. There was an old rug on a plain quarry-tiled floor. There were no polished brasses, fruit machines or juke box, no piped music. Ralph's cat lazed in front of the fire-place. At the end of the room, through an archway, Nona saw arm-chairs before a window with a view of the sea, and a glimpse of Griselda in one of them.

'Can I help you?' Ralph got up from the table where a couple of men nodded their welcomes and returned to their dominoes.

'Are you cooking?' Nona asked.

'Griselda is,' Ralph sighed, as though he rather wished she wasn't.

'What d'you want?'

Nona ordered jumbo sausages in batter all round, and chips. Griselda emerged through the archway, sniffing her disapproval.

'What you little things need is proper food,' she said, a gleam in her eyes as if she could just picture it. 'Simple salads and a soup, a selection of cheeses and some decent bread . . .'

'Oh, get on with it!' Ralph said, as though he'd heard all this before.

Griselda sighed, and went.

'She won't be long,' said Ralph. 'Come and sit down.'

They settled round the fire. The cat jumped into Sharon's lap. Nona stared past the wall telephone, with the coast-guard's and lifeboat service's numbers underneath it, to a sepia photograph of some military fellow who was once, according to the plaque beneath, the Prince of Wales. She tried imagining Griselda cooking sausages in batter. It had never occurred to her that in the hours between waking in that tent of hers and retiring to it at the end of the day, Griselda *worked*. Ralph arranged a fresh shovelful of coal on top of the glowing embers of the fire.

'Is anything the matter?' he asked, unexpectedly.

Perhaps it shouldn't have been unexpected, for Sharon looked even more woebegone than usual, Poppy was in a right dream, Bryn actually sat still for once and even Cody was quiet.

'We're fine!' Nona said. She wondered what she looked like.

'In trouble, are you?' Ralph said.

Ridiculously, Nona found herself, like Mum before her,

71

on the verge of tears. Astonished, because she never cried, she bowed her head and fought furiously with her weakening lower lip. Somewhere beyond her private battle, she heard Sharon pouring it all out and she wasn't in a position to stop her. She realized the men round the table were straining to listen too. She'd got to get a grip on herself. She was being stupid...

'The Great Herself has been at it again,' she heard Ralph say.

'What, down at Nyth-y-dryw?' called back one of the men.

'That's right,' said Ralph.

The man got up and came over. He wore a butcher's striped apron, and big, brown shoes. His face was creased with indignant lines. 'She's trying it on again,' he declared. 'That wretched woman! You give me five minutes. I'll nip out to the van and get my things. We'll sort this out, you see if we don't!'

'Emlyn's the landlord's agent,' Ralph explained, while he was away. 'You've come down at the right moment. He's just the man you want.'

Their lunch appeared, wrapped up in newspapers. Griselda dumped it down and went back through the archway. Nona emptied the purse to pay for it. Emlyn returned with a huge, battered folder full of bits of paper and maps. He slammed it down on the table and began rummaging through.

'Your case is clear...' His scrubbed hands, huge like hams, thumped down on a map. 'Look at the boundaries, just look you! It's plain as day! Come on. I'll ride you down. I'll take the map round and get the key for you.'

They found themselves bustled outside. The thing was taking on a pace of its own and even Nona, struggling for control again, couldn't stop it. Emlyn stuffed them into the back of a red-and-white van, with TAURUS MEATS, painted on the side. They crouched on the sawdust floor, between shelves of bacon and slabs of lamb, and Emlyn shut them in.

'Good luck,' they heard Ralph call, as they drove away.

Down at the cottages, Emlyn let them out again. They brushed the sawdust off their clothes. Emlyn took off his apron, smoothed down his hair, clutched his folder and grinned.

'I'll enjoy this, I will,' he said. 'Now you go home.'

Nona wondered what Mum would say. She took the take-away lunch inside and explained as best she could, making sure Mum knew that it was Sharon, not her, who'd spilled the beans. Mum, surprisingly, said nothing. She unwrapped the packages onto plates she'd been heating in the oven, scraped the last chips off the newspaper and sat everybody down. She ate with the rest of them, but she was very quiet.

Just as they finished, there was a knock on the door. Sharon went to see, and it was Emlyn. He came in, grinning with pleasure at what he'd done, and apologizing for disturbing the meal. He slapped the summerhouse key down proudly onto the table.

'It took a bit,' he said, 'but I got it in the end. I've been up and had a look at it. From the dust I'd say she's had it locked up for a good few years. If I were you I'd have tea up there this afternoon. Let her know what's what. You'll be all right now. But if you have any more trouble, mind, you know where to find me.'

They didn't have tea up there. Mum couldn't face it. In fact, she said she couldn't face going out of doors at all, in case she bumped into Miss Parry.

'You've got to go out sometime,' Nona said.

Mum didn't answer. She turned on the radio instead. She lit the wood-burning stove. Bryn was forgiven for his deadly arrow. Cody fell asleep on Sharon's lap and Sharon moaned, more to herself than anyone else, about not having a television.

Nona went upstairs and sat on the window-sill, as though on guard duty. Emlyn's words rang in her ears. 'You'll be all right.' She didn't believe it. She guarded the front path all afternoon, waiting for Miss Parry to come back.

10

It was an ominous week, waiting for something to happen that never did. On Saturday morning, worn out with it all, Nona could have done with the chance to sleep in, down in the snugness of her bed. What she got instead was the revving and turning of the postman's van outside.

'Once I'd have slept through articulated lorries,' Nona thought, remembering the old days. 'Now I wake up at a measly little van. How quickly things change!'

She dragged herself out of bed. Downstairs, she found a letter from Susie Lennox waiting for her. She opened it, read its contents. Even more than last time, it seemed to come at her from a million miles away.

'I haven't told a soul where you're staying,' Susie Lennox wrote. 'No one's got a clue. I'm glad you ran away. I'm glad the new school's okay.'

Everyone was still asleep upstairs. Nona found notebook and pen, and struggled into her new wellington boots. She'd go down to the beach, write back to Susie, take a walk on her own.

Down on the beach, the man with the red handcart was harvesting the morning's high tide. Nona walked behind the sea wall, hoping he wouldn't notice her. She didn't want to say 'hello'. At the end of the wall, she climbed over the stile onto the cliff path. She followed it all the way to the secret beach.

It was good to be back. And there was no wretched boy

this time, though she did find, underneath the bottom step, that five huge bars of chocolate had been added to the hoard. She put the boy out of her mind, and found a shelf of rock where her feet could dangle above the water. She got out her pen, propped her pad on the rock and wrote:

'*Dear Susie . . .*'

To her surprise, the letter wouldn't come. What could she say? '*I've met this nice girl. Her name is Beca. She's good at all her school work, which sounds a drag I know, but she can run like the wind. I've got this nice teacher. Her name is Mrs Thomas . . .*' She could go on endlessly like that, but it wasn't really her news, and she hadn't the heart for it. She pushed aside the pad, and stared at the sea . . .

'Mum won't go outside,' she said at last. 'She's been like it all week. I said to her, 'We're out of money,' but she won't go to the Post Office or anywhere, and I've had to get credit up at Bella Pugh's. She's afraid of seeing Miss Parry, that's what it is. But it's been a week and nothing's happened yet. I passed Billy in his truck yesterday and he smiled, so perhaps it'll be all right, like Emlyn said.

'Poppy's started dreaming again. Once she's woken up, she's too scared to go back to sleep, and then she comes in to me and both of us lie awake until morning. They're trying to get her out of sucking her thumb at school. It's a waste of time, if you ask me.

'Sharon's driving me mad—as usual. Bryn drives me mad too, but at least he doesn't moan. Cody's so sweet. I don't know where we'd be without him. He looks so pretty, with his curly hair. Mum says we let him get away with things, but she's as bad as the rest of us. She says he's her last baby. She wants me to write the funny things he says in my word book, so we don't forget them. I don't know what Mrs Thomas would make of the words Cody uses!

'It's great, collecting words. It cheers up even the most awful scenes. Like when Miss Parry was screaming at Mum, I thought of the word *rant*. It just came into my head and I put

76

it in the book and now I'm using it all the time. It's a bit like collecting pebbles on the shore. You pick them up and put them in your pocket and feel them there, all smooth and nice. You get them out and look at them again. *Rant, rant, rant...* That's one of the things Uncle Brady always used to do.

'Mum's bruises and burns are better now. It's a shame about Miss Parry. In other ways, Mum's easier to get on with than she's been for ages. She even let us go down to the Mermaid Inn to watch the telly last night. It was great. We felt almost normal, almost like the rest of the world. Griselda was down there, by the window in her chair. She never said anything of course. Emlyn was there with his pal who farms the headland. The handcart man was down there too. He's always got a different girlfriend with him. They never sit beyond the arch, like Griselda does and Ralph sometimes.

'Ralph gave us free lemonades. I don't know why. He's always very kind. I forgot to worry about Miss Parry for a whole hour! Ralph said Mum should come down with us one night. Fat chance of that. She's always kept to herself, but since last week she's been worse than ever. Of course she doesn't want Uncle Brady finding us, but he's not going to do that, is he? Not now.

'There was a mist last night, when we got home. It was there, too, after school, just on our bit of the common. The air was damp and grey and there were shapes, bushes, a bit of the summerhouse, poking out of it. There were fingers of it curled round branches and over the rushes in the middle of the common. I'd never dare walk out there. The ground is so wet that when the sun shines on it, you can see silver pools. Ralph says wild irises grow out there in the summertime. I don't suppose we'll be around to see. I have to keep reminding myself this is just a winter let. It's not our home. There'll be another move. Ralph says we wouldn't believe the wild flowers that grow out there. And the creatures. Glow worms, dragon-flies, lizards, rabbits, even otters and snakes.

'I went exploring after school. Thought I'd go down past that dead tree, take a look at that caravan and those tin sheds, be on my own for a bit. But I was scared. When I got near that tree it looked just like a ghost. I turned round and ran back. Sharon was waiting for me. She was cross because I hadn't gone straight in with her to make the tea.

'I wonder if Sharon and I would have got on better if we'd had the same dad? Mum says I take after her, but I sometimes wonder about my dad, and if I'm like him too. Mum makes me feel guilty if I ask her things. And she never answers. I hate the way she *puts away* what she doesn't want to think about. I hope she's wrong, about me being like her. I wouldn't want to do that too.

'Look, I'm going to have to move. You've nearly reached me now. Why King Canute thought he could keep the waves at bay, I'll never know! You've got a life of your own, haven't you? I bet the King Canute thing never really happened.'

Nona shifted back. The sea was finding every nook and crevice beneath her now. She propped her notebook on a new rock and wrote, not at the front with 'Dear Susie' but tucked away on the last page under the heading, 'To the Sea': *I want to cup you in my hands and watch your sparkling drops squeeze out between my fingers like salty tears.*

Embarrassed at herself, she shut the book. What was it about the sea? Why did she feel as though it really was alive, did understand? She put the pen away.

'I'll write to Susie another day,' she thought as she turned and—because the low rocks were covered by the tide—climbed up the steps and back the way she had come.

When she reached the big beach again she felt happier, unburdened somehow. She saw the man with the red cart, still paddling. His long scarf dangled in the water, and the bottoms of his trousers were wet, but he didn't seem to care. He was struggling with a bird's cage now, which was enmeshed in brown weed.

'Can I help you?' she called.

'Thanks,' he said.

Close up she found that he had ice-green eyes with wrinkles round them, and brown skin and a golden earring. She held the cage steady while he untangled the weed.

'Have a nice day,' he called after her, when the job was finished, and she was half way over the wall again.

He never knew, nobody could have done, that she wouldn't have another one for a long time . . .

11

Sunday morning began with the sound of a truck on the track, the slamming of doors, shouting of voices and barking of dogs. Nona stuck her head between her bedroom curtains and yesterday's *nice day* might never have been. Poles and rolls of wire and a big metal gate had been thrown all over what Miss Parry liked to think of as her 'bit'. Billy was hauling tools off the back of the pick-up truck and Cledwyn was struggling to help him. Billy began pegging out a narrow strip from the front gate of Nyth-y-dryw along to the edge of the common. The black dogs barked from the back of the truck.

'What's going on?' Sharon stumbled into the room. She pulled the curtain back further, leaned over Nona's shoulder.

'I don't know,' Nona said.

After breakfast, Nona and Sharon rushed back upstairs to find out what was happening now. Mum buried her hands in the washing-up and said she didn't want to know, while Bryn said he was going to get those Parrys with his bow and arrow. Poppy, like Mum, chose to pretend that everything was all right. She got out her shells and made patterns with them on the living-room floor.

But everything was not all right. From the window, Nona and Sharon watched Billy, red-faced with exertion, banging poles into the ground, unrolling fencing and barbed wire, even installing a metal gate to let his own truck on and off the 'bit'. Cledwyn watched him from the truck. The dogs barked. The whole area outside the cottages, right up to the old boathouse wall, had been fenced off, leaving just a narrow strip by which they could get from Nyth-y-dryw onto the track.

It took Billy all morning to finish, and they watched him all the time. When he had, he threw down his tools, jumped over the fence and began to make his way up their front path. Cledwyn set the dogs free, and they bounded after him. They reached the front door all together. Billy banged upon it with his fist.

Nona almost fell downstairs in her unsuccessful effort to get there before Mum. She stared into a hot, wild face that had smiled so reassuringly, only a few days before. '*You can't trust the Parrys when they're being nice,*' Mrs Lark had warned.

Mum, white as death, stared too. Billy held his writhing dogs by their collars, while his screaming gave a whole new dimension to the word *rant*. Mum's language wasn't always all that hot, but she was stunned—they both were—by the words that flew out of Billy's mouth. Nona'd never seen such anger. Not even from Uncle Brady. She'd never seen faces bulge before, eyeballs stick out, red veins throbbing. She thought maybe Billy'd die. *Hoped* he would.

They weren't ever to threaten his sister again, Billy said. Weren't ever to send that butcher fellow round to bully her again because she might look big and strong but she was fragile really, and she lived alone, and she'd got a heart. If his sister died, he said, he'd get Mum, Nona, Emlyn, all of them for murder. Not manslaughter, mark you. *Murder*, see, because they were wicked people who meant to do her harm.

His sister had been kind to them, Billy yelled. Hadn't she given them tea? Hadn't she let them tramp all over her 'bit,' up and down to school, up and down every day?

They were English, he yelled. *English*, with no right to any bit of land round here, let alone his sister's precious summerhouse, let alone her 'bit'. Why didn't they go back

81

where they belonged? If they ever even *spoke* to his sister again, he screamed, he'd *kill* them . . .

Mum made a pot of tea. A big pot, with enough in it for everyone. She ladled sugar into all the cups and poured the stuff and began to talk, very fast and as if nothing had happened:

'We're going to make coconut cakes!' she declared. 'Nona, you'll nip up to Bella Pughs's, won't you, and get the things we need? They'll still be open, if you hurry up! Oh, and I've written out an advertisement for their front window. You could take it too. I thought I'd do home typing, like in the old days before Uncle Brady's. We can't live on Social Security payments for ever, you know!'

Nona knew what Mum was doing. Recognized the voice, everything. 'What a good idea,' she said—it obviously wasn't the moment to remind Mum that the purse was bare. 'I'll get my bicycle. Of course I'll go.'

'What are you two on about?' said Sharon, who'd never put a brave face on anything in her life. 'Cakes? Typing? What are we going to do about . . . ?'

Nona, letting herself out of the front door, didn't know what they were going to do about . . . Nor did she want to think about it. Not just now. Not squeezing along the bit of path that had been left for them, not cycling away from all that barbed wire.

She passed Griselda coming out of the women's toilets with her sponge bag and towel. Waved to Ralph on the sea wall calling, 'Here, Offa, here!' after his rampaging cat. She got off the bike and pushed it up the hill. Got back on again at the top and rode through Jerico to Bella Pugh's, humming a little tune as she went to keep her spirits up.

When she got home, the little Wren's Nest looked like a fortress under siege. Nona squeezed along the path, trying with difficulty to keep the shopping off the barbed wire.

'Thank goodness you're back,' Sharon said, when she got indoors. 'Mum's been singing and she never sings. I sometimes think she's a bit mad. And as for you...'

Nona gave the eggs to Mum who was, indeed, singing. Bryn ran down the stairs to report that somebody was coming along the track. Nona went up to see. It was the man with the red hand cart. When he got close enough to see their barbed wire, he turned it around. Nona watched him all the way back to the Mermaid Inn, watched Ralph come out, watched their sticks of arms pointing and waving.

'Why don't you come down into the warm?' Mum called. 'Come and help us with the cakes.'

'I'm doing my homework,' Nona lied. She'd never be able to look at coconut pyramids again without remembering this day. 'I'll come down when I've finished.'

'You'll miss your chance.'

'I won't be long.'

Nona watched clouds thickening, out over the sea. She watched the first fine mizzle as it hit the common. Watched Emlyn Hughes' 'Taurus Meats' van as it stopped at the pub and the men climbed into it. As it bounced along the track, towards the house...

When it got as near as it could manage, the van stopped. The men got out. They stood, staring at the mess of wire and fenceposts in front of them. The rain washed down their faces. Emlyn Hughes went to the front of the van, got out his tools. Then, with grim indignation, they set to work, cutting wires, tearing out posts, throwing the gate into the bushes.

Nona sat very still, watching them as she'd watched the other, equally determined man. Sharon came clattering up the stairs, and so did Bryn. They all saw the last posts being pulled out and Emlyn Hughes, maps and deeds in his hands again, marching over next door's bridge and up to its front door.

Sharon rushed back downstairs. 'Mum, Mum, you'll never guess what's happening...!'

Mum's voice answered sharp and quick. 'I don't want to know!'

'But Mum . . . !'

'Sharon, not another word! Let's switch on the radio. Let's see if there's a play to listen to.'

Nona heard a loud burst of radio, a twiddling between stations, then the senseless drama of a half-finished play. Ralph and the hand-cart man, by now drenched, clambered back into the van among the meat, to wait for Emlyn. The play, coming up through the floor-boards, had begun to make sense by the time that Emlyn reappeared. He came straight from Miss Parry's bridge to theirs, straight through the gate, straight up their front path.

'Nona, will you answer it?' Mum called, urgently.

Nona came downstairs. Mum's face was pointy and sharp. She'd had enough.

'It's Emlyn,' Nona said. 'Shall I ask him in?'

'No!' Mum said, with a determination that matched any of the men's, who'd been so busy outside her house today.

'Is your mam at home?' said Emlyn, when Nona opened the door.

'She's got a headache.' It was the usual excuse. It tripped off Nona's tongue.

'I'm not surprised,' he said, not knowing. 'Anyone would have a headache with *her* next door. Look, tell her not to worry. We've put the old bag right, once and for all. She hasn't a leg to stand on, and she knows it. Tell your mam, tell her that *everything's all right.*'

He beamed with simple pride at what he'd done. It was so uncomplicated to him. 'He's just like Bryn who thinks that we can get them with his plastic bow and arrow,' Nona thought. 'He's not that different even to Billy. It's simple to him too . . .'

'Thank you,' she said.

'It's nothing.' Emlyn smiled confidently. 'She'll probably try to get me for it, but I can handle her. I'll *enjoy* it.' He wiped his wet face with his hands and turned to go. 'Like I said before—anytime.'

Nona watched the van turning on the reclaimed patch. She waved the three men off as they drove away. Went back indoors and shut the door.

'Turn the play up, will you?' Mum said.

Nona listened to the patter of the rain outside. It sounded so noisy, even light rain, on a tin roof. The play ended, but she never heard what happened. Mum finished the cakes, but she couldn't bring herself to eat one.

She was wondering what the Parrys would do next.

12

ENGLISH BASTARDS GO HOME.

That's what it said on the crumbling boathouse wall when Nona woke up next morning and drew back her curtains on a pure and blameless October day.

ENGLISH BASTARDS GO HOME. Carelessly splattered with blood-red, ragged paint strokes that were lit by the morning sun...

'What are bastards?' Poppy said.

'We are and you told them.'

'I don't know what you mean...' Poppy climbed into Nona's bed.

'We all had dads who went away,' Nona said, wearily. 'I had one, and you and Bryn and Sharon did too, and now even Cody hasn't got a dad any more.' She shut the curtains tight.

Poppy pulled the covers over her head. 'Why does it say GO HOME?' she said from underneath them. 'Where do they want us to go? We haven't got anywhere else.'

'It's only paint, Poppy. It doesn't matter. We'll get it off.'

'Why don't they like us?'

'I don't know.'

'They must have done it in the night. Those letters are awfully big. They must have used a ladder.'

'Come on, Poppy, it's getting late...' Nona pulled her out from under the covers. 'I'll find your clothes. You wake up Sharon. Tell her she won't have time to fuss over her hair, if she doesn't get a move on. Don't look like that! Things always seem worse on Monday mornings . . .'

Just when it was time to go to school, there was a knock on the front door. Mum was still upstairs. She too had drawn her curtains again. She'd got back into bed, pulled the covers over her head, like Poppy had done, and curled up in a ball so that Nona's heart ached dully for the Mum who'd slept with outstretched arms and smiling. She answered the door.

Miss Parry's smile was as gloating as a wicked child's. She smoothed down her skirt, picked a speck off it. The delight in her eyes was more than she could conceal. Her pink hands smelt of bleach again, as if she'd had to soak them to remove the paint. Behind her, parked so as not to block their view, Billy and Cledwyn waited next to the wall.

'My Billy's come for me. It's my day for doing out his house, see. Would any of you *children* . . .' she said the word as if she had another on her mind, ' . . . like a ride up to school?'

Nona didn't bother to answer. She slammed the door. It was a game, wasn't it? Miss Parry toyed with them like a cat.

'That wasn't her?' said Sharon, astonished at the nerve. 'What did she want?'

What she wanted, Nona thought, was to witness pain. 'She's out for the day,' she said as briskly as she could manage. 'Mum'll have the chance to get the wall cleaned before she comes back. Isn't that good news? I'll go and let her know.'

It wasn't, however, as simple as all that. At the car park, huge, red letters were emblazoned on the toilet wall, and when they got up to Jerico, the same message was everywhere, even on the steps up the side of the chapel barn. Somebody had had a busy night!

'Look how thick the paint is, look how big the letters are.

We'll be stuck with that message for the rest of our lives,' Sharon said, so miserable that even the company of King Offa couldn't comfort her.

'No, we won't,' Nona replied. 'We'll be leaving here at Easter. It's only a winter let, you know. We can stick it out till then.'

'I feel so ashamed,' Sharon said, her eyes moist with misery.

'Lots of kids are in the same boat as us,' Nona said, struggling not to get cross with her. 'You can be sure it's no different here to anywhere else. There's nothing special nowadays about being bastards.'

'But we're the only ENGLISH ones . . . !' wailed Sharon.

Nona left Sharon to it. She didn't want to shout at her. Not today. Not in front of everyone. Some people just wouldn't be consoled, would they? She reached the school gate, and Beca waited for her.

'Are you all right?' said Beca.

'Of course I am!'

But all day long, instead of the work that she was meant to do, she day-dreamed wildly about the fathers that they didn't have, wondering where they were and what had gone wrong and why they didn't have them any more. Then, after school, when they went up to the shop, she was sure that none of the other shoppers would meet her eye. But perhaps it was she, who didn't want to look at them. Perhaps it was her *imagination*. Mrs Bella Pugh looked at her straight enough, from across the check-out desk. And Emlyn, in his van, waved as he drove by.

When they passed the barn beside the chapel, they found that the steps had been painted over and the words no longer showed. Further down the road, ENGLISH BASTARDS had been crossed out and PARRYS had been painted over the top of them. When they got down to the common, everything but the word GO had been scrubbed from the toilet wall.

Back at Nyth-y-dryw, however, nothing had changed.

The message was still there, and the curtains still were drawn. Mum was sitting in front of the fire, spotlit by that awful lampshade. Her hair fell over her shoulders. Cody slept upon her lap. The room was hot and airless.

'You should see the village, Mum,' said Sharon, with relish. 'There's red paint everywhere!'

Nona could have throttled Sharon sometimes. 'Don't listen to a word she says, Mum. It's not that bad, really it's not. She's exaggerating. Honestly.'

But Mum wasn't listening to *either* of them. Her face was pink, moist, sleepy. Her eyes were glazed. Nona crossed the room and opened the kitchen door. Cold air came rushing in. Nona breathed it, thankfully. There was something nasty about the closeness in the living-room. Mum seemed to wake up. She raised a hand, pushed the hair back off her face. Nona took the shopping out to the kitchen, where not even the breakfast dishes had been done and a pile of wet laundry waited to be hung out on the line. 'Is *she* back?' she called.

'I don't think so,' Mum answered her.

'Sharon and I had better make a start, then, on the wall.'

'Oh Nona, I'm sorry . . .' Mum tried to shift Cody without waking him . . . 'I should have done it. I slept in late, but I thought I'd still have time before you came home. I don't quite know what's happened to me today.'

'It doesn't matter. Come on Sharon.'

But Sharon had had enough. 'No,' she rebelled. 'I won't. I'm sick of the way you're always bossing me, and anyhow I've got my homework to do.'

'I've got homework too,' retorted Nona indignantly, 'but we can't leave the wall like that.'

'Do it on your own, if you're so keen,' said Sharon, and she headed up the stairs.

Alone in the near darkness, with Miss Parry not yet returned, Nona had scraped all but ENGLISH away. Pausing to rub her sore hands, she saw a light bobbing along the track. She stared, surprised. A lantern? Yes, it was a lantern. She watched its orange leer come closer. She shivered. It had what looked like a *mouth* and *eyes*. Seemed to be lit by a dancing flame. It made her think about the Ku Klux Klan. About nationalists who burned down English cottages. It made her want to cover up that ENGLISH. They didn't burn them with the English in them, did they? She wouldn't put it past the Parrys to get involved with things like that.

The flame flickered close now. Perhaps that was who it was: Miss Parry, lighting her way home. Nona heard crunch, totter, crunch, upon the track. She heard a singing voice. Then the flame lit up the boathouse wall. The singing stopped.

'They've done it down here too, have they?' Griselda said, her fur coat falling open to reveal a mass of jewellery.

'Yes,' said Nona, surprised to see her, and weak, too, with relief.

'No trick,' Griselda said. She held up the orange pumpkin lantern. Her black-lined eyes and bird's nest hair could have been witch's eyes and hair. 'Just a treat. I bought you some sweet apples. Here you are.'

Nona stared at the bag, uncomprehendingly. She didn't move.

'Hallowe'en,' Griselda explained. 'Didn't you realize?'

They'd made masks that afternoon. Written silly poems about witches brews, but she hadn't noticed anything they'd done at school today.

'I thought you might need cheering up,' Griselda said.

'Oh. Yes. Thank you.' Nona took the fruit. Griselda dipped inside her coat and produced a bottle of stout as well. 'Ralph sent this,' she said. 'It's for your ma. He thought she might need cheering up as well.'

Nona didn't know what to say. She took the bottle too.

'Weather'll be turning now,' Griselda said. 'It always does, after Hallowe'en. It'll be winter before you know where you are.'

'Yes, I suppose it will.'

'Pumpkin's for you too,' Griselda said. Then, steady and firm and unexpectedly, 'Don't let the old hag get you down.'

It wasn't often people looked at you straight like that. It took Nona's breath away. Griselda wasn't a witches' brew of make-up and hair, after all. She wasn't just an oddity who camped on a common, but a person just like herself, a person who understood what she must be feeling. Suddenly, Nona wanted to ask, while it was possible, why she lived on the common in a tent, who she was, how long she'd been there, how long she planned to stay.

But Griselda, having done her bit, turned to go. Her high heels scraped on the track. 'Goodnight!' she said, and Nona didn't dare call her back. Her dark bulk lumbered away.

Nona picked up the lantern. Felt its warmth against her raw hands. Griselda never turned and waved. She just dissolved into the night. Nona, clutching the gifts, decided it was too late to scrub any more. As she made her way back over the bridge, she heard Griselda's voice fading down the track:

> *Hobgoblin nor foul fiend*
> *Can daunt his spirit:*
> *He knows he at the end*
> *Shall life inherit.*
> *Then fancies fly away:*
> *He'll fear not what men say:*
> *He'll labour night and day*
> *To be . . .*

Nona must have left the front door unwittingly ajar, for Mrs Lark just pushed it open and walked in.

The girls and Mum were seated round the fire. 'Another of those wretched radio plays'—Sharon's words—was up loud, which explained why none of them had heard the car. Nona was warming meaty lumps of hand before the fire. It

91

was a night, obviously, for visitors—just when Mum wanted to be left alone!

'I've come to persuade you up for a cup of tea,' Mrs Lark said determinedly. 'Beca's worried that I shouldn't interfere, but I wanted you to know we're not all like the Parrys in Jerico.'

Mum half-rose, startled, from her chair. 'I couldn't possibly . . .' she began.

'Nona could come too,' said Mrs Lark as if she realized it would make a difference. 'Just for an hour. What do you think, Nona? You and Beca could do your homework together.'

The thought of copying Beca's immaculate work was not without appeal.

'We're pleased to have another family in the village, English or not,' Mrs Lark was saying. 'This isn't a Welsh thing, you know. The Parrys speak for themselves. We're all so ashamed. You *will* come up, won't you? I've made a cake . . .'

Poor Mum looked trapped.

'Why don't you go?' Sharon said, who longed to switch channels to the Top Fifty Show.

'You really mustn't shut yourself away,' Mrs Lark said anxiously.

'The little ones are asleep,' Sharon urged. 'And Poppy's never any trouble. She'll go up when it's time. It'll be all right.'

Mum looked at Nona, as her last hope. 'I *have* got loads of homework,' Nona said. 'And I haven't had a chance to start it yet. I wouldn't say "no" to doing it with Beca . . .'

Pale and limp, as if she didn't have any fight left in her, Mum was bundled into Mrs Lark's car. Nona sat next to her on the back seat. They were driven along the track and past the few vehicles outside the Mermaid Inn—somebody's tractor, the 'Taurus Meats' van and a pale green car—and up the hill. In the village, blinking and surprised, they entered a world of street lights, glimpses of television sets through windows, boys mending motorbikes.

'A place where other people live!' Nona thought, suddenly excited, awoken, hungry for the outside world.

Mrs Lark's kitchen was awash with the smell of fresh cake. Beca sat at the table, her books in front of her, and a model of a ship and tubes of glue that Nona was sure had nothing to do with homework.

'You haven't been introduced to Owen, have you?' Mrs Lark said.

'Owen, this is Mrs Davies. You must have met Nona at school...' The boy came out from behind the door. Nona froze. It was no consolation that he looked as horrified, shocked, embarrassed as she surely did herself.

'My husband's out visiting tonight,' Mrs Lark was saying. 'It's a lonely life sometimes, being the minister's wife... Owen, don't just stand there. Take that *expression* off your face and put the kettle on.'

He didn't look at all like Beca or his mother, with his brown skin, and dark hair. But all the same, Nona thought, she should have known. He was tall like his father. And it was what you'd expect from a minister's son, skiving off church in his Sunday best, down on the secret beach where he hoped nobody would see.

'I'll let you copy my French,' Beca was offering, 'if you'll help me with Mrs Thomas's essay. I don't know what to write about.'

'What? Oh yes...' Nona turned her head.

'*Owen*,' Mrs Lark said again. 'Aren't you going to put the kettle on...?'

Nona sat down. Owen did as he was told. Mrs Lark took Mum's coat and sat her down as well. Owen gathered up the bits and pieces of his model ship, which Nona realised had been meticulously cut out by hand.

'I'm going upstairs,' he announced, without looking at

Nona at all. 'Got to get on with my Greek.'

'Owen is going away to school next year, away to Father's old school,' Beca whispered when he'd gone. 'He'll need Greek there, and so Father's started him. He hates it. Poor Owen.'

Nona opened her book. Poor Owen indeed! 'They should be sending you,' she said. 'You're good at languages. Now what do I do about . . .?'

Mrs Lark threw a cloth over half the table. She got out plates, and cups and saucers, set down the cake, made the pot of tea. Mum seemed to settle. A proper, *ordinary* colour began to creep back into her face. Mrs Lark cut the cake and poured the tea. Beca and Nona bent over their homework. Across the table, Mrs Lark talked about being a minister's wife, and recipes for cakes; about life by the sea and how nice everything was.

'She doesn't seem quite real, Beca's mother,' Nona mused. 'She's very kind and everything, but she's like an advert for brown bread or soap or a better sort of gravy. I bet that Owen's plan-ning to run away. I bet that's what his hoard's all about. Maybe Beca's happy with it, but it wouldn't do for me, all this apron stuff and baking stuff and golden plaits and making apple pie . . .'

'We ought to go,' Mum said at last.

'Won't you have another cup of tea?'

'We really mustn't. Sharon, you know.'

'Of course. Well, come on. I'll take you down.' Mrs Lark found the car keys. 'I have enjoyed this, you must come again . . .'

'I will,' said Mum, surprisingly, as if she really meant it.

When they turned in the car park they saw, distantly, that all the house lights were on. *All* of them.

'Whatever's Sharon up to?' Mum said, surprised. 'They're meant to be *asleep*.'

Mrs Lark drove through the car park, and onto the track.

Half way down it, something—someone—rushed at them out of the night, then halted, blinded by the headlights. It was Sharon. Sharon with the bicycle! Sharon with her hair in a right old mess and her coat flapping and eyes puffed into slits.

'Mum, oh Mum ...!'

Mum was out of the car and Sharon, bicycle discarded, was upon her.

Mrs Lark jumped out too, and Nona. None of them could make out what Sharon was saying. 'You've got to speak clearly!' Mum was shouting. 'I can't understand you! Sharon!'

'Uncle Brady's been,' Sharon managed, shuddering. 'He came ... oh Mum, he came with Billy! They knocked on the front door and I saw who it was and I wouldn't let them in. I tried, Mum, I tried! I did my best, honest I did! But they came round and pushed the back door in. Oh Mum, you know how rickety it is ...'

'Uncle Brady ...?' Mum said. 'With Billy? But how ...?'

'I don't know how! I don't know anything!' Sharon sobbed. Mum shook her.

'Sharon! Stop it! Where are they now?'

'I don't know that either ...' Sharon wailed, quite unable to stop. 'Mum, oh Mum ...! Uncle Brady's taken Cody!!'

Nona pedalled furiously up to the house. Mum and Mrs Lark were somewhere behind, still trying to comfort Sharon. In her mind's eye, Nona pictured Uncle Brady's metallic lime-green car parked next to the 'Taurus Meats' van. She'd *seen* it. Driven past it. Hadn't realized. What had been the matter with her?

She threw down the bicycle when she reached the hedge, and raced over the bridge. It was her fault, all her fault. She, who'd encouraged Mum to leave Sharon in charge ...

On the doorstep, she found Bryn and Poppy howling

together as if they couldn't make up their minds which was worse, going back in or coming out. Two frozen, terrified bundles in thin pyjamas and bare feet . . .

'It's all right, it's all right,' Nona heard her voice as if it belonged to someone else. She bent down to them. 'Please don't cry. It's all right . . .'

The outside light came on next door and the front door opened. Miss Parry appeared in her dressing-gown, the light shining upon her hair. Nona never forgot the parody of a halo it made around her head.

'I've got to get this into perspective,' she thought. 'She's not the devil, this woman, she's not. This is just ordinary wickedness and I mustn't be afraid.'

She waited for Miss Parry to tell them that if they didn't make less noise, she'd get her Billy, set the dogs on them, call the police. But Miss Parry didn't say anything. They stared at each other. Miss Parry looked the way she'd done when she'd handed them the chocolate cake. Mum's and Sharon's voices could be heard, crying, close now, on the track.

Miss Parry smiled.

PART TWO

Footsoldiers

13

The road down from Jerico bent and the ocean came into view. Mr Lark strode on without so much as raising his head, but Owen stopped and stared with the wonder that he always felt when he came round this corner. His gaze took in the crumpled, orange bracken above the beach, and foamy heaps of waves upon the sea. Ahead of him, the road sliced through the granite cliff. It was sheltered here, but he could see the wind's trail dancing up the sand, across the car park, towards the shadows around Nyth-y-dryw. The sun was bright, but winter was blowing in from the sea. Leaves were shaking off the willows. The common had exchanged its greenery for a hundred different shades of brown. Owen had a sense of the whole world humming with the changing seasons, busy and *alive* . . .

'Hurry up!' Mr Lark called. He'd stopped now, turned. In the shadow that the cliff made, his dark outline pointed like an indignant exclamation mark. His long, black coat was buttoned against the wind, right down his legs. His hat was rammed on tight. 'Lot's wife was turned into a pillar of salt for stopping on the way!' he chuckled drily. 'You wouldn't want that to happen to you now, would you?'

Uncomprehending, as he always was on these dreaded Saturday afternoon walks when his father cracked his mild, theological jokes, bared his inexplicable soul, came out with the guidance that he felt his son needed; furious too that a special moment had been spoiled, that his father appeared not to see what he could see, Owen dug his hands in his pockets, pretending he hadn't heard. A gull, above his head, cried out what he already knew; that there was a sky in which to fly, a world to see, that there was more to life than following in his father's footsteps.

'I said hurry up, son!' Father called, sharply now. Owen knew that he wanted to get back to the security of his study. He had no time for the sea, and the walks were a duty.

'All right! I'm coming ...' He hated being called 'son'. Maybe it was because it made him feel so precious that he knew he couldn't help but disappoint. But it was something else too. He and his father were members of a private club who went on brooding marches, while his father thought his thoughts, and he, Owen, trotted behind. A private club. And back at home there waited Mother and Beca who made the tea and polished the chapel. Strangers who did other things, and couldn't have joined the club, even if they'd wanted to.

'Sea's like a hungry cat ...' His father was thinking his thoughts out loud now. They'd reached the beach, crossed the car park, clambered up onto the wall. 'Just look at the way it pounces at that sand! All nature's like that, waiting to get you when you least expect it ... Waiting to eat you up ...'

Owen looked. Down on the beach, Harry Llewellyn hauled his hand cart along the edge of those waves, care-free, picking at what the tide brought in. He didn't answer his father. Just followed him along the wall, wondering why he didn't shut himself up in a monastery, safe behind closed walls, if he felt like that.

Harry was struggling with a lump of wood now, a dead, salty bit of what had once been a tree. Owen would have liked to help him with it, but he knew his father wouldn't approve. Harry Llewellyn wore an earring and womanized, and everyone knew he lived like a wild beast in that place of his, and that he was a poacher and a rogue.

Father was starting up the cliff path now, getting

through the walk in record time. Owen hurried after him. His limbs ached with keeping up. He thought how Beca would have enjoyed a trot like this. She was so different from him, but then girls were. He couldn't understand them. They were more than a world apart, and they frightened him. He often wished that Beca had been the boy. She'd know what to say when Father railed against all the things that bothered him. She was good like that.

Owen's long bones ached. They always did these days, and Mother said it wasn't surprising when you thought how tall he'd got, and how quickly too. His narrow chest was bursting. Beca would have kept up with half the effort he was making. But their father never asked her.

They were level with the track now, that cut down to the secret beach. Owen was thinking that he'd have given anything to be down there, when he saw a flash of a tiny figure between the brackens. It was Beca's new-found, wretched friend with the closed face and the secret eyes. He was sure of it.

He should have felt sorry for her, after what had happened down at Nyth-y-dryw the other night. But all he felt was jealousy because she was free to go off on her own, anger because—again—she'd chosen his special place, anxiety lest she found his secret store.

Father had reached their turning-point now: the first of the Hundred Steps up to the Head. He was holding his hat on tight, his hair streaming under it. Owen struggled to join him. His father's gaze passed him by. It stretched beyond the beach, car park, pub, track. Like the late afternoon sunlight, it got as far as Nyth-y-dryw, where the side wall was lit, and the little bathroom window.

'Sun's gone as far up the common as it will, now,' Mr Lark announced, seriously. 'Give it a week and they'll have had it for the winter. They're going to be cold down there.'

Owen wanted to ask what had happened the other night. It was all so secret. He was sure his parents talked about it when he and Beca weren't around, but all he'd found out was the gossip in school; that Billy Parry had found the little kid's dad asking about Cwmgwyntog Common in a pub in town; that he had helped to snatch the child back, and the mother was beside herself, and the rest of them hadn't been in school all week.

'We'll go back now,' said Father.

'Are you going to help them?' Owen asked.

'I would if I could.' Father turned his head away. 'But there's probably nothing, now, that anyone can do . . .'

And with this, he hurried back down the path.

'There must be *something* we can do . . .'

Mrs Lark looked up from her pile of mending as her husband reached for the iron chapel key from the hook behind the door. Tea was over. Beca was in her bedroom, working. Owen was gathering together bits and pieces of model boat to take upstairs. Mr Lark was going over, as he always did on Saturday night, to get Sion ready for the morning service.

'It'll be a custody matter, and we don't know the ins and outs,' he said.

'But I feel responsible!' Mrs Lark pricked her finger in her distress, staining Owen's school shirt with the slightest blood. 'If I hadn't asked her up, the children wouldn't have been left alone. Maybe none of this would have happened.'

'Boys need their fathers—perhaps he's better off where he is,' Mr Lark said. Then, as if this had reminded him, 'Owen, where are you going? Aren't you coming across the road to help me, son?'

Owen trailed up the chapel path, his plans for a quiet hour of model-making postponed. His father put the big key in the lock and opened up. When they went in, Owen could smell the polish on the pews. The communion table gleamed, and the lacquered wooden floor-boards. The brass lamps

101

shone, as if they were made of gold. The big stove had been blacked. Mother had done the flowers on the piano. She was good with flowers, Mother was, but Father, as if loveliness frightened him, always complained that she did it 'too fancy'.

'Let's set out the hymns,' Mr Lark said. He put a list of hymn tunes on the piano, ready for the morning. Owen fumbled for the box of numbers, impatient to get the job done and return to what he really wanted to do. When they'd finished slotting them into the right places on the board, they hung the whole thing up beneath the gothic lettered text that pronounced, big enough for all the world to see, LOVE AND SERVE THE LORD.

Owen stared at the words gloomily. He supposed that was what his father did when—always in the middle of the night—someone phoned and asked if the minister could go round. It was what he did when they hadn't enough money to buy new clothes, or pay for this blimming school where he wanted Owen to follow after him. LOVE AND SERVE THE LORD! It was what he did when the chapel was only half full and those who came were old, and none of them—including Owen himself—understood what he said.

'You put out the hymn books. I'll do the stove, and then we can go.' Mr Lark watched the shifting, dark-haired boy, so like himself, he thought, at the same age, rushing up and down the pews, impatient to get the job done. He lit the stove, which would warm the place by the morning. Then he let them both out. The sky was dotted with stars. He hurried back indoors with his head down. You couldn't trust the way the sky made you feel, any more than you could trust finery on a woman or the lure of the ocean or the bright lights of the Mermaid Inn.

'Come along, Owen,' he said, anxious for the son who didn't know yet what a fearful place the world could be.

At three o'clock in the morning, when the family was asleep, Owen—clutching half a bottle of communion wine from the back of the pantry—made his way down the road with his head tilted back as if to drink in the stars, each and every one of them.

It was a sharp night. His breath came out in white clouds that haunted the air above his head, and then disappeared. He shivered happily, slapped his long arms around his body. He was glad he'd got a sleeping-bag down at the beach. Glad for his matches. This was a night for fire.

He followed the bend in the road beyond the holiday cottages, creeping beneath overhanging trees, waiting with anticipation for the first glimpse of the black sea. And there it was, and he was down the road, across the car park, down the dark, shining beach where the tide was drawing out, over the low rocks that he'd have known if he'd been a blind boy, and back *home*.

Leaving the wine upon the bottom step, he crawled underneath and got everything out. There was wood for the fire, the matches, even—cheating of course, but it did help—firelighters. He broke open a slab of chocolate while the fire took off. Drank the wine which might have made the stars spin, but maybe they were doing that anyway.

He loved the black rocks and the breaking sea, the flashes of white wave-tops in the dark, the smell of salt on pebbles. He got inside his sleeping-bag and snuggled into the beach's familiar curve. He lay back and watched the stars and listened to the sea. After a long time, he got out his journal and began to write.

Writing in the journal wasn't easy. It was done in code, and it took him all his time to work it out. It looked like the biggest load of drivel in the world. But every twentieth word was the real message; hidden among the stuff about 'Mum made pie for tea', were the things he really wanted to say.

Tonight, however, the words wouldn't come. Maybe it was the wine—it needed a clear head to hide the messages properly. He chewed his pen and stopped and started and stared out at the sea. Finally, exasperated, he wrote plainly what he wanted to say, in the good light of the fire. Codes were stupid, anyway. They were all right for little kids and secret agents and if there really was a danger of having what you'd written found and read. But nobody, not that po-faced girl, *nobody* would ever think to look where he was going to hide his stuff from now. For the real reason he'd come down here was to move his hoard . . .

When the fire had nearly died and he was in danger of his early-rising father finding that he had gone, he packed up everything and climbed, with the sure-footedness of one who'd done it before, straight up the cliff behind him. The place beneath the bottom step didn't feel safe any more. Not since what-was-her-name had found him there. He struggled up and down with his things, poking them bit by bit into a long rift in the cliff which never, no matter what time of year, came out of the shadows. When he'd just about crammed the last thing—his journal—in, he sighed with relief. It would be dry, safe, hidden in there—or so he hoped. He scrambled up onto the grass at the top and lay regaining his breath.

'If I get back quick, I might even catch a bit of sleep!'

He made his way down the cliff path as fast as possible, and along the sea wall. In the car park, King Offa stalked him curiously. It was an impossible task, getting past the Mermaid Inn without that cat of Ralph's knowing about it! But he obviously decided there was no harm in Owen, for he didn't follow him up the road.

Back at home, Owen climbed up the side of the garage, across its flat roof, over his protruding bedroom sill, and in through the window. He got undressed and into bed, hoping that he didn't smell of woodsmoke, wine or the sea. He hooked his hands through the wooden bars, lay upon his back and fell asleep.

Next door, the floorboards creaked. He was just in time.

14

It was the first morning of a late half-term Owen had thought would never come. Instead of enjoying himself as he wanted to do, he raced about the village with handbills to put up about some chapel meeting, and instructions from Mother to have finished by half past twelve because Uncle and Aunty Lark were coming to lunch. With the last bill, to go outside the Mermaid Inn, he hurried down the beach road. He knew why he was running so hard. It wasn't because of what Mother had said. It was to drive from his mind Uncle's phone call first thing that morning, and what Father had said about it:

'Something wonderful has happened, son. Uncle Lark has offered to pay your school fees. You'll be starting next September, and we'd almost decided that you wouldn't be able to go.'

At the sea wall, Owen encountered Harry Llewellyn struggling with his hand cart which was made of cupboard doors, nailed together and painted red, and attached to the wheels and handle of an old pram. It overflowed with pickings from the tide. For him, at least, it had been a good morning.

On top of everything else, he had loaded a piece of furniture. Owen couldn't make out what it was. It had rows of tiny drawers with glassy knobs on them. Its varnish had curled off. It was quite bleached. It wobbled frantically, but Harry seemed determined to keep it.

'You wouldn't help me, would you?' he called. It was the

first time they had spoken. 'Pay you fifty pence . . .'

'What is it?' Owen said.

'It'll be a dental cabinet . . .'

'A *what*?'

'It's lovely, isn't it? Look what the sea's done to it. Look how those cut-glass knobs have been worn smooth as pebbles. There'd have been shiny metal instruments in all those drawers, once upon a time. Bits of drills and hooks and things. I wonder if I'll ever get them open.'

Stuffing the last handbill into his back pocket, and putting everything to do with Uncle and Aunty out of his mind, Owen held the cabinet while Harry steered the cart through the car park and onto the track.

'What will you do with it?' he asked.

'Oh, something will suggest itself.' Harry laughed, and shrugged.

They passed Griselda's tent, shaking in the wind that blew through the willows, which were bare now. It shook the cabinet as well, and Harry had to stop the cart. Owen helped him. They straightened everything, and trudged on.

Owen had always known that Harry lived somewhere on Cwmgwyntog Common. But he'd never thought much about exactly where. They were half way down the track now. The common's reeds lay as flat as the hair on some wet dog's back. Harry stopped. Owen saw a parting between the reeds.

'That's where we've got to go,' said Harry. 'Fox's track. We might have to do some carrying, if it's too much of a bog. I can usually get the cart through, but we're a bit weighed down today.'

With Owen pushing from behind, they got the cart right out onto the common before the wheels gave out, sinking into the mulch beneath them.

'Oh, well,' Harry said, eyeing Owen's thin, gangling body, and then the cabinet. 'Do you think you can manage?'

Owen flushed. 'Of course I can!'

They got the cabinet off the cart. Hauled it until they were in the trees by Nyth-y-dryw, where they put it down and Harry pointed out the ruined, ivy-covered wall of what had long-since been another cottage. They got it as far, next time, as Nona's dead, stark tree, stripped of its bark, and then, finally, up to some rusty, corrugated, moss-covered sheds.

'Well done! That deserves a bit more than fifty pence,' Harry exclaimed, fishing about in his pocket. 'We've got it home!'

Owen took Harry's money. He looked around him. It was funny what some people called a home... They were out from the trees. The ground was covered with rambling ivy, dead bracken and nettles. Like something from a fairy-tale—half-covered with the enchanted growth of a hundred years—stood a ruined caravan with three, unfairy-like, breeze block steps up to its door.

'That's ... where you live?'

Harry laughed at him. 'Home from home, that's right!'

Owen stared at the caravan in unbelief. It was so old. So overgrown. Nobody could live in there.

'There's a track up to the road behind the sheds,' Harry said, as if to prove that this was civilization, really. 'I get in and out on it by van, though you wouldn't notice anything from the main road, with the trees and all. I've even got electricity down here, so I'm quite comfortable. I work in the sheds. Help me get the rest of the stuff, and I'll show you.'

They struggled back to the hand cart. Two trips and the job was done. The bits of rope, bottles, tin cans, scraps of driftwood were all stacked outside the sheds, waiting, as Harry put it, for 'something' to be done with them. Peeping up between blades of dying undergrowth, Owen saw other bits and pieces that were obviously waiting too, and looked as though they'd been doing it for a long time.

'We won't leave our cabinet like them,' Harry said, following Owen's stare. 'We'll get it inside right away.'

A tin door stood ajar. Harry struggled to open it further,

muttering as it creaked that he was *sure* he hadn't left it like that. Owen hardly took in what he said. An altogether foreign smell, flat and musty, had come out to greet him.

'Come on,' Harry said, as if he hadn't noticed it. With Owen's help, he hauled the cabinet into the dark.

At first Owen could see nothing. His nose quivered with animal wariness. He tripped over a heavy tub and something wet splashed him. His jacket caught on a hook and tore. Between them they got the cabinet to the far end of the shed and set it down. Owen's eyes began to accommodate the dark. He turned to see what the tub had contained.

A white ghost hovered, just behind him ...

Harry flicked a switch. There was a quiver, a hiccup, then a long, fluorescent tube burst into life. The white ghost turned into a huge chunk of chicken wire wrapped up in—what was it?—clay and strips of sacking? It stood on a floor which was covered with pale dust and buckets of mucky water and pots of paint. Owen examined his wet trouser—at least it wasn't the paint—and his jacket which had been torn by the chicken wire. On the walls all around him were shelves full of pots, dusty tins, books, tools, pens and pencils, a shotgun and some nasty looking snares, chunks of wood, even a glowing aquarium with tropical fish. From the roof hung coils of rope, old lamps, strips of seaweed, a rusty bird's cage.

'What do you think?' said Harry, unwrapping the bandages of sacking to reveal the top half of a glistening, long-haired woman with enormous breasts. The woman and the sacking were wet. She was putty coloured.

'Clay, see,' explained Harry. 'I have to keep her wet, or I can't work the stuff.'

Owen stared at the clay. It had dried out on the woman's hair, which was crumbling at the ends. The musty smell was even stronger now. He breathed in its fine dust, coughed. The stuff was everywhere.

'I didn't wrap it properly this time,' said Harry. 'I'll have to do those bits again.' He touched the woman's hair, which fell into his hand. She's a figurehead. You know, like they had on the fronts of sailing ships. She's a special commission for a maritime museum. I'll make a mould from her and then I can run off as many as they want.

'Run off?'

'In fibre-glass, boyo.'

'Fibre-glass?'

Harry began to explain what fibre-glass was, but Owen hardly heard, so lost was he among everything around him. The world of Father and his handbills, Mother and the visiting Larks, was a million miles away. He began to walk about, smell, touch, pry; Harry's voice went on and on while Owen explored the whole shed from end to end. Eventually, he returned to Harry, who stood in front of a wrinkled screen, which had probably come out of the sea as well. Harry was saying he'd be making fairground horses next. Owen's interest was caught by the screen. It had once been decorated with dolphins or mermaids or seals; the thing was so worn it was hard to see. Owen put his face up close to it.

And two eyes met his. *Real* eyes, not mermaids' ones. Glistening eyes they were, peering at him through holes in the screen.

'Are you all right?' said Harry.

The eyes met Owen's and didn't flinch. It was he who looked down first—and saw wellington boots protruding underneath the screen.

'I . . . I mean . . . I . . .'

'You look pale. It's too stuffy in here, you need fresh air. The trouble is I'm used to it. I don't realize . . .'

But before Harry got any further, Nona Davies stepped straight out. She wore a cardigan and a pair of holey jeans. Her face was white as the clay dust and Owen knew, from the tilt of her chin, that she'd decided she'd give herself up rather than be told on by him. Grudgingly, he admired her for it.

'Well . . . !' Harry's words dried up. 'No wonder the door

was open when I thought I'd left it shut!'

'I'm sorry ... I didn't open the door ... I was just walking and it swung in the wind and I was curious. I haven't touched anything. Really, I haven't ...'

Her voice faltered. She couldn't look either of them in the eye. She was a funny little thing; so grave—private somehow and cautious—that Owen could have believed, despite the size of her, that she was years older than him.

'We never hear you from our cottage,' she said, as if in justification. 'I came along before. I thought all these sheds were ruins ... I never realized anybody lived here ...'

Owen sympathized. Who would have realized? 'Oh, I'm very quiet,' Harry explained. 'My van's parked up the track, and the wind blows any noise I do make the other way. Don't look so worried. I won't eat you up.' His eyes softened. 'How's your Mum ...?'

She didn't like him asking that. Again, she couldn't meet his eyes. 'Oh, she's fine,' she muttered, and she smiled a silly smile, which reminded Owen of Aunty Lark when she was saying one thing and thinking another.

Aunty Lark!

'What's the time?' he cried out. 'Oh, good grief! Mother's expecting me back for lunch ...!'

Harry dug out a watch, on half a plastic strap.

'A quarter past one!' wailed Owen, and Nona was all but forgotten.

'It's my fault,' Harry said, looking for his jacket and van keys. 'You must let me drive you home.'

'Thanks,' Owen said. He wasn't going to argue about it. How could he have let this happen?

They hurried outside. Harry shut the doors properly, so that they wouldn't swing again. The old world had come back so quickly, that Owen didn't know what had hit him. But he *did* know what he'd be in for when he got back home!

'You come again,' Harry was calling to Nona who blinked in the daylight as if she, too, couldn't quite keep up

110

with the pace of things. 'Any time you want. Don't be afraid to ask. Have a bit of clay, if you like. Make yourself something with it.'

She ran off from them, through the trees towards Nyth-y-dryw. Owen followed Harry up to the van. He wished he didn't have to go home, late or not. He wished he could have a bit of clay as well. They climbed into what looked like a series of large, gun-metal dustbins welded together. Owen tried not to think about Uncle and Aunty Lark. Harry reversed, turned and aimed them for home.

'I make model ships,' Owen said, trying to hang onto something that was slipping away from him. 'I'd like to show them to you.'

'You must bring them down,' said Harry, as if he wasn't just being polite. They lurched up the track, dodging low-hanging trees. 'Bring them tomorrow, if you don't have anything else to do. I'm always around, just so long as you let me get on when I tell you to.'

They reached the main road. Harry shot along it at his uttermost speed. He turned by the signpost, drove past the school and pulled up right outside Owen's front gate. It had all happened so fast. It couldn't have been more than five minutes since Owen had looked at Harry's watch. He jumped out onto the road. He was coming in to land after a long trip out across uncharted oceans to foreign parts.

'See you, then,' he said.

'See you,' Harry replied and drove away, his exhaust popping right back up the road.

Owen swung open the gate and began up the front path. Despite everything, he whistled. For what had Harry said, that had put worries in the shade?

'You could have a go if you wanted to, with a bit of clay. Have a go tomorrow, if you come down.'

And what had he replied?

'Thanks. I will.'

15

Father's Aunty Lark was a straight-backed paragon, with a passion for knitting and male voice choirs. His Uncle Lark was without any passions at all, as far as Owen could see. He had a ski-slope of a nose, loose skin on his neck, and pale blue eyes which seemed to have no lashes.

These eyes hooked upon Owen now, as he came in through the door and all of them sat around the table, lunch finished in front of them and Mother pouring cups of tea.

'Your meal has frozen,' she complained, her face pale and her voice sharp, for she never was her usual self when Uncle and Aunty came visiting. 'Where have you been?'

'On the beach,' white-lied Owen, 'I didn't realize the time.'

'But you *knew* Uncle and Aunty would be here,' she said. 'Really, Owen, you're without excuse! You don't deserve any lunch at all. Apologize to Aunty and Uncle straight away!'

Owen sat at his place, where a best dinner plate heaped full of roast potatoes and good Welsh lamb congealed in scummy gravy. 'I'm sorry,' he muttered—and he was, in more ways than one.

'Couldn't you heat it up for him?' Beca dared to plead on his behalf.

Maybe Mother would have done, but 'Of course she couldn't!' Aunty chipped in, who'd never had children of her own, and couldn't remember being young and hungry. 'He might be growing up...' her eyes flickered over his expanding frame, 'but he's lucky your mother hasn't taken it away!'

Owen tried to shrink down in his chair, as if to avoid the way Aunty took him in from head to toe.

'I hope you're working hard, as well as going to the beach,' Uncle Lark leaned forward and said, 'it means a lot to your father to see you go to the same school as him.'

Owen muttered something about 'doing the best I can'. He shrank down even further.

'We've brought you some little gifts,' Aunty said, when he had eaten his cold lunch and his plate was taken away. 'We've all been waiting for you to come in so that we could hand them out. These silks are for you, Beca. You must embroider something nice with them before we come again. We shall ask to see. And Owen, seeing as where you're going, this is for you...'

She leaned across the table proffering a brown paper bag. 'Thank you,' Owen said, knowing even before he opened the thing that it contained a piece of her knitting, and when he took it out that the colours on the scarf had to be those of the dreaded school.

'You must be so excited,' Aunty said, poking beneath his polite smile with her beady eyes.

Beca saved him from answering by scraping back her chair and beginning to clear the table, without even being asked. Aunty, who couldn't bear to sit around if there was women's work to supervise, sprang to her feet. 'Here, let me...'

Father got up too. It was time for him and Uncle to adjourn. Once Owen would have been left behind because he was a little boy, but now...

'Won't you join us, Owen?' Father said.

'We've got to get to know each other better...' Uncle blinked at him with those lashless eyes, 'since you'll be living with us while you're at school...'

Owen followed them into the sitting-room. A smoky

fire had been lit in Uncle's honour. Armchairs were placed around it. The three of them sat down. Uncle Lark and Father began to talk. Father tossed back his hair and made circles with his hands, the way he did when he got into the pulpit. Uncle listened, like nobody else who Father knew. Father looked relaxed and happy. He'd always been closer to his uncle than his dad, who'd wanted him to use his long legs for Wales on the rugby field. It had been Uncle who'd understood him wanting to become a minister instead.

Neither of them noticed Owen any more, which suited him fine. He snuggled down in the deepest armchair, nearly dropping off to sleep. He day-dreamed about going down to Harry's shed again and trying out that clay, about exploring the rest of the common. It wasn't the lost lunch that he could almost smell, but the damp grasses and decaying leaves. It was the white dust that was still in his nostrils. His fingers itched to get at that wet sacking, that smooth body of clay ...

When the washing-up was done, Aunty reappeared with the knitting that was her trade-mark. Beca dutifully brought in her new silks, and a piece of canvas that Mother had found. Mother collapsed, worn out by the weight of all the advice that Aunty had given her, particularly on the bringing up of Owen.

'I've just been telling Mary,' Aunty said, moving with ease onto a favourite subject. 'A proper chapel should have a choir ...'

The afternoon wore on. The fire burned low and one by one, the adults fell asleep. Owen fingered in his pocket the five pounds that Uncle had given him 'to start a fund for school books,' turning over and over as he did so his grand plan to run away. It was always the same when Aunty and Uncle came. He always returned to it.

Owen had conceived the plan when Father had first broached the idea of him going away to school. Father had stood in front of him, positively glowing at the proud thought of his son at his old school, and Owen had known without ever having seen the place, that he couldn't go to it, or live with Uncle and Aunty. He had begun to scheme.

Running away was a funny business. You could plan it for years and never do it and it didn't matter, because the planning was enough. Owen felt *safe* now that he had his store, knew his sleeping bag, money and food were waiting for him. Despite the time wasted on Greek, despite all his father's expectations, he knew that the dreaded school wouldn't get him. And if, as now, the assurance faded, he could buy chocolate or a map or a torch and take it to the secret beach and get everything out, write up his journal, make more plans...

'Where are you going?' Beca whispered as he tiptoed out. He didn't answer, just put his finger to his lips, just whispered, *'Cover for me,'* knowing that whatever she thought of the risks he took, she would.

It would get dark soon. Owen set off briskly for the beach, knowing that he was mad to think he'd get away with it, but that he couldn't have stayed in that stuffy room a minute more.

Half way down, he thought he smelt burning on the wind. The sun had gone and the common, with its flanks of cliff on either side, was quiet and empty. Maybe the Parrys had lit an early Guy Fawkes bonfire for that little runt Cledwyn. It would have been just like them to get theirs in before everyone else.

Down in the car park Owen realized that he'd got it wrong. He couldn't smell the smoke any more because the breeze, as always, blew the other way. But looking along the track, what he saw made his heart skip a beat.

Flickering against the distant trees, flames were jumping out of Wren's Nest's chimney! Handfuls of black smoke, spangled with red bits, were shooting up into the air and no

115

darkness could hide them...

Owen hammered on the door of the Mermaid Inn. Ralph answered it. He'd obviously, like Owen's family, been asleep. King Offa stretched himself, sleepy too, beneath his feet.

'We've got to call the fire-brigade!' Owen yelled, making for the telephone on the wall. 'Wren's Nest's burning!'

'What?'

'It's on fire! Wren's Nest is on fire...!'

The 'Great Fire of Cwmgwyntog Common', as the village persisted in calling it, was an embarrassment to Owen for ever more. Ralph, as was his way, phoned not only the fire brigade but half the village, bringing car after car of fire fighters down the hill. The fire brigade sent out two engines, all for what turned out to be, in the words of the chief, 'a simple chimney fire' that was over the worst by the time that they arrived. Even Mother, Father and Beca, with Uncle and Aunty in tow, arrived to 'see what we can do'.

Nona's mum stood down at her front gate, fielding offers of help until she looked as though she could drop, and offering awkward apologies for all the trouble caused. 'It was an accident... We don't get the sun in any more and I was worried about keeping us warm... It's so dark and damp, and I thought... We're quite all right now, really we are... There's nothing to worry about...'

The firemen tramped in, snuffed out the last of the fire, and tramped out again. Gradually, with nothing to do or to be seen, people drifted off. The fire engines departed.

Mother and Beca were the last to go. Father had taken Aunty and Uncle back up by car, but Mother, who wanted to make sure things really *were* all right, said that she would walk. Owen, hiding in the bushes and dying a hundred deaths, listened while she explained to Nona and her mum that it was he who'd thought the place was burning down and had called for the fire brigade, and that she felt respon-

116

sible for putting things right.

'It's bad enough to have a chimney fire, without all this fuss as well,' she said. 'You must have a dreadful mess inside, after all those men tramped in and out. Can't we stay and help you clear it up?'

From over the garden wall an unexpected voice humphed its disapproval. 'They could help *me*, if they wanted to do something useful,' Miss Parry muttered from somewhere in her garden. 'It's about time those chapel people spared a thought for me. All this fussing over newcomers! They should live next door to them! They don't think of no one but themselves when they light those great big fires of theirs. They don't think where the wind blows all their soot and muck, or what it's like having half the village and all those fire engines mashing up my bit . . .'

'Why, Miss Parry,' Mother began, but before she got any further Miss Parry had gone in and slammed her door. She'd said her piece and didn't want to know what anyone else had to say.

'We can manage,' Nona's mum said. 'Thank you for offering, but really we can.'

'I've been meaning to come down,' Mother said, lowering her voice as if she thought Miss Parry still might hear. 'Has there been any news of the little boy?'

There was a pause. 'My Cody's staying where he is,' Nona's mum said quickly. 'It seems the best. Thank you for asking. We've got to get in now. It's getting cold . . .'

Owen heard Beca and Mother as they went past. 'That's how Nona is at school,' Beca was saying. 'It's not just me. She won't talk to anyone. You can't tell what she's thinking. Even in Mrs Thomas's classes, she just stares at the wall . . .'

Their voices faded. Owen climbed out of the bushes. The ground all around him was a quagmire and his feet squelched as he picked his way out of it. He did turn once to look back at the house. He saw a yellow window full of light upstairs, and Nona silhouetted. He knew, despite the night,

117

that she could see him, the boy who'd sent for the fire-brigade, who'd brought all the village down. She drew the curtains quickly and he turned away and shivered. More than ever now, she'd got it in for him. They couldn't get it right, could they?

16

When Nona came down next morning the first grey log of the day was already on the wood-burning stove, beads of sap rising on it and moss curling. Mum, in coat and wellington boots, was closing the iron door and twisting the ring that let the air in, forcing yellow flames from the barren log rather like rabbits from a magician's hat.

'We'll have to watch that chimney from now on!' Nona eyed the yellow flames anxiously, her mind still on last night's fire.

'Oh, it'll be all right,' Mum said. There was something careless about her, now that Cody had gone. Something empty and ghostly that made Nona shiver inside. 'I've got to get on with my typing. You'll give everybody breakfast, won't you?'

Most mornings nowadays, Nona awoke to the sound of the front door shutting and Mum sneaking beneath the window on her way up to the summerhouse where she'd set up her typewriter and was, apparently, working on her first home-typing commission.

Nona would have been relieved that Mum was doing something about their finances, if she'd believed that was what was going on. Instead she thought Mum wanted the excuse to get away from them—more than that, to close her mind to what had happened.

For when Nona tried to talk about what Uncle Brady had said in the letter they'd received—*Don't think I'll ever let you have Cody again'*—or to say that Emlyn Hughes had offered to 'help' or that Ralph had given her the address of a good solicitor, all Mum would say was, 'I can't think about it now. I'm busy. I have my typing ...'

'Do you *have* to type today?' Nona said. 'We hardly have any food. We ought to go to town.'

Mum sighed. 'I can't go to town,' she said. 'I'm too busy. You'll have to do it.'

Nona sighed as well. Everybody else went shopping with their mums at half-term. Why'd they always got to be the ones who had a rotten time? 'You might have lost Cody, but you've still got us, in case you hadn't noticed!' she thought.

'There's only two pounds in the purse,' she said out loud, 'and I can't draw out your Social Security from the Post Office, so you'll have to come.'

The town bus was twice-daily, thirty years old, blissfully ignorant of the advantages of suspension. It had about half as many seats as were needed. Mum, with Bryn wriggling on her lap, sat at the back, wedged between brown old men with trays of eggs and baskets of vegetables, who conversed over her head in their mother tongue.

The rest of the family had to stand. It was a relief when they were all tipped out in front of the stone Town Hall where, behind the council offices and police headquarters and rows of plaques commemorating the deaths of lifeboat men, a huge, breezy, white-tiled market hall was teeming with activity.

Mum got the money from the Post Office, then disappeared with Bryn and Poppy, saying she couldn't abide the crowd. Nona did the shopping and made Sharon carry it. Usually, Sharon would have complained, but since Cody'd gone, she'd been a different girl. Dreamy, just like Poppy. Ghostly like Mum.

At Emlyn Hughes's stall, they bumped into Harry

Llewellyn buying bacon pieces from a stripey-aproned butcher's boy.

'Poor old you!' he said to Sharon, looking at her bulging carrier bags, and then at Nona as if he realised how bossy she could be. 'Now me, I only have to shop for one, and that's bad enough...'

A girlfriend came through the crowd and took his arm. 'Shop for how many, you old goat?'

'Well, sometimes for two...'

She laughed at him, and they moved away. What she saw in him—what any of his girlfriends saw—Nona couldn't imagine. He looked so dishevelled and old and gaunt. But when he passed her by he raised his sea-green eyes and winked at her.

And perhaps there *was* something about him after all. Perhaps he wasn't *that* old. Sharon didn't comment, after he'd gone. She didn't even ask Nona who he was, and when Nona told her anyhow, she didn't answer. The last thing Nona heard, as they disappeared through the crowd, was the girlfriend's voice:

'Aren't they the ones whose house burnt down...?'

House burnt down indeed! Nona shook her head as she bought bacon pieces too. 'Uncle Emlyn said you had a fire last night...' the butcher's boy began.

She moved on to the bakery. Everybody there seemed to know as well. It got her free bread, even though she said she had a home to go to. She took her bread and marvelled at the speed at which news travelled.

Sharon followed her, still without complaint. When they passed the fruit stall she didn't whine for oranges. When they struggled between rails of clothing she didn't put in a plea for what everyone else at school was wearing. Nona wondered if she'd ever be her old self again.

'Hi there, Sharon!' The crowd brought someone forward, from Sharon's class at school. 'I heard about your fire. What happened?'

'It was only a chimney fire!' Nona said crossly, on Sharon's behalf. 'It was really nothing.'

'That's not what I heard—you had two fire engines down...'

'Only because Owen Lark phoned the fire-brigade!'

'They say Miss Parry did it.'

'Did what?'

'Set your house on fire, of course.'

They met Mum in the teashop next to the Post Office, all of them crowded with their shopping, around a table that was only made for two.

'I wish we'd still got Uncle Brady's big green car,' said Poppy, as if his wasn't an unmentionable name. 'I wish we didn't have to get these bags on the bus, and then carry them all the way down the hill, at the other end.'

'I wish we could play on the swings and slides,' said Bryn, who'd been tied to Mum's side ever since they'd come into town, as if she feared that he, too, might be stolen.

'I wish we could stay at home,' said Mum.

Nona heaped her cup with sugar 'to cheer her up'. Sharon stared off into space. 'Aren't they the ones,' two women at the next table whispered all too loudly, 'who tried to set the Parry woman's house on fire...'

Bryn got out his new, Welsh dragon-shaped water pistol and hit each of them, in turn, in the eye.

It was a relief to get home; to shut the front door on the outrageous outside world, put on the kettle and swear never to go out again.

'I can't say what I wouldn't like to do to Bryn sometimes,' said Sharon. 'He's so embarrassing.'

'I can't say what I wouldn't like to do to that Owen Lark!' Nona said.

'He probably thought that he was helping.' Mum emptied shopping bags all over the kitchen table.

'Funny sort of help,' said Nona, putting tins away and glaring pointedly at Sharon, who turned away from them and sank into a chair next door.

'It always is a funny sort of help,' said Mum. 'It's better to be left alone.'

Like a form of mockery, there was a knock on the front door. Mum groaned. 'Sharon can get it,' Nona quickly said. 'She's not doing anything else.'

Sharon went. When she returned, Ralph came in behind her.

'Whatever is it?' Mum looked awkward, trapped. She didn't want to see anyone. She'd had enough.

'I've been waiting for you to come in,' Ralph said. 'I've got a proposition to put to you. It's about King Offa.'

'King Offa?' said Mum.

'He's not really my cat,' explained Ralph, spreading out his hands. 'I found him in my car when I moved down here. Somewhere on the border he must have got in, when I stopped for petrol. A real messy stray, he was.'

'Oh,' said Mum, in a voice that would have put off anyone else.

'I'll be straight with you,' said Ralph, undaunted. 'We don't hit it off. He gets bored on his own. He needs a family. He'd be a great guard and you could do with one with *her* next door. He's a right old warrior. Would you like to have him?'

'Would we *what*?' Mum said, as if she couldn't believe what he was saying.

'He's devoted to your lot,' Ralph urged. 'You must have noticed the way he follows them up and down.'

'But we couldn't afford to feed another mouth!' Mum exclaimed. 'It's hard enough as it is.'

'That wouldn't be a problem...' Ralph had anticipated this. 'Emlyn says he'll help with scraps. It won't cost you a penny.'

'*Please, Mum, please...!*' burst in Sharon unexpectedly. Her eyes were suddenly sparkling, the way they always used

123

to be when she wanted something badly.

'Please . . .' Bryn and even Poppy joined in too.

'But we can't!' Mum protested.

'Why not,' argued Sharon, 'if we don't have to pay for food?'

'He's outside,' threw in Ralph. 'Come and have a look at him.'

They all trooped outside. Offa sat on the path, every inch the proud warrior, refusing to look at them until they invited him in. Sharon plucked him up and held him close and made extravagant promises to Mum about *never* being unhelpful again. Bryn and Poppy joined in.

'Nice to see them happy, isn't it?' Ralph said, conspiratorially.

'They've looked so miserable ever since that little chap of yours went away.'

And suddenly Nona realized what he and Emlyn were up to. They were doing what they'd tried to do before. They were trying to be kind, and it was very simple to them. The kids at Nyth-y-dryw had lost their brother—they were giving them a cat instead! Oh, she wanted to shout at Ralph for thinking anything could be as simple as that. But maybe—with Sharon at least—maybe, this time, they'd got it right. Who was she to say? Maybe this wild and strange and kingly cat would make some difference . . .

Mum must have thought the same thing too. Either that, or she didn't have the energy to say 'no'. For, unexpectedly, she said, 'Oh, all right. If you're really sure you want to give him away. We'll take him. Thank you very much.'

Nona couldn't believe her ears. Sharon clutched King Offa possessively as if she'd never let him go. But Offa wasn't having that. He jumped out of Sharon's arms and strode in independently. Bryn and Poppy, like courtiers, followed him.

'Thank you, Mum,' Sharon said, 'oh, thank you . . . !'

'Thank Ralph,' Mum said, shakily. 'Not me.'

17

Owen got up early. It was Saturday, which meant Greek, and he didn't feel as though he could bear it today. He dressed. It was hard to explain, even to himself. He felt restless, wide awake. Larger than life. It was the end of a half-term spent almost entirely down at Harry's. His absences from home had engendered a whole string of lies, and the lies now bred within him positive rebellion. He didn't want to struggle with a stupid, defunct language any more! The thought of Greek made him want to burst. He wouldn't do it, oh he wouldn't!

Not knowing quite what he did want to do, Owen crept out of his bedroom and down the stairs.

'You're up early, son!' Father opened his study door.

'Oh,' said Owen. 'I couldn't sleep.'

'Where are you going?'

'I . . . I just thought I'd sit out, and watch the sun rise.'

'We'll do it together, then . . .'

Rebelliously, Owen scuffed his heels against the wall as they sat looking beyond the village, up at the mountain. White dots of sheep were moving about up there. The first hints of sun were in the sky. In half an hour, the whole mountain would be ablaze with it. They'd be able to pick out almost every dip and dell and clump of boulders and snaking lane up there.

'I'm going back in,' said Owen. What point was there in sitting here, with Father at his side?

Over breakfast, Owen asked his mother, 'Would you, Mother, would you say you are a *happy* person?'

Mother looked surprised. 'Well, yes,' she said, automatically. 'Of course.'

'But were you happy when you were *my* age?'

'I had a little hat with feathers in it, when I was your age,' Mother said, remembering. 'Such a pretty thing, but it meant too much to me. Things always do when you're young. You're so full of foolishness and hope. I wouldn't be your age again for anything...'

Owen would have asked her, if he'd dared, if she'd ever felt angry and rebellious. But it was a stupid question. She wasn't like that.

'I'm going upstairs to make the beds,' she was saying now. 'Put your knife and fork and plate in the sink, won't you, when you've finished?'

'Greek in half an hour,' mumbled Father, heading for his study.

As soon as they'd left the room, Owen stole an apple and some toast and slipped out of the back door. It was as if there was no choice and that he *had* to go. He cut down the back garden, across the school playing field, over the main road, towards the mountain.

He didn't know what had come over him in just the space of a few short days. He'd always managed to do the things he wanted, but he'd done them secretly. Now it was almost as if he didn't care. He felt like an animal running wild, as if the house, the family, could no longer contain him. He was too big, too loud, too alive even for the little, secret beach today. It was the mountain he wanted, with the hills rolling to the Severn Bridge and England and the rest of the world beyond. Only the windswept, open mountain would do...

It was a nice day. Bright and fresh, though with a hint of rain to come, out over the sea. It took him an hour to get up where he wanted to be and then, in his best school sports shoes, he began to run—not fast and tidy like Beca, but in huge, loping, wolfish strides. He didn't know how long he ran, dodging around bogs and over stones, laughing as he added ruined trousers, socks and shoes to the catalogue of misdemeanours that the day was running up.

But it was what he'd come here for. And at last, exhausted and aching and his anger loosed, he could *breathe* again. Only then, collar turned up against the wind, did he allow himself to collapse upon a blue lump of granite at the side of the lane.

He was on the brow of a small hillock. Below him lay the sea and the headland rising out of Cwmgwyntog Common, and Jerico, sprawled along the main road. He tried to pick out Harry's sheds, but a cyclist caught his eye instead, struggling up towards him from the village.

Everybody came up here; walkers, kids from school, parties looking for picnic spots with a good view. But Owen had never seen a cyclist trying it before. The lanes were too steep. If you wanted the outside world you went along the main roads, and if you were looking for a good day out you'd never lug a bike up here.

The cyclist must have realized that by now. He was off his bike and pushing. Grey clouds scudded inland, over his head. It was like that by the sea, weather changing all the time, nothing certain. The cyclist had nearly reached Owen now. His covered head was bowed with the effort he was making. The huge bundle on his carrier was tugged by the wind.

Owen marvelled at his stamina. He was close enough now for Owen to hear him puffing. 'Good morning,' he greeted him cheerfully. The cyclist looked up, surprised. So absorbed had he been that he hadn't noticed Owen until now. Owen saw his face, red from exertion, wet from crying.

It was Nona Davies.

Owen couldn't believe it. Nona's eyes were round and horrified and she, obviously, couldn't believe it either. There

127

were probably five hundred children living in Jerico who could have chosen to spend this bit of their half-term holiday up here. So why did it have to be her—again? It was almost as though ...

'You're following me,' she got in before he could. 'Everywhere I go, you're there as well. Why can't you stop it?'

He glared into her indignant face. 'It's not *me* who's following *you!* Why can't *you* go away? Why are *you* always following *me?* It's ridiculous—a little kid like you ...'

'I'm not a little kid, I'm thirteen!'

'Oh yes, then why are you crying like a baby?'

'I'm not crying! Don't you know what sore eyes from the wind look like?' She stared with old woman's flinty eyes that certainly looked as though they'd never break out in tears.

'Well,' Owen conceded, 'maybe you're not crying. But where do you think you're going on that bike?'

'It's nothing to do with you!!' The eyes *blazed* at him now.

'Then there's no point warning you about the weather,' Owen said. 'No point telling you it gets even steeper at the next hill. No point ...'

'I don't need your advice! We've had enough of you! And next time you see our chimney smoking, don't think you have to tell everybody, and if the next hill's steep, you don't have to tell me so. *You can just leave me alone!*'

She got on her bike and without so much as looking back at him, freewheeled down the other side of the hillock, until it began to rise up to the next ridge. Owen watched her struggling. He got out the apple from his pocket and ate it. Then he ate the toast. She pushed her bike right up that slope, and disappeared over the top. Owen tried to put her out of his mind as well. But he kept imagining her coming up from the village, struggling with a bike that he'd never have had the persistence to get up that far. She was tough, all

128

right. And where *was* she going . . . ?

'She's not running away!?'

It was too awful, to think that she just might be copying him in this as well. Owen threw his apple core away. The sea below him had turned the colour of dirty washing-up water. Heavy spots of rain fell onto his head.

'I think I'll go home,' he said.

It was hard to feel wild and strong and free in a down-pour of rain. And the rain around here was wetter—Owen was sure of it—than anywhere else he'd been. He got up from his stony resting place. Lunch was over. Within minutes he was walking through a slate-grey, downpouring afternoon, with no shelter in sight between here and Jerico. He turned once, to look behind him. No return of Nona Davies. The rain came down harder. Cut down to size by the elements, his rebellion over for today, he left her to it and trudged back home.

18

The rain blew noisily onto the back of Nona's anorak. She felt it dripping off the bottom edge onto very sodden trousers. The view in front of her was one of uninterrupted gloom, a long road over undulating hills which were the back way to England. A long, grey road along which she had to go to get Cody back.

The bundle of Cody's clothing fell off the bike into a puddle. Nona dismounted, picked it up, tied it on again. She wiped the rain out of her face. This was ridiculous! She'd known it all along. She wouldn't get beyond these hills, let alone to London. Not on a bicycle. Not without money for food, and places to stay and a map to show her where she was going. And how would she get Cody back again if she *did* reach London? What would she do with him? She couldn't bring him home on the bike. They were bound to be caught, bound to get into trouble. There were no hidden back ways outside London, no empty hills like these, into which they could escape. Oh, it was stupid, *stupid*, coming up here. What was she doing?

The rain came on heavier. The clouds were so low that she couldn't see the ocean any more, or the houses of Jerico. She'd have gone back, but she couldn't bear the thought of Owen Lark crowing, 'I told you so,' as she went by.

She got on her bicycle and struggled on. Maybe it wasn't stupid. Maybe if she wanted it enough, she'd get there. Maybe, somehow, Cody would know that she was coming; he'd be waiting for her and when she saw him it would be all right—she'd *know* she'd done the right thing.

The wind blew at her. The bicycle shook like a winter leaf. The road sloped down again. She began to freewheel. It twisted and at least the weather was behind her, wind, rain, gravity rolling her on towards a horizon that never lightened.

A crossroads came into sight, with a telephone box and a signpost which warned against a steep alternative route down to Jerico: DANGEROUS! PERGYL! NOT SUITABLE FOR HEAVY VEHICLES!

The words stopped her. She couldn't bring herself to pass them, or the lane that branched off by their side. She hated warning signs. The hills, Jerico, Cwmgwyntog Common, the whole of her life, even the wind and rain, had DANGEROUS! hanging over it . . .

Defiantly, she shouted not only at the elements, but at rotten Uncle Brady, Sharon who was all over that wretched cat now, Mum who'd buried herself in typing . . . *'I don't care if it's dangerous! I've got to show Cody that someone in our rotten family cares!'*

But they were empty words, and she knew it. The road went up again and she didn't have the strength. She untied Cody's bundle, flung down the bicycle, shut herself away from the weather in the telephone box. Opened the bundle and buried her face in Cody's wet clothes.

The smell of him still lingered. Poor Cody, who Mum might never even see again—perhaps he wasn't waiting for them, perhaps he was all right. Uncle Brady wasn't always angry and horrible. He could be nice, occasionally. Perhaps Cody didn't even miss them . . .

At last, Nona raised her head. It was pointless trying any more to cry. The tears just wouldn't come, she could feel the dead weight of them, all stuck inside. Bleakly, she emerged from the telephone box, fumbling as she did so for her word book and pen, as if putting something down was her only hope of consolation. But the word she wrote was washed straight off the page by the lashing rain...

Swearing she'd never use the stupid book again, she got back on her bicycle. By surely the bleakest telephone box in the whole of Wales, she gave up, and aimed for home.

'So what if it's dangerous!' she thought, as she passed the warning sign. 'I don't care. Nothing matters. It's *over* ...'

She freewheeled past stone walls and huddling sheep. The wind blew across the open mountain side, cutting into her. The bicycle shook as it plunged down. Her hands and face were completely numbed by the cold and rain. Time seemed to have lost its hold on her. This might have been an hour or a split second or forever.

At long last, the lane fell upon Jerico, straight as a Roman road, with no regard for obstacles. Nona saw roof-tops below her. She hurtled towards them, surely on the verge of flight. 'Even if a car came up here now,' she thought, exhilarated, 'I wouldn't care...!'

A van appeared. And it was one thing to *think* you didn't care, but at the last minute, beyond thinking, Nona swerved to avoid it and careered across the lane, over a turfy wall, down into a dip which was full of bracken and thick, moorland grass. She did not land on her head. She lay on the bracken with her bicycle on top of her, its back wheel spinning beside her ear.

The van pulled up. The noise of it sounded very far away. Nona heard the door go and a voice cursing. The man's face was too close as he bent to pluck the bicycle off her—or was it that she was too confused—for her to see him properly. He got her out of the ditch. 'Thank God you're all right,' he said. He got her to his van. They were half way through the village before Nona realised from the golden earring that he was Harry. He was tight-lipped, silent, grey. She'd frightened him. His hands upon the steering wheel were shaking. She was shaking too.

'Perhaps I ought to take you to the hospital,' he said, at

last. 'I'm useless about things like this. I don't even know what to do when I cut my finger...'

'I'm sure I haven't b-broken anything...' Nona's voice trembled at the thought of hospital. 'I'm sure I'm all right.'

'What were you playing at?' he said.

'I d-don't know. P-please don't tell my mum...'

He took in the muddy sight of her. 'You'd better come down with me and get yourself cleaned up, then... Don't worry. I won't let her see you shaking like that. I dare say she's got enough to worry about without you.'

Harry took down rows of washing which hung over his tiny stove, and cleared magazines off a split horse-hair sofa. He moved a stenching pot of what looked as though it might be stew to the side of the stove. Then he filled a kettle at a brown sink which was choked with washing-up, bent down, opened the fire door, blew fresh life onto the sticks inside, put the kettle on top.

'Don't just stand there. Come in.'

Nona wasn't shaking any more, just numb. 'I'm sorry,' she said, for all the trouble that she was causing.

'Don't you worry.' Harry looked her over, carefully. 'You're safe, that's what matters, and you won't do it again, will you? Come on. Sit on the sofa where I've made a place for you. Hang up your wet anorak. That's right. Wrap yourself in that blanket. The fire'll be up soon.'

Nona sank onto the sofa. Harry cleared a pathway through the newspapers on the floor. The kettle on the stove hissed. A wren outside began to trill. Nona watched it, on the ivy that wreathed the window-frame.

'Quite a contrast, isn't it?' Harry sighed. 'Everything in its place out there, and doing what it's meant to. I wish I could say the same in here!'

He piled books onto a table, unsettling paints which fell onto the floor. The kettle whistled and he dug down in the sink for a teapot, and in a corner cupboard for a packet of tea.

While he made and poured the tea, Nona looked around the caravan. He was talking now about clay dust on his chest, and how he oughtn't to live down here in such a damp place. He was talking about the homes he'd had before, the jobs he'd done, the places he'd travelled to and why—despite everything—this was the best of them. Nona's eyes fell upon a postcard of a ship, carving its wedding-cake whiteness through blue skies and seas.

'I only worked the tables...' Harry brought the postcard down. 'But I had a fancy uniform. All white it was, with gold epaulettes. I looked a treat. I was younger then, you understand. No damp for me then, but sunshine all the way.'

'Owen Lark's got a ship like this,' said Nona, turning the postcard over, to find its name. 'He made it himself. Cut out all the bits by hand.'

'I've seen his boats,' said Harry. 'He's got a clear eye and a steady hand. Nice boy. Very quiet. You don't like him, do you?'

Nona wished she hadn't brought the subject up. 'I don't *know* him. It's just one of those things. We got off to a bad start...'

'I bet that wren out there *marvels* at the mess we make of things,' said Harry wistfully, as it began to sing again.

Nona wondered what he was thinking of. She was sure it wasn't her and Owen, or the brown sink full of washing up, or the paints all over the floor and the blue-coloured stew with bones in it. She drank her tea. It was getting dark outside; not the approach of night but another bout of rain.

'I ought to go...' She rose to her feet. 'Mum'll be wondering what's happened to me.'

'I ought to go too,' Harry said, 'and get on with some work.' He unhooked her anorak, wiped off the mud and helped her into it. 'I'll straighten out your wheel and bring the bike round soon.'

'You won't tell Mum?'

'As long as you don't do it again!'

Harry followed Nona down the breeze-block steps, struggling into a huge pullover with unravelling sleeves. They went their different ways. Nona heard the scraping of the shed door.

'Bye then,' he called.

'Goodbye.'

The rain was blowing in handfuls up from the beach. Nona pulled up the hood of her anorak, screwed her face tight against it again. What a world it was, all choked with the messes people made and sinks full of washing-up and driving, endless rain and danger everywhere...

She was half way across the common before she realized she'd missed Nyth-y-dryw. The ground squelched beneath her feet. She turned to get back and her boot went straight in. She had to pull it out with her hands. The wind blew and the few reeds that hadn't flattened rippled around her, like the waves on another sort of sea. 'People lose themselves in bogs,' she thought, and the brief lull of Harry's caravan seemed a long way off... 'Just like on the real sea. They get sucked in and nobody finds their bodies again, or knows what happened to them.'

She began, frightened, to try to find the track. The word *desolation* came into her mind. It was the word that the rain had washed from her wordbook, but it wasn't that easy to get rid of. Her feet sank everywhere she put them down. When, at last, they stumbled upon the track, she didn't know how they'd got there. And in front of Nyth-y-dryw, Billy Parry's pick-up truck was parked, as it usually was on Saturday afternoons.

Nona slipped past it and home. An unopened letter from Susie Lennox waited for her, poked into the gilt frame of the living-room mirror. She left it there. She couldn't see the point of keeping up with Susie any more.

'Where have you been?' asked Mum, who sat before a pile of wet logs that she'd collected for the fire.

'Oh, nowhere in particular,' she said.

19

On Monday morning, it was back to school. Mum waved them off with 'I've survived another half-term, and I'm on my own again,' written all over her face.

'You know where she'll be all day, don't you?' Sharon said, as they looked back at the already-shut front door. 'She'll be in the summerhouse with her feet up, listening to the radio. I don't know what's got into her. I wish she'd do the house or get the washing done for a change, or clean out the fridge and that rotting bowl of fruit.'

Nona shrugged. She didn't bother to point out that Sharon could have helped Mum, if it meant so much to her. She stayed head down all day, with eyes that said she wasn't 'at home'. Beca Lark gave up on her. Even Mrs Thomas left her alone. After school, she went up to the shop. She paid for the bag of tea things but Mrs Bella Pugh, behind the till, couldn't get a word out of her.

'She's such a bright girl, usually,' she said to the Evans lad from up the Vron, who stacked the shelves. 'She don't mean not to answer, I expect. Poor little thing, she'll have got something on her mind.'

When they arrived home, Mum was breaking branches all over the floor.

'Is it home-time already?' she said, shaking bits of bark out of her hair. 'I hadn't realized. Have you brought anything in for tea?'

Nona went into the kitchen. She piled the breakfast things into the sink.

'I've been typing my fingers to the bone,' Mum said as lightly as she could manage. 'Sorry about the mess.'

Nona didn't answer. She put a saucepan on the stove, and began to make a potato stew...

That night was cold. Even with an extra blanket, Nona couldn't sleep. She got out of bed, drew back her curtains. The sky was clear and starry. There'd be a frost. She could almost smell it. She watched the ocean glisten beyond the dark pub. She knew what she wanted to do.

As quietly as possible, she dressed, crept down the stairs, found her boots and the torch Mum kept by the meter box and her anorak. Then she let herself out. The door shut with a little click. She waited. No curtains fluttered, nobody had heard. She tiptoed down the path, through the creaking gate, over the stone bridge. Beneath her feet she heard the full stream carrying away the weekend's rain...

On the secret beach, the tide was up higher than she'd seen it before. She arranged herself on the bottom step. Sat and waited for the words to emerge, for she'd come to tell her troubles to the sea. The white waves flashed their encouragement at her...

'Tell us, tell us...'

She sat still as a stone, and no words came out.

They were all inside, the words about how Mum was behaving, and how it made her feel. But she couldn't bring herself to say them. What was the matter with her? Why couldn't she tell the sea that Cody wasn't going to come home? Why couldn't she say how pointless everything had become? She couldn't even tell the sea how bad she felt about Beca Lark, who tried so hard to be friends, and who she couldn't look in the eye since Cody had gone. 'It's not her fault,' she thought, but she couldn't say it.

She waited, but she couldn't say a thing. She even

scooped up a handful of the sea and washed her face with it, but it was pointless. She couldn't even cry. The awful numbness was still there. She got up to go.

'Wait, wait . . .' the sea called after her, and she felt as though she'd let it down, betrayed their friendship in some way. She fumbled for the steps, and in the dark her boot stubbed something. In her hurry to get away, she nearly didn't bother to stop. It was only just in time—just before the tide got to it—that she changed her mind and stooped to touch the hard cover of a book . . .

She stood on the bottom step, turning Owen's rain-swept, fallen journal over in her hands. 'We had pie for tea,' it announced, in the torchlight as she rummaged back through the pages, looking for something better. And then she found it. Right at the back, several blank pages on from all the rest. 'I'm the wrong boy inside the wrong body,' it began. 'I'm not like the rest of them. I never get the chance to be the sort of boy I really am, except down here. It's as though I'm living out somebody else's life instead of mine . . .'

Nona slammed the book shut. She could have written those words herself. They were more than she could bear.

'What is it?' whispered the sea. 'Tell us . . .'

She rammed the journal into her anorak pocket, and fled straight up the track. Away from the sea she took herself; down the cliff path, right behind the sea wall where the frost was settling on the common. All she wanted was her silent bedroom, where she wouldn't hear the waves any more. She'd think about the book later, read it properly, talk to the sea another day when she was herself again—if she ever was herself again! She passed the pub, shivered her way across the icy car park. And then, something caught her eye . . .

The small, frosted-glass window on the seaward side of the ladies' toilet was lit up, not brightly but enough to cast a square of light on what had been dark ground when she'd passed this way before. She came level with the door. This was lit up too. A smudgy haze swirled out of it. She smelt something in the air.

'What's going on in there ...?'

She didn't even care. She didn't want to stop and *certainly* she didn't want the light—she wanted sheets of dark sleep pulled up tightly over her head. And yet she found herself turning from her race back home, taking a look—or so she told herself—just to check that everything was all right ...

And so it was that she found the candles. Twenty-nine of them. They were lined up along the floor, underneath the basin, on top of the cisterns, underneath the water-pipes. Nona stood and counted them, astonished. Twenty-nine dancing, tiny flames transformed bare walls and dingy, graffitied doors and cobwebbed ceilings into something glorious. And as they danced, they winked at her.

Nona stood rooted to the spot. Her frost-nipped face warmed before their golden light, and her eyes filled with unexpected tears. They just came out of her like that. And it was as if the flames, in this Cinderella of a place, had been lit especially to melt them out of her. More tears appeared; gentle tears, soft tears. They ran straight down her cheeks. So long was it since she had wept, that she'd forgotten the strange pleasure it could bring. She gave herself over to it in the candle-light, and it was the way that babies and small children cry, opening their mouths wide and everything rushing out in a desperate stream.

'Oh, Mum, oh Cody ...! Oh why, why, *why* ...!'

The candle flames danced before her breath. Some of them blew out and snakes of smoke coiled up to the ceiling. Nona bowed beneath them, like a baby in a cot, or a womb, or a paroxism of colic. For the pleasure was changing to something else. Her mouth became square and the tears hard like rocks, hot like anger. The cries that came out now were sand-paper raw. They were dredged up from dark and dreadful places and she would have stopped them if she could ...

When, at last, Nona opened her puffy eyes to find herself upon the floor, a paraffin lamp had been placed by her side, and Griselda crouched over her in a fluffy zip-up bedsuit with her fur coat thrown over it.

'That's the best bit of crying I've seen for a good long while!' she pronounced, impressed. 'Even better than what I can do ... Now, are you finished?'

Embarrassed, Nona scrambled up. She couldn't speak, her throat was too worn.

'It's all right. You don't have to answer me ...' Griselda helped her onto her feet. 'Come and have a swig of something for that throat of yours.'

Griselda's lamp lit their way across the car park. It lit hoar frost on the willow branches and the wooden platform where her tent was pitched. It lit her sleeping-bag, pillows and eiderdowns laid out on the platform next to it.

'I usually sleep out when it's clear like this.' Griselda hung her lamp upon a tree. 'Can't bear to miss the stars.'

'But don't you freeze?'

'I've never been much of a one for an indoor life. When I was a little girl I slept on a balcony, all weathers round. The maids strung up a green tarpaulin to keep the snow away. I remember the smell of it, even now. They thought I was mad, of course, but I always had my way. I used to love it out there, hearing the night sounds, watching the sky.'

Griselda shook off her boots, climbed into her sleeping-bag, indicated that Nona should help herself to eiderdowns. 'Fresh air won't give you bugs and sicknesses,' she said. 'I've never had worse than a sore throat in my life.'

Nona pulled an eiderdown around herself. Griselda reached for a thermos flask and poured out what smelt, deliciously, like coffee.

'You must talk to your ma,' she said, as she handed the steaming stuff across. 'If I were her and you were mine, why, I'd be *devastated* if I found you crying the way you were just now. You owe it to her.'

Nona sipped the bitter coffee, which had something in it, she was sure it did. She pretended she hadn't heard what Griselda had said. 'Where do you come from?' she asked. 'You must have been rich, with maids and all! How long have you lived down here?'

'Oh, I don't really come from anywhere,' Griselda said. 'Not any more. I'm here and I live a day at a time. When the wind blows I shut myself up tight in my tent, and when I need to earn a bob or two I work for Ralph, and when it's frosty I watch the stars and light all the candles in the ladies' loo ...'

'The candles ... You ...?'

'Of course,' Griselda said. 'Who else would it be? I light them to keep the pipes from bursting. Haven't you seen them before? I wouldn't be able to stay down here if the toilets didn't work. They mightn't be up to much, but they're all I've got. One may live in a tent, but one's got to keep oneself clean. One has to have *standards*.'

Nona laughed out loud.

'You sound like you're feeling better,' Griselda said.

'Yes,' replied Nona. 'I think I am.' She drained down the last of the coffee mixture, and returned the cup.

'Real coffee, that is,' Griselda pointed out. 'None of that mucky instant stuff.'

'With something in it?' Nona's arms and legs were beginning to swim.

'With something in it.' Griselda slid right down her sleeping-bag. 'Now you should go. Your ma might worry, whatever you think of her. And isn't there school in the morning ...?'

This was undeniably true. Nona forced herself to abandon the eiderdown, which she threw over Griselda's snuggling form. She climbed off the platform. 'Turn out the lamp,' Griselda called, as if Nona were one of those maids.

Nona reached the lamp and snuffed it out. The common was thrown back into darkness, except for the sheen of the

141

frost and the little light the stars threw down.

'See your way, can you?' Griselda called.

'Yes, thanks. Goodnight.'

'Goodnight. And think about what I said. Talk to your ma ...'

Nona crackled across iced puddles all the way along the track. Griselda listened to her footsteps fading. Then she listened as the wind got up, as it blew clouds across the stars she used to watch from that balcony beyond her bedroom, when she was a little girl ...

In the morning, Nona couldn't wake up properly. She heard the others getting ready for school, Mum coming up the stairs, a cup of tea being placed beside her bed. She told the time from the clock beside the cup of tea, but even then she couldn't stir herself.

It was the missed sleep, wasn't it? Maybe, too, the little something in the coffee? She examined herself, as best she could. Were there signs of a hangover? Did a headache lurk, as well as her still raw throat.

'Come on! Nona, wake up!'

Sharon stood over her, plucking the bedcovers off her delightedly because she—for once dressed and breakfasted on time—had the upper hand.

'Go away! Leave me alone! Stop it!'

'It's twenty past eight! You'll be late for school ...'

'I'm ill!'

'You're what?'

Nona was never ill. Everyone knew that. 'Give me back my bedcovers,' she said thickly. 'Go away. Tell Mum I'm not going to school.'

Sharon conveyed the message. Mum came up and felt Nona's head, which was warm, but it would have been after a few hours tucked under all those bedcovers.

'Perhaps you ought to have a marigold pill,' Mum said uncertainly. 'Shall I draw back the curtains? Do you want breakfast before I get on with my typing? Will you be all right on your own—the others have gone now—?'

The weariness in Nona's body came from the crying, she suspected, rather than any germ that a marigold pill might combat. Unable to move, apart from to spit it out when Mum wasn't looking, she ached all over as though she'd climbed a mountain or rowed across the bay.

When Mum had gone, she shut her eyes again and slept long. When she awoke, it was to a better day. She lay and looked at the melting frost on the window. Her throat was less painful, and so were her aching limbs. She decided to get up.

When she got downstairs, a letter lay with the breakfast things on the kitchen table. It was addressed to Mum, but Nona read it. She had to open it out. It had been crumpled into a ball. It informed Mum that as she was a fortnight late with her urgent typing, and as, too, she had been *warned*, the job was being sent elsewhere. Could she please return everything straight away.

Nona folded up the letter. She was about to put it with the pile from Susie Lennox, and all the unopened bills, but she changed her mind. Mum, as Griselda had said last night, needed talking to. She forced down a fresh cup of tea and then, letter in hand, went to find her. She didn't much feel like it, but what choice was there?

Up in the summerhouse, Mum sat before a typewriter which hadn't even been taken from its case. She wore her dressing-gown, with a coat thrown over it, and a pair of thick woollen gloves. Her hair was piled untidily on top of her head. The radio was buzzing. Nona turned it off.

'Ah Nona, better are you?' Mum said, not looking at Nona at all, but at her own reflection in the summerhouse window.

'About this letter . . . !' Nona brandished it at Mum.

'Do you think I'm pretty?' Mum said as though she hadn't spoken, and she put a hand up to her hair.

143

'We can't live on Social Security for ever. What are we going to do?'

'My mother always said I wouldn't get a nice boy if I didn't take care of my hair ...'

Mum let it down and spread it out, just like Sharon would have done. She ignored the letter. Nona's hand, which held it, began to shake. Mum looked at her in the window. She smiled a silly smile, and her frightened eyes pleaded to be left alone. Suddenly, Nona didn't know what got into her, but she wanted to hit those eyes, pound that pasty, pointy face and *make* Mum talk about getting Cody back, about the typing and the money and what they were going to do ...

And then she thought it. *'This is how she made Uncle Brady feel. It wasn't all his fault. When she smiled like that, she made him want to do it, just like she's making me ...'*

'Oh, Mum!' She trembled at the thought that *she* could be like Uncle Brady, for it wasn't ordinary people who did things like that, it was wicked people—wasn't it? *'Please* can't we talk?'

'I never was good enough for any of them,' Mum said, not to her but far away. 'Even Mother was sorry for me, because I wasn't pretty like her. And as for Dad ... I'm glad they're dead and can't see what became of me.'

Nona left the summerhouse. She shut the door, and Mum didn't even notice, just started on about what the house needed was more trees to keep prying eyes away ...

Back in Wren's Nest, Nona began clearing up. She wasn't angry any more. Just frightened, because she hadn't seen Mum like that before. She hung up washing in the bathroom, picked up Bryn's pyjamas where he'd stepped out of them in the middle of the floor. Picked up her anorak ...

Out of it, like a ghost come back to haunt her from last night, fell Owen's journal. She held it between her palms. Some sort of fellow feeling lay between these covers. It might be an unlikely source. It might not be her business to pry. But she needed fellow feeling just now.

She sat down, found the back page again, and read right down it to the end.

20

'Nobody at our house ever has time for *fun.*'

Owen Lark was fashioning a lump of clay after the shape of Harry's head. It was Saturday morning, the second in a row that he'd been down. Things had suddenly gone his way. Father had been off on funeral and preaching trips and there had been no Greek, and no special walks. Sure enough, Father had found out what he'd been up to, and banned further visits. But as soon, today, as he'd struggled into his coat and hat, and Mother had gone out to wave him down the road, Owen had been off, across the icy playing-field.

'You'll be in dreadful trouble!' Beca called, who would never do a thing like that.

'I don't care!'

He didn't, either. It would be his birthday in a month or two. Boys of his age took out girls, and got away with drinking in pubs. Most of what they did made his few hours learning about clay look completely harmless...

'*I didn't hear you—what did you say?*' Harry shouted from the other side of the shed.

'My father's idea of fun is Uncle Lark and funerals,' Owen shouted back. 'My sister's is being top of the class. My mother's is making jam and mending socks. We never have a good time. We're always too busy to go out together anywhere, except to chapel.'

Harry put aside the huge globe that he was working on, and crossed the room. He stank of resin. His face was white

146

with dust. It was going to be a right pain getting the thing out of his shed, and it'd need a crane to lift it onto the transporter. He was fed up with the wretched job, he'd be glad to see the back of it. 'What do you mean by *fun?*' He stood over Owen, picking slivers of fibre-glass out of his hands.

'Well,' said Owen, looking from Harry's work to his, 'this is fun, isn't it?'

'What a boyo you are!' laughed Harry. 'This isn't fun, it's a blimming nightmare!' He looked at Owen's lump of clay. 'Do I really have a nose like that?' he said. 'Don't tell me—I probably do! You know, you really are getting there...'

Owen turned the model from side to side. He'd *get there* if it brought his whole family's wrath down upon his head. He would. He didn't care.

'I was going to see a film tonight,' said Harry, 'but my girl didn't fancy it. Do you want to come along? Seeing as you never go anywhere.'

'All right.' Owen grinned at him.

'Good,' said Harry. 'Meet you on the main road, then, at six o'clock. If I can get this bit of *fun* out of the way...'

Nona was cycling past the toilets, with a carrier full of washing that she was taking to the launderette, when Griselda emerged with her sponge-bag and towel. It never would have occurred to Nona that, without make-up, she could have looked so different.

'*Haven't seen you all week,*' Griselda yelled, her scrubbed face shining. '*Are you better now?*'

'*Yes.*' Nona's bicycle wobbled. '*I'm fine.*'

'*Good.*' Griselda wobbled too, on her dinky high-heeled shoes. '*Then you'll come out with me tonight.*'

'*Come out?*'

'*Shakespeare, at the crummiest flea-pit in the whole of Wales!*' Griselda yelled. '*Too good to miss! We'll catch the cinema bus, and come back on the half-past-ten.*'

147

Nona hesitated. Mrs Thomas had said that they all should go, but the days when she listened to Mrs Thomas were well and truly over now, as if words and poems and stories had been swallowed up by the dreadfulness of real life. But how could she say 'no'? Griselda was so adamant. And how could she too, when something inside her, despite everything, wanted to say . . .

'Yes!'

'That's the spirit!' Griselda's face shone like a little girl's. 'We'll take a picnic. I always do. We'll make a night of it. Girls out on the town . . . !'

Nona pushed her bicycle up the beach road. Below her, Griselda waved. What had she let herself in for?

'Make sure you dress up!' Griselda yelled.

Something got into Nona. She *did* dress up. She brushed her hair till it shone and stole out with Mum's sequinned party frock from the Uncle Brady days underneath her anorak, and a pair of pointy shoes with bows on them—the sort of shoes they always used to wear before they came down here.

'Griselda's taking me to the cinema,' she told Mum, who was stacking logs, again. 'She'll bring me back on the half-past-ten. I'll see you later.'

Sharon scowled, because she wasn't going too. Bryn, with his most disarming grin, said he'd like to see Sharon get him into bed. Mum said, 'Yes, dear,' where once she would have made a fuss, even if Nona had been going as far as Ralph's.

Nona shut the front door, before Mum changed her mind or Sharon commenced her inevitable protests. King Offa followed her down the path. Over the bridge they saw, parked on the 'bit', the Parrys' pick-up truck with Cledwyn in it, looking the other way. Offa growled, low and throaty.

'Want a lift anywhere?' Billy called, friendly as anything as he came out of next door's gate with his sister by his side.

'We've got room for another one.'

He looked like an ordinary sort of chap. Miss Parry, too, smiled nice as pie. Her hair was newly permed, every little wave in its proper place. 'I've been meaning to warn you about that Emlyn Hughes and those bits of meat he keeps giving you,' she said, conspiratorially. 'You be careful with him. He gets wild rabbits from Harry Llewellyn, and you never know where they've been. But worse than that, he gets *cats* and other bits of dirty beasts. Everyone knows that round here. You tell your mam.' Offa slunk away. You could tell, from the disdainful angle of his head, that even he knew a lying trouble-maker when he heard one.

'I think I'll walk,' said Nona.

'Suit yourself.' Miss Parry climbed, with Billy and Cledwyn's help, into the front seat. They drove away. Nona could imagine them saying, 'We try, we do, but they're so unfriendly.'

Up at the car park, still putting the Parrys out of her mind, she came upon Griselda, extracting herself from the bushes. It was a clear night, despite the distant boom of a fog-warning out across the water. Nona could see that Griselda had done a real job on herself.

How did she manage it? Her hair was so lacquered that it didn't move an inch. Her arms glittered with bangles, her neck with golden chains. Her ears drooped beneath the weight of earrings the size of Christmas tree decorations. The smell of her perfume nearly knocked Nona flat at fifteen paces. She forgot the Parrys, instantly.

'I've made up the picnic.' Griselda waved a basket at her. 'What do you think? I do like to eat *properly*. We've got soup in the thermos—I cooked it myself—and cold chicken and french bread, roasted chestnuts wrapped in foil, a lump of cake, some Brie, some grapes and a small game pie ...'

Nona couldn't believe it! Beneath the laundered napkins—how *had* Griselda managed them?—she saw a bottle of something called 'Old English Vintage Elizabethan Mead' and another one of fizzy cherryade.

'Where will we eat all this?' she said.

'Why, in our seats, on our laps, of course,' Griselda replied.

'But supposing it's not allowed...?'

'Not allowed...?' Griselda pondered this idea as though it were a novelty. 'Well, no one's ever stopped me yet!' She wrapped her fur coat round herself determinedly, and clutched her basket tighter. 'In any case they're philistines round here. They'll all be in the boring pub with Ralph, drinking boring beer and eating *chips*. You mark my words. The place'll be empty...'

They had the worn and faded Circle to themselves, apart from a dogged smoker up at the back. Griselda marched right down to the front and began unpacking the picnic on the empty seats around them. She put the cherryade on the battered rim of the balcony.

'We can eat with Falstaff and Pistol at the inn...' she said, oblivious to her surroundings. 'Become footsoldiers round the campfire on the night before Agincourt...'

She flung off her coat. Anything less like a footsoldier had never yet been seen. Uncertainly, Nona struggled from her anorak, spread out her own modest sequins. Griselda put the mead reverently on the rim too—'for drinking King Henry's health after the battle'—and sat down, arranging her frock around her as the lights dimmed. She'd brought a beaded gossamer stole which she flung round her shoulders as if she were at the opera. Nona wanted to ask her why she went to all this trouble for a night out in a place like this, but, '*My, you look a treat!*' a voice behind them boomed, before she had the chance.

They both turned round. Harry Llewellyn bore down upon them with Owen Lark by his side. Nona froze at the sight of them. Owen was dusty, with white particles of clay even in his hair. But Harry, mad as Griselda, wore a velvet

150

jacket, and a waistcoat embroidered with flowers and birds, and a silk cravat stuck with a gold pin with a dark stone in it.

'All dressed up too, I see?' Griselda said tartly.

'That's right.' Harry grinned at her. '*And* I've brought a picnic too.'

'No girlfriend then, tonight?'

'Been stood up, but never mind. Owen's come with me instead.'

He began to unpack his cans of beer, and a newspaper full of fish and chips.

'Go away!' Griselda flapped at him as though he were a fat, buzzing bluebottle. 'This is our picnic. You can't sit here!'

'*Shut up, will you!?*' the lone smoker shouted from the back. 'Some of us want to *hear* this film!'

Griselda rose indignantly, to tell the smoker that no one wanted to hear it as much as her. She flung wide her arms to make the point and the Agincourt mead went over the edge. A solitary cry rose from the Stalls. They all stared down from the balcony upon a shocked usherette, who'd been in the right place to save it!

'No drinking in this cinema, see . . . !'

Smugly, she tucked the bottle under her arm and marched away. Harry fell back laughing. 'You'll have bought the best, of course,' he said. 'Oh dear, you'll have no choice but to share our beer!'

Griselda opened her mouth to protest that she *did* have other choices, but the smoker at the back was beginning to look like a footsoldier himself. Reluctantly, she sank down.

Harry, as if anxious not to push his luck too far, removed his picnic to the row behind and settled, with Owen in tow, just behind Griselda's head.

'If I sit here, you can forget about me, and if there's anything you want . . .' he leaned forward and whispered into her hair, 'you can just ask.'

Nona almost forgot him in the end, apart from the smell

151

of vinegar from his chips which, mingled with Griselda's perfume, made her wonder once or twice if she wasn't going to faint. She forgot Owen too. For the film took over.

She hadn't expected much. Certainly hadn't realized that this ancient king from a bygone age would turn out to be so real. And he *was* real! Though he mouthed words that people nowadays would never say, he could yet have been a football yob screaming from the terraces, or a soldier in a modern war, or a Billy Parry or an Uncle Brady . . .

Nona got out her all-but-forgotten notebook, and dead Shakespeare's words and phrases fell like stars onto its pages. Griselda watched her, even Harry and Owen behind, but she never noticed them. She cried when Pistol died, let Harry's beer pass her by at Agincourt, almost—briefly—understood why men went out and fought like that, and women welcomed them home again as heroes instead of fools. She longed for Henry when he courted the French princess, was only dimly aware of Harry behind her, whispering things into Griselda's hair. When it was over, the picnic lay hardly touched.

'Oh well, never mind,' was all Griselda said, and after such a fuss bringing it too. Without complaint, she packed it away. It was as if she, too, was waking from a dream. She didn't even protest when Harry offered to take them home. What had got into her? They stood outside the cinema, the four of them enclosed by the fog that had crawled in from the sea, and all she said was, 'Thank you. That would be nice,' as if she'd forgotten that he was a bluebottle who needed shooing away.

Nona, who would have chosen otherwise, clambered into the back of Harry's van with Owen. She was glad not to have to walk down to the Town Hall for the bus, because her fancy shoes were pinching her. But it was awful sitting next to him, unable to meet his eye because *'I'm the wrong boy inside the wrong body,'* and the other things he'd written, wouldn't go away.

To her relief, Owen was dropped off first. Then Harry drove them down to Wren's Nest. Next door's blinds stirred. Griselda laughed at the sight of them.

'Goodnight, Nona,' she said, waving through the window at the blinds.

'Goodnight,' said Harry too, leaning across Griselda to open the door and let Nona out.

'Thank you for taking me,' said Nona.

They drove away. Miss Parry let her blind snap shut. Nona watched the tail-lights fade into the fog, thinking about the picnic she'd never eaten, the film she could have seen right through again. Suddenly it was lonely, standing out like this, with the foghorn booming distantly and the party over as though it might never have been. She felt like the only girl in the world. The house lights were out. She wished that somebody had waited up to hear about it all.

21

Owen, who would have liked nothing better than to return to sleeping parents, crept into the kitchen to find his mother, hair about her shoulders and in her dressing-gown, darning grimly beside the stove. She looked up as he came in. *'Your father's in the study. Shut the door behind you as you go.'*

Father looked the way he used to do before a spanking. Owen, relieved that he was too old now for that sort of punishment but dimly aware that there were worse things that could be done, approached the fire-place where Father waited as stiffly as though he'd been standing there for half the night.

'You've been down at that man's?' His voice was whip-thin. He didn't say Harry's name, although he knew it.

'Yes,' said Owen, trying to feel brave, though unsuccessfully. His father didn't get truly angry often, but when he did...

'Why?' his father asked him coldly.

'H-Harry's showing me how to model with clay. He says I'm good with my hands. I'm making this head, you see...'

'But I told you not to go again!'

'I know you did. But I like it down there, Father. You can't imagine how it feels to be good at something for a change. And Harry's not as bad as you think. He's not at all like people say...'

'When I got home tonight,' his father silenced him, 'your

154

mother was worried to death. She'd been all over the village, even down to those filthy sheds. She said there was no sign of you anywhere. You hadn't even been back for tea...'

'We...we went to the cinema.' Owen hung his head. 'I just wanted a night out, like everybody else has on Saturdays. Harry thought I'd been home for tea. It's not his fault. I sat on the beach instead, because I knew Mother wouldn't let me out again.'

'So,' his father said, in a voice that shrivelled Owen inside, 'you wanted a night out, and disobeyed your Father to get it, and worried your Mother sick, and set your sister the worst example to grow up into when it's her time. You *wanted a night out!*'

Owen muttered unintelligibly about not having done anything wrong, not really.

'Well, you won't do it again,' his father declared, his voice trembling and his hands shaking slightly. 'You won't do any of it. Not even sitting on the beach, and certainly not the model making.'

He pronounced the words 'model making' as though they were the root of all the trouble. He crossed the room and pulled out a box from underneath his desk and, to Owen's astonishment, it contained his model boats, all thrown in, any old how. 'You will write your mother a letter of apology,' he said. 'You will not go out on your own again, apart from school, until Christmas Day. There will be no more model-making.'

Father lifted out one of the boats and, before Owen could really grasp what was going on, he crushed it in his huge hands, then tossed it onto the fire.

'*Father, no ... !!*'

But Father's hands were already ripping the next boat, throwing it, too, onto the fire, starting on the next now, as if a lifetime of self-control was finally too much for them.

Owen lunged forward but his father was too big for him. With his great arm holding Owen away, his free hand broke the last, the best, the biggest boat as if it were so many sticks, then tossed it onto the fire. The whole lot went straight up, the rigging fizzed, the light, dry wood bursting into quick flames like the easy tinder that it was.

'No, no, no . . . !!'

'If your right arm offends you, cut it off! If your eye offends you, pluck it out..!' Father's usually mild face was flushed. His eyes gleamed remorselessly.

'I hate you, Father,' Owen screamed. 'You don't deserve my love. I'll never love you again.'

Up in his room, Owen sat tentatively on a corner of his bed, as if afraid that the whole lot—the room and house and world too—might well collapse around him. He'd known, of course, that he'd get banned from going out again. The way he'd been carrying on, it was inevitable. But he'd never thought that his father would burn his precious boats. Not the boats he knew his son had taken so long and so much care in making.

Owen would have cried if he could, but his heart was hard. He wouldn't run away *yet*. He'd punish them first by his hatred, *then*, when they couldn't stand it any more, he'd punish them some more by running away. And he'd make a good job of it too. None of the Boys' Own stuff he'd planned so far, but a real, military operation where none of them would find him again.

Without taking off his clothes he climbed into bed, locking his hands, as he always did, through his bed-head bars. His head felt something beneath his pillow. Of course, *of course*, Father hadn't known he kept his first, his worst and favourite boat in his bed. Letting go of the bars, he pulled out the hammily-made old crate and held it against himself, as though it were a beloved child.

'He didn't get you. Oh, he didn't get you . . . !'

It was easier, less painful now to close his eyes. Father thought he'd crushed him, but he hadn't done it yet. His thoughts went back to Henry's fight at Agincourt. That was the spirit!

He drifted towards sleep with the day, bits and phrases from the film, the clay, Harry, Griselda, Nona, spinning through his head. He remembered Harry turning his clay model round and round, and the sight of Griselda sweeping the mead over the balcony, and the smell of her perfume. He remembered the glitter of Nona Davies's sequinned frock and shiny hair; Nona Davies who'd pushed him in the sea, cycled doggedly up that windy hill, come out, chin protruding, from behind Harry's screen.

His last clear thought was of her. It wasn't of Father burning his boats, or Mother's worried face, or Beca's voice, whispering through the wall, 'Owen, are you all right?' As he drifted off, he wished he hadn't lost his journal, wished he could write his thoughts down. He knew what it was about Nona Davies that got to him. She was only his little sister's one-time friend, only a kid, but she was a loner too; more than that, she was a *fighter*. There was something wild and desperate in her that he recognized in himself. She'd *do anything*. You could see it in her. She was like him, underneath the hard eyes and the silly smile, drowning in her family . . .

Nona had a hard week of it. Even telling the sea about Griselda's behaviour at the cinema didn't put it right. Sharon sulked, partly on account of Nona's night out, which had left her—as she put it—'in charge of Mum', and partly because Bryn and Poppy, fed up with the way she kept Offa to herself, were fighting for control of him. Mum shut herself out of it in the summerhouse, writing off letters, apparently, about jobs. The house was its usual mess. There was hardly any food in the cupboard, and not much that could be done about it until Mum could be persuaded to go to the Post Office to get their money out.

Nona was worrying about Christmas now. All the shops

had been dressed up for weeks, and rehearsals for carol services at school were under way. How, she asked herself, would they pay for presents and a tree and all the Christmas food? It seemed a long week, listening to, 'Mam's started on the Christmas puddings,' and 'We're going to my nan's like we always do . . .' There was no sign of Griselda, to cheer her up. Her tent was closed and Saturday night seemed long ago.

On Friday, after school, Nona met Ralph on the sea wall. The waves were crashing onto it, white as the sky. She was watching them, not caring if they splashed over her as well.

'You've got to respect the sea,' Ralph warned, plucking her back from where she stood, too near to the edge. 'It won't respect you.'

Nona followed him towards the pub, wiping flecks of foam off her school coat as she went.

'Enjoy yourself the other night, did you?' he said.

'Oh, yes. Thank you, I did.' It still amazed her, the way everyone knew your business. She thought she'd never get used to it.

'Let's hope you've brought Harry and Griselda back together,' Ralph said. 'I always thought it'd be something simple like this.'

Nona stopped in her tracks. *'What did you say?'* She stared at Ralph.

'Your little trip,' Ralph repeated slowly, as though she were a fool. 'Let's hope it's brought them back together.'

'Together . . .?' Nona had never, by a glimmer of a clue, thought of them in any way *together . . .* 'What do you mean?'

'Griselda's Harry's wife,' Ralph said. Then, as if to make it doubly clear, 'Harry's Griselda's husband. Didn't you know?'

It was the most ridiculous, outrageous thing Nona had ever heard. She stared through Ralph and saw Griselda swotting Harry away as though he were a troublesome fly. She saw Harry with his girlfriends, in the market, in the pub. And then she saw him whispering into Griselda's hair, the

158

pair of them turning up with their picnics, all dressed up, as if it were something they'd done before. She saw the two of them in Harry's van, with the tail lights disappearing down the track...

'I didn't realize,' she said, and she *was* a fool. 'I wondered why Griselda stayed down here, but I never thought... What happened to them?'

'Oh, I don't know that.' Ralph shrugged. 'Harry has his girlfriends, Griselda has her annoying ways. But who can really say? I'll tell you one thing, though. Griselda's the only person I ever met who's truly been cut off without a penny. Stinking rich she was, apparently, but she left her family for Harry. Seems like a stupid idea to me, but there you are!'

They began to walk again. 'Do you really think they'll get back together?' Nona said.

They reached the pub. Ralph winked. 'Who can say? But until last Saturday night they wouldn't even pass the time of day...'

When Nona came level with Griselda's tent, she remembered what she'd said, about the maids. She tried, unsuccessfully, to imagine her in a posh house with chandeliers and a big staircase and a library and ornamental gardens.

She tried to imagine her on Harry's arm, or living in his caravan, though not with any more success. She found it easier to see her on the balcony, beneath the green tarpaulin in the snow. She wondered why people fell in love.

She wouldn't give up a proper home, if she had one, for anything...

22

Time moved remorselessly towards Christmas. Mother
made a large fruit cake and mince pies and and a variety of
other Christmas favourites, which she froze for the big day.
The grand Jerico lights were, as tradition demanded, lit up by
Father who—happy as Scrooge—stood on a wind-swept
podium between Santa Claus and Mrs Bella Pugh decorated
as Snow White. The shop illuminations began to look
tawdry, so long had they been up.

Owen maintained a stoic, sulking silence, impervious to
all approaches of festive cheer. He did what he was told, but
always with a black coldness in his eyes which the season did
nothing to melt away. His stare went through things as
though they weren't there. He was delighted with the effect
this had, especially on Father.

'I was too hard on him,' he heard him muttering to
himself, down in the empty kitchen. 'I'm not cut out for
dealing with people. I always get things wrong.'

'You wouldn't admit that to me, though, would you?' Owen
whispered from the stairs, where he sat much of the time
now in self-appointed exile. 'You wouldn't ever say you were
sorry.'

Beca came in, Mother behind her who'd been into school
to play the piano for the carol concert practice. Owen heard
them fling off their coats, cry for soup to warm them up,
complain about the strong, cold wind.

'Nona's written a brilliant essay on Henry V,' he heard

160

Beca say, when Father asked her about her day. 'Mrs Thomas says she's the best writer of the lot of us and she's going to enter it into the inter-schools Eistedfodd. She says you never know where you are with Nona Davies. One minute she looks like she hasn't heard a thing, and the next she's turning in top-class work...'

Owen saw Nona after school next day, distantly among the younger girls, huddling against the wind up by the school path. The weather was wild and bleak. These were days for scuttling home and staying indoors.

'My Uncle Emlyn really fancies that mam of hers,' Aidan Hughes confided, to the lads at large. 'He takes her meat, you know, for that cat of theirs. What he says she needs is a man.'

'He should watch it, he should,' said Rhys from up the Vron. 'She's funny, that one is. My cousin Dilys says so. D'you know what she did in town the other day? She went into the Post Office, right up to Dilys's counter, and she just stood there and wouldn't say a thing. Dilys kept saying 'Yes?', just like you would, and then she burst into tears. They couldn't get her out. In the end Dr Williams had to take her home.'

'She'll get herself put away,' Alice Pugh from the shop chipped in. 'I don't know what your Uncle Emlyn sees in her. Whenever she's on the street she looks a real untidy mess.'

'It's because she's got to do everything on her own. It's like Uncle says...' Aidan grinned, the answer was so simple. 'She needs a man!'

Nona hurried home fast, not so much because of the wind—which exhilarated her—but because Cledwyn, on his way down for tea at Miss Parry's, had attached himself to Bryn.

'Good job Sharon's had to stay late at school,' said Poppy, looking to where the boys fought each other against the school fence. 'She can't stand that Cledwyn.'

Nona looked at Cledwyn too. Who of them could? 'I feel sorry for him all the same,' she said. 'He can't help being a Parry. It can't be very nice, having Billy Parry for a dad and *her* instead of a mum.'

Poppy stopped for King Offa, who'd appeared, wind-swept as the day, to bring them home. Nona left them running round each other, Poppy cooing delightedly because she'd got Offa to herself for once. She struggled off the school path and onto the road.

'Goodnight,' Owen called, as she passed the Larks' gate. Nona hadn't seen him, not to speak to, since the night at the cinema. She'd been down on the little beach a couple more times, but he never was there. Her thoughts went, guiltily, to the journal. She ought to find out where he kept it, and put it back.

'Goodnight.'

She still had trouble looking him in the eye. Hurrying on she thought of Mrs Thomas instead. She thought of the essay that had caused so much fuss, and how there were only a few more days of term. They still hadn't made any Christmas plans. She thought of Christmasses before, especially the ones at Uncle Brady's with the big, synthetic tree and the telly on most of the time and all that booze and the turkey in the kitchen weeping blood because Mum hadn't cooked it properly.

'I can't wait to get it over with! Things will be better in the new year. We'll only have a term, and then we'll be off again. And we'll find a *real* home next time we move...'

She was half way down to the beach now, the wind beating at her face, with a threat of rain in it. Looking down upon the brown common, she saw Griselda's tent, tightly shut up and resolute despite everything.

'You'd think it had been fastened into that common with concrete!' she thought.

When she got to the car park, she saw black smoke and bits of sparks rising from Wren's Nest's chimney, to be whooshed away by the wind into the trees behind.

'Oh, *please*,' she thought, 'not another chimney fire...'

She ran all the way along the track. She could imagine not just the chimney but the house on fire and Mum not noticing. Above her, dark clouds blustered in from the sea, but there were no lights on at Wren's Nest, or in the summerhouse above.

By the time she got to the gate, she could see that Wren's Nest wasn't on fire. No flames flickered at the windows. The sparks from the chimney had died down. She hurried up the path. Perhaps everything was all right, after all.

As soon as she entered the house, however, she knew that it was not. She stood in the dark hall, and she couldn't say why, but she didn't want to open the living-room door. There was no sound of Mum anywhere at all. She braced herself and opened it.

The room was hot as a summer's day; that sticky, thundery heat, which meant that the wood-burning stove had been overstacked. And it was full of trees.

TREES.

At first, Nona couldn't understand. A forest of trunks and bare branches seemed to spread in front of her, the wood-burning stove glowing beyond them like a camp-fire in a glade. She switched on the blue plastic light. Even then she couldn't, immediately, believe what she saw, which was trunks still laced with ivy; branches and twigs meshing and entwined; so much wood cut down, dragged indoors and stacked up until it had become an indoor forest. And then she realized. The log collecting had gone mad, hadn't it?

'*Mum, Mum*...' Nona pushed her way across the room. Mum wasn't by the fire. She wasn't in the kitchen or the bathroom. Perhaps she was upstairs. Perhaps she was in bed, exhausted from what she'd done. Nona dragged the nearest logs back from the fire. She shut the stove door then, fearfully, mounted the stairs.

'*Mum, are you all right?*'

Mum sat before her dressing-table mirror. She wasn't dressed, but her face was made up. Her dressing-gown was over her shoulders, and she was striking matches, holding them up to lighten her reflection, then dropping them on the floor.

'*Mother was right*,' she said, shaking out her hair. '*I'm not pretty at all!*'

Nona plunged over Mum's bedside photographs which were smashed all over the floor. But she wasn't in time. It happened so quickly. The next match went into Mum's hair, and there was no stopping it. Mum's hair fizzed and flamed. Smoke rose, stinking, from it . . .

When Nona got the eiderdown over Mum's head, one side of her hair had gone and her face was scorched. When Nona pulled the eiderdown off again Mum still smiled, as though she got pleasure from what she saw. Pain didn't seem to have touched her. She looked as though nothing touched her, as though nothing would touch her again . . .

Nona flung open the window, to let the smell of burning hair away. She scattered the rest of the wretched matches out upon an astonished Bryn and Poppy who had made it, finally, back home.

'Hey, Nona! What are you doing?'

Bryn and Poppy's faces were blue with coldness, their hair damp with rain. Neither of them had warm enough coats and where was the money coming from to do anything about it? Nona spun round at Mum, like the wind which was cleaning out the room.

'What's for tea, Mum? Did you go to the shop today, Mum? Have you written to a solicitor about Cody yet, Mum? If you don't pull yourself together, you'll lose us *all*. Dr Williams will come and take you away. Is that what you want? Is it? Mum, you've got to pull yourself together!'

Mum stared blankly. Nona had never seen her face shrunk so small, like a baby now with just a little fuzz of hair, and eyes desperately pleading for the things that babies needed. The sore side of Mum's face screamed for special help, and Nona didn't know what to do. Voices called to her up the stairs; Bryn and Poppy's worried, frightened voices from the forest beneath. For once, she wished that Sharon was here. Trust her not to be around on the one occasion when she was needed!

'I'm feeling very cold,' Mum whispered. 'I've felt like it all day. Do you think I might have 'flu?'

'Lie down, Mum,' Nona said, shutting the window. 'I'm going for help.'

Outside, rain was now pouring from the sky, but she hardly noticed it. She made straight for Harry's. Maybe he'd have some proper antiseptic cream, instead of all that herbal stuff of Mum's. Maybe he'd have bandages too. It was pitch dark now. She followed the path round the side of the house, down into the common, past the dead tree. Harry was home, thank goodness. She saw a light in the caravan. She climbed the steps and, drenched, knocked upon the door.

A girl peered out at Nona. Not the Griselda Nona had half-hoped to find, but a new one.

'You've got a visitor,' her voice complained.

There was an awkward pause while Nona wished herself anywhere but here. Then Harry opened the door. He was wearing a huge shirt that came down to his knees, inside out and back to front. His hair stuck out all over. He was not a pretty sight. He looked embarrassed.

'What do you want?' he said.

'I...We ... It's *nothing*.' Nona backed down the steps.

'Nothing?' said Harry. 'Are you all right?'

'Yes, I'm fine ...' All she wanted was to get away. 'I'll call another time.'

Harry began to cough. The wind and wet had got at him. 'Get back in here and shut that door,' Nona heard the girl call, not funnily like Griselda would have done, but

165

crossly. Nona wondered why he'd got her there, and not Griselda.

'Goodbye,' she called.

He shut the door, reluctantly. He knew something was wrong. She heard him coughing inside, and hurried off quickly before he changed his mind. She passed the dead tree. The wind whipped her wet hair across her face and oh, she couldn't bear the thought going home; she was so tired of everything. She almost wanted to lie down on the soaking common, feel the rippling reeds wash over her like another sort of sea, let them take her down, down . . .

By what means she never knew—or how long it took her—she found herself on the garden path. The stones beneath her feet were covered in puddles and she must have been gone for quite a while, for Sharon was home again. She was standing by the front door, yelling, 'Nona, where are you?'

Nona came round the side of the house. 'I'm here,' she answered.

'Are you all right?' Sharon must have thought she looked a real sight, for she came up to her and took her arm and it was a brief truce.

'What's been happening?' she said. 'Where have you been? I can't get a word of sense out of Bryn or Poppy, and as for Mum . . . You'd better come upstairs and see who's taken her over, seeing as you weren't here . . .'

23

Nona went through the living-room, and up the stairs. She imagined Mum's bedroom taken over by Dr Williams—tipped off by Miss Parry, of course, who'd seen everything with her binoculars—busily packing to take Mum away. She imagined the smell of burnt hair lingering, and piles of clothes everywhere, imagined the distant see-saw whine of the ambulance hurrying down the hill to cart Mum off. She could almost hear Mum crying, as she began to realize what was happening . . .

The little bedside lamp was switched on, illuminating Mum's head on her pillow. Mrs Lark sat by her side. Mrs Lark! She was bathing Mum's face with cotton wool and cold water. The bedside light shone on her hair. The sleeves of her frock were rolled right up, and her lightly freckled arms were bare. As Nona came in, she pulled down her sleeves, and put the bowl and cotton wool aside.

'What . . .? How . . .?'

'Mrs Lark brought me down,' explained Sharon. 'She dropped several of us off after the carol practice, because it was so late.'

'Good job I did,' said Mrs Lark, getting to her feet, and looking for her coat. 'Now, I'm quickly running Bryn and Poppy home for tea. I'll be back soon. They shouldn't be here, not with things like this.'

Complete exhaustion washed over Nona and, surprisingly,

an incongruous hunger that could have done with tea as well. 'Is . . . is Mum going to be all right?' she heard herself say, in a voice that seemed to come from far away.

Mrs Lark looked down at Mum again. 'Her temperature's up,' she said. 'Her face doesn't look too good. I'll come and sit with her tonight, and you two can get your sleep. We'll go for Dr Williams if she gets worse, but don't worry, I think she will be all right.'

When Mrs Lark came down later, she brought with her—as if she knew what Nona had been thinking—a minced beef pie and a dish of mashed potatoes. While the girls ate, she dragged outside all the mad, waving branches that Mum had brought in. Nona watched her at work. She seemed so energetic and determined. Nona had never seen her like that before.

'I'll have to go again, to get the little ones to bed,' she said, when all that was left in the living-room was the mess of broken twigs and bits of bark all over the floor. 'This can be cleared up in the morning, before you go to school.'

'I'm not going to school,' said Nona hotly. 'I'm staying right here to look after Mum. It'll only be Christmas nonsense—everyone going on about their presents and what they'll watch on T.V., and another practice for that wretched carol concert, and the stupid Junior School nativity play.'

'I don't want to go either,' chipped in Sharon. 'I'm staying to help too.'

'Oh, no you're not!' said Nona.

'Oh, yes I am . . .!'

Even after Mrs Lark had gone, they argued on. And when she returned for the night with her sponge bag and dressing-gown, they still hadn't given up.

'You two look exhausted,' she said. 'Go up to bed. It *is* late, whatever you do tomorrow.'

'It's not really that I don't want her,' Nona tried to

explain, when Sharon had stormed away. 'It's just that Mum wouldn't like both of us missing school. And Sharon makes fusses all the time, and she's so *noisy* ...'

'You should go up too,' said Mrs Lark. 'You need your sleep as well.'

Nona couldn't imagine her thoughts stopping for long enough to let her sleep. 'I haven't made you up a bed,' she said.

'I'm going to sit up with your mother,' Mrs Lark said. 'Don't worry about me. Go on. I'll be all right, and I'll wake you if she needs you ...'

In bed, with the light switched off and the curtains drawn back so that she could look beyond the window bars down at the sea, Nona's thoughts weren't of Sharon, whose heavy breathing she could hear through the wall, nor of Poppy and Bryn, nor Harry in his caravan, nor Griselda's tent—all dark now. For she felt as though she and Mum and Mrs Lark, next door, were the ones who really mattered, the ones with the spotlight on them, like a company of players on a lonely stage acting out their allotted parts in a secret war, battling with a script that they couldn't even understand ...

She dropped off to sleep and the living-room was a forest again, a stage-set forest with crudely painted, cardboard trees. She tried to get out of it and Mum's voice was calling her: 'Help me, Nona! Help me! There are snakes down here ...' Somewhere distantly she was sure the wind got up. She wanted to get out of the dream but it wouldn't let her go. She was drawn back through the forest. There were pits, barbed wired with PERGYL, DANGER written over them, and small brown snakes slinking through the grass. Suddenly, Miss Parry laughed at her from the branch of a tree, sitting up there like a pantomime Cheshire cat, with eyes as big as brass-rimmed binoculars ...

She woke up. The day outside was bright. There was

sunshine on the sea and on Griselda's tent and the side of
the toilet block; sunlight that never got as far as Wren's
Nest any more. Nona struggled out of bed. It must be late.
She stumbled in to see Mum next door. Mrs Lark was
slumped on duty by the bedside. She shifted stiffly in her
chair as Nona came in, managed a tired smile.

'She's had a night of it,' she whispered. 'But she's settled
now. Shall we have some breakfast?'

Downstairs, Nona prepared for the three of them the last
of the porridge. They ate it before the ashes of the fire, which
had spilled all over the carpet. Poor Wren's Nest looked as
bleak as Nona had ever seen it. Without the family filling it,
they had an uninterrupted view of dirt and untidiness, awful
messes not just from the forestation of the living-room, but
from neglectful weeks.

'We had it so nice when we first moved in,' Sharon said,
despondently.

After she'd been persuaded to leave for school, Mrs Lark
cleaned out the ash and relit the stove. Then she and Nona
sat in companionable silence, like two footsoldiers on the
morning after King Henry's war, thought Nona.

'You know what we *could* be doing?' Mrs Lark said,
tentatively.

Nona did indeed!

While Mum slept, she and Mrs Lark cleaned the living-
room from top to bottom, sweeping and beating with the
window wide open to let the dust out and the fresh air in.
Nona even washed the curtains, sooty from the day of the
chimney fire, and hung them out in the bright sunshine. Mrs
Lark made lunch. She took some up to Mum on a tray.
Mum's eyes were open and bright now, perhaps too bright.
Her cheeks were pink.

'I've come to the end, Nona,' she said, as if she didn't
realize that it was Mrs Lark. 'I can't go on.' She pushed the
lunch away.

'She's still not well at all,' Mrs Lark said, when Mr Lark

170

brought Sharon down after school. 'Her temperature's going up again...'

In the night, it went up even more. Nona insisted on sitting with Mum this time, and Mrs Lark slept in Poppy's bed. Mum was flaming hot and she kept shouting things. Her burn looked frightful, puffy and raw and Nona was sure they'd have to give in, and take her to the hospital. She woke Mrs Lark, who got up immediately. She bathed Mum's face again with cold water and sat by the bed, holding her hand.

'We'll get the doctor if we have to, but let's wait a bit longer and see. I'll sit with her. You try and get some sleep...' Nona woke at dawn and Mum was better. Her temperature was down and her face less raw. She was propped up on her pillows, and Mrs Lark combed what remained of her hair.

'What did I tell you?' she said, looking up from the task. 'Doesn't she look better?'

Nona nodded, relieved. Mum smiled wanly up at her as her face was washed for her, and her hands.

'You take over and I'll make a cup of tea,' Mrs Lark said.

When she brought it up, they drank together, again in companionable silence, but as though a whole war and not just a battle had been won this time; a whole drama played out and the curtain-call now ready to be taken.

'I ought to go,' Mrs Lark said, regret in her voice as if she, like Nona, didn't want the moment to end. 'I've got a family to take care of. I dread to think how they're getting on up there! Mr Lark will come down later, and we'll keep the rest of you for another night—or longer if you need it.'

'Thank you,' said Nona.

'Thank *you*,' said Mrs Lark.

'What've you got to thank me for?' said Nona, surprised.

'For the privilege of helping, of course,' said Mrs Lark.

Sharon went to school again, saying she might just as well go back to the Larks' afterwards, seeing as Nona so obviously didn't need her. Nona and Mum were on their own until the middle of the morning, when the living-room window-pane was rattled, and Harry's face peered in. Nona opened the front door.

'I've just been shopping,' Harry said, 'so I got some things for you too.'

Nona took the box he handed her. It was full of luxuries like tins of salmon and ham, and coffee beans, and doughnuts with fresh cream, and bottled apple sauce. 'Oh, thank you ...!' she said, not knowing how they'd pay for it all.

'I *knew* something was wrong the other night,' Harry said, not noticing the falter in her voice. 'I should have come straight round. How's your mum now?'

'My mum?' said Nona, cautiously.

'This is a village!' Harry laughed at her. 'You can't keep it secret if someone's ill. By the way, Emlyn asked me to bring you this ...' He handed her a lump of something in a polythene bag, which felt too heavy for Offa's usual bits of meat. 'He says it's a spare off-cut of Welsh lamb but, from the feel of it, I'd say you've got a leg-and-a-half in there. He says to wish your mum well and to let him know if there's anything he can do.'

Nona pushed the meat back at Harry. 'We can't pay him ...' She went bright pink, and thrust the groceries back as well. 'We can't afford all that meat, and we can't pay you either.'

'*Pay* us?' Harry pushed it back at her. 'It's nearly Christmas, you silly girl. The food's a *gift*.'

'I ... we ... I mean ...'

'Look, I've got to dash ...' He didn't stay to savour her embarrassment. 'If ever you're in trouble, do come round. Don't be put off by my stupidness another time ...'

Ralph brought down sausages and chips and bottles of stout and lemonade for lunch. Mr Lark appeared briefly in the afternoon, with a get-well painting from Poppy, and a quarter pound of chocolates in a paper bag from Bryn. Mum cried when Nona brought them up, so Nona didn't tell her about the Welsh lamb and the shopping, not yet. Mum lay still in her bed. She was quite awake now and Nona ventured, 'About the other day...'

'The other day?' Mum frowned. 'Oh dear, I can't remember the other day...'

She looked upset, as if the struggle to remember hurt, and Nona changed the subject, guiltily. Mum obviously wasn't well enough to talk about it yet. She made a bit of tea, and hung up the freshly ironed curtains. In the evening, Mrs Lark called.

'Is she well enough? Can I go up?'

'Yes, you can.'

Their voices murmured above her. Nona opened out the door of the wood-burning stove and lit a candle, as they'd done on the first night. She felt warmed through by so much kindness. Safer than at any time since Cody had gone. Above the candle-light, she saw the place where she'd hidden Owen's journal. She got it down. Suddenly she wanted to talk about it all, and not just to anyone, but to someone who felt like her. Astonished at her nerve, she opened the book after Owen's last entry, and wrote one of her own.

When Mrs Lark came down, she'd filled more than a page. 'You won't need me tonight,' she said. 'She's *much* better. I'll come down in the morning.'

When she'd gone, Nona went up to see. Mum leaned against her pillows, with a shawl around her shoulders. She looked the way she'd done after the births of Poppy and Bryn and Cody, peaceful and sleepy and content, as if there never would be a storm again.

'The others are staying with the Larks,' she said. 'They say I need to rest and they'll keep them so that I can. Isn't that kind of them? And they've asked us up for Christmas Day. What do you think, Nona? It would be a relief not to have to struggle through it on our own...'

173

'If that's what you want, Mum,' Nona said, as she always did.

'I think I do.'

'Then that's all right with me...'

24

A real storm blew in from the sea on Christmas Eve, not the usual old wind and rain, but a hint of hidden powers, a small lifting of nature's veil to glimpse its raging real self. Up in the village, trees broke, slates were thrown off roofs, Mrs Bella Pugh's shop sign came off, the roads were awash with sheets of water. The mountain became invisible. Down on the common, Griselda's tent was all but blown away, and a torrent rushed off the escarpment behind Nyth-y-dryw, filling the stream until it rose level with the stone slabs, and threatening to spill right over Miss Parry's 'bit'.

The storm blew all day, and half the night. Nona stood at her window, wondering about Griselda and if Harry's caravan was all right and whether Mum managed to sleep through. Mum did sleep through and in the morning, when she awoke, it had subsided. Owen, at his bedroom window too, put off plans to run away until the weather quietened down. Sharon slept contentedly, for it was Christmas Eve and she liked it at the Larks'. But Bryn tossed and turned and longed for morning. And Poppy lay, eyes open, longing only to go home to Mum.

Presents were opened after breakfast in Owen's house. Father wanted to get started early, what with three extra children for whom gifts had been wrapped. Owen sat with his lap full of a book from Beca and socks from Aunty Lark, chocolate Father Christmasses from Mother and a rugby ball from Father. He was surrounded by a ripping and squealing in which he played no part. Mother and Father, watching him, knew that even Christmas hadn't melted his stony heart.

'I must get the turkey in the oven,' Mother sighed, putting down the lace handkerchiefs that Father bought her every year. 'We've only an hour before chapel and I haven't even stuffed it yet. Beca, come and help me with the potatoes. Sharon will you do the sprouts?'

'Of course I will.' It was only to Nona that Sharon complained; all the Larks thought she was a 'lovely girl'.

'You could take Bryn in the garden with the rugby ball,' Father said to Owen. 'I might come out too, if I have the time. See if I can't point one of you in the direction of the school team.'

'Later, maybe.' Owen opened the topmost of his books, and held it up in front of his face.

Nona went down to the beach early, to tell the sea that it was Christmas Day. When she came back, Mum was out on the path scattering cake crumbs for the wrens, all dressed up for the occasion in clean jeans and her best cardigan. She looked up when Nona opened the gate. The fresh clothes didn't bring her hair back, or make the dark rings around her eyes look better, or the burnt side of her face. But at least she was smiling, at least she'd made an effort for the day.

'Christmas treat for the birds!' she called, shaking out the tin and returning back up the path. 'Are you going to join me? I've made a pot of tea.'

In the living-room, the tea resided on a cold hearth beside two unopened envelopes. Mum, not ready for a real fire again, had plugged in a fan heater which she'd found in a cupboard, and the living-room was acrid with the smell of burning dust. Nona sat down. Despite Mum's bright attire, it was hard to believe that it was Christmas morning. It was so still. She'd never woken on Christmas Day without the shrieks of the rest of them all about her.

'Funny, isn't it?' Mum said, as if she was thinking the same thing.

'We'll see them later.'

'Yes.' Mum sighed. 'I haven't bought them much. Just a few sweets hidden under the bed. And for you too. I haven't wrapped them yet. Let's open the cards.'

Nona's was from Susie Lennox—and she didn't feel so guilty when she read it, for all the unopened letters stuffed now in the back of the drawer.

'Don't be cross because my mum found your address,' Susie wrote. 'She said it was right that your Uncle Brady should know, and telling him the way she did was for the best. I hope you'll forgive me and write again. Cody seems very well. He came to our house the other day to play, and Mum cooked your Uncle Brady dinner. She says he's doing a grand job, all on his own like that. He's taking us all to the pictures next Wednesday afternoon. I've made a new friend at school. Her name's Judy and she's not as nice as you, but all the same. She's coming too...'

The other card was from Cody. Mum's face didn't show a thing. She just examined it, turning it this way and that to make out the writing, then held it up for Nona without a word. It was a playgroup effort with a wobbly print of a Christmas tree and an uneven distribution of glitter and the words *Happy Christmas* neatly printed by the teacher and a pile of scribble inside, amongst which the word *Cody* could just be made out.

'He's clever for his age.' Nona swallowed hard. 'Fancy writing his own name.'

Mum shut her eyes. 'Let's get out of here,' she whispered suddenly. 'Let's go up to Sion for the Christmas morning service.'

It was the least likely thing that Nona could imagine Mum wanting to do. But, 'Anything you say, Mum...' she said. And she plucked the card off Mum's lap, and put it up on the shelf, then screwed up Susie's letter, and threw it at the dead fire.

Owen knew the instant Nona and her mum walked in, because all around him ripples of interest spread out, and heads almost but not quite turned. You could feel the presence of newcomers in a place like this, like the wind blowing in through an open door. Owen saw his mother get up from the piano, and walk down the aisle, smiling her welcome. Sharon, Poppy and Bryn, by his side, turned to see what was going on and sure enough, 'It's Mum and Nona,' they said, and they all began to shuffle along the pew to make room.

But Mum and Nona weren't going to sit themselves right down on the front row. They weren't up to that, and Owen didn't blame them. Out of the corner of his eye he saw them settling in, right at the back. He saw Father stooping to shake Mum's hand, he saw Mother returning to her place. She began to play a carol, her head bowed beneath the brass lamps, her white cuffs moving up and down the keys as 'O Come All Ye Faithful' rose to the last musty corner of the roof and even the berries on the holly seemed to cheer up at the sound of it. Father waited till she'd finished, then he marched up the aisle and climbed the pulpit steps. Quickly, Owen unwrapped the cellophane from a peppermint, which he popped into his mouth.

The service began.

Nona'd never been to a chapel before. She marvelled as Poppy, Bryn and Sharon sat still as mice up at the front. The pews were so hard and Mr Lark was up now, talking, and he might have been speaking in Welsh, for all she understood.

Nona wished they'd start carolling again. It had been nice, despite all she said about 'Christmas nonsense', to join in with the rest of them. The Evanses from up the Vron were in front of her, and Farmer Pryce who owned all of the headland above the cliff path and drank with Emlyn down at Ralph's. Emlyn was there, and all the other Hughes's too, and all sorts of folk that Nona knew by sight—the dinner ladies from school, the newspaper agent, the people who ran the launderette. They were all staring at Mr Lark with goggle eyes, and Nona stared at him too. His huge arms were waving. His eyes were bright. He thumped his fist. He was saying something about losing Paradise and Nona felt Mum nodding at her side, and knew that she was thinking about Cody.

Mum, all things considered, didn't look too bad. Her ruined hair was covered with a hat which she'd bought in an Oxfam shop for Sharon, who hadn't wanted it. She'd never worn a hat before—her hair had always been her crowning glory—but this one, demin patchwork with a floppy brim, suited her very well, even though its style was out of date. It matched her jeans.

After the service, Mum and Nona slipped out quickly, because Mum didn't want to be wished a 'happy Christmas' by half of Jerico. Mrs Lark, who seemed to understand, gave them her back door key. They left her behind, in the thick of all the seasonal greetings, and let themselves in to her quiet kitchen. It was only briefly quiet. Poppy and Bryn came bursting through the back door after them, and Mum rose, full of pleasure to see them. They clung to her. Even Sharon was smiling as she gave Mum a glass-and-gilt brooch which she'd bought in Bella Pugh's.

After the Christmas roast, with all its embellishments, Nona went for an afternoon walk. Mum seemed warm and safe and happy in the Lark's big armchair. Beca was spreading out a board game for the rest of them. Nona couldn't face Beca's game. She felt too tired for it, too tired for anything, apart from being on her own.

It might almost have been summer on the way down to the beach. Yesterday's storm had blown itself out, and Nona

179

could see walkers on the cliff path and children running up and down the sand. She decided to go home, to take a chair outside the cottage and watch the wrens with their bits of cake. She imagined protecting them from King Offa while he settled on her lap and purred them both to sleep ...

'Give this to Griselda, will you ...?' Ralph called to her from the doorway of the Mermaid Inn. Nona saw Harry behind him and the new girlfriend, and Emlyn Hughes still in his chapel suit. Ralph held aloft a package, tied in brown paper and covered in stamps.

'You mean she's staying in her tent, on Christmas Day?' Nona took the package from him.

'In her tent? Not a bit of it! She's hidden herself away in the ladies' lavatory,' Ralph exclaimed indignantly. 'I invited her in for lunch, but she wouldn't have it, stupid woman. What do you do?'

Nona took the package to the toilet block, where a notice had been hung on the ladies' door:

THIS TOILET HAS BEEN CLOSED
UNTIL FURTHER NOTICE.

But the door wasn't shut, and right across the car park wafted the smell of ... food!

Nona hauled the package in. Griselda huddled over a primus. Candles had been lit again, and the floor was covered with her eiderdowns.

'Come in! Sit down! Happy Christmas!' Griselda yelled, as if she didn't have a care in the world. 'What's this? A present? I know where it comes from! I know what it is!'

She ripped open the layers to reveal another fur coat. 'They cut me off without a penny, and then they send me coats!' she exclaimed, throwing the thing down onto the toilet floor. 'Funny things, families! I suppose they think I'll freeze to death. Where are you off to? Sit down, I said ... You're just in time to eat.'

Nona would have explained that she'd eaten already but,

'Nobody wants to eat alone on Christmas Day,' Griselda shouted as she scraped stew off the bottom of a bubbling pot.

'You should have eaten in the pub with the rest of them,' Nona said, instead.

'There's somebody outside,' said Griselda. 'See who it is, will you?'

The somebody was Owen, who'd left home too, because Father had promised he could go out again on Christmas Day. He stood outside the window, drawn by the smell of food and Griselda's shouting.

Nona leaned in the doorway, staring at him with her secret eyes.

'It's Owen Lark,' she called.

'Well, invite him to join us!' Griselda yelled from within. 'The more the merrier!'

Nona looked Owen up and down. *This is your chance to start again,* something inside her said. *Your chance to put things right.*

And she *did* want to put things right, didn't she?

'Join us, if you want to . . .' She smiled at him, and when he smiled back she knew that he wanted to be friends too.

Griselda brought out the eiderdowns, and bowls of turkey stew. 'Get this down you,' she demanded, settling herself on the ground with her back to the sea and the Mermaid Inn.

Nona laughed at Owen's expression as he sat down by her and took his bowl. She knew how much he'd eaten already! Griselda handed her a bowl as well, and she started to pick at it.

'Come on, come on!' Griselda admonished them both. 'There's a home-made Christmas pudding afterwards. None of that plastic stuff Ralph's cooking! Come on, you're letting it get cold!'

While they both made the effort, the afternoon began to slip away. Birds above them fell quiet. Shadows began to sneak into the common. Cars drove away. The voices of walkers faded up the hill. When, at last, their plates were clear, and the Christmas pudding had been eaten too, Griselda sang to them:

> *Once in royal David's city*
> *Stood a lowly cattle shed*
> *Where a mother laid her baby*
> *In a manger for his bed ...*
> *With the poor and mean and lowly*
> *Lived on Earth our Saviour holy ...*

'We'd better go,' said Nona when the song, too, had faded away and the only sound left was the beating of the waves upon the empty shore.

'Father will be wondering where we are,' Owen said.

'Wouldn't you like to come up and have Christmas tea with us?' both of them said, awkward at the thought of leaving Griselda on her own.

'You think a ladies' toilet isn't a fit place to celebrate the birth of so high and holy a king!' Griselda had arisen to collect their bowls. She stood now with her dirty dishes in the doorway ... 'That's the trouble with you kids nowadays. You've got so blimming much, you fail to understand the point of simple things!'

Mrs Lark's special Christmas tea was a sight to behold, but *impossible* to eat if you'd just crammed down your second dinner!

'I don't know what's wrong with you,' she complained, when all the rest of them had got down from the table, and Owen and Nona still pushed turkey-and-stuffing sandwiches around their plates. 'I've spent hours getting this ready. There's trifle still to come, and Christmas cake and iced macaroon biscuits. I thought you'd be hungry after all that fresh air.'

'It's lovely,' Nona said, wearily.

'Yes,' said Owen, pushing away his plate.

When at last they got down, Mum said that perhaps it was time to go. She'd sat with Poppy on her lap and Bryn, unusually still, at her feet all afternoon, close as they could get. They jumped up, delighted as she spoke, and you could see that they wanted to be back home with her again.

'You can stay till later,' Mrs Lark said, as if she hadn't noticed. 'Christmas night's still only half over. Don't feel you have to go.'

'I want to take the children home,' Mum replied, as emphatically as any of them had ever heard her. 'I've been missing them.'

Even Sharon rushed upstairs excitedly to collect her things, and only Nona was left behind, standing in front of the fire with its light brightening up her hair.

'You've done so much for us,' Mum was thanking the Larks. 'You've both been so kind.'

Mr Lark turned over his hands, as if he didn't know what to do with them. Owen, behind him, smiled bitterly. Mrs Lark flushed, pink with goodwill. 'We'll come down tomorrow to see if there's anything you want. You mustn't expect to be better all at once. You mustn't overdo things.'

'I'll drive you down,' Mr Lark said, as the rest of them came back down the stairs.

'Goodbye, Nona.'

'Goodbye.'

'Goodbye.'

'Thank you for everything.'

'Goodbye Poppy, Bryn. Sharon you've been wonderful. A credit to your mother, you are . . .'

The last to say goodbye were Nona and Owen. They stood amid the pile of shoes around the kitchen door, while voices and footsteps and farewells faded down the path.

'Perhaps I'll come down,' Owen said. 'if that's all right with you? Meet you on the little beach one afternoon?'

'I'd like that,' Nona said.

PART THREE

Rabbit Stew

25

For several nights, Nona noticed light coming up the stairs and the sound of Mum moving about, and she called, 'Are you all right, Mum?' and Mum called back to her, through the floorboards, 'Yes, I'm all right. Go to sleep. I didn't mean to wake you.'

One night she went down, and Mum was pacing from side to side of the room, though she stopped before the mantelpiece when Nona walked in.

'I'm sorry,' she said. 'You don't have much peace with me for a mum, do you?'

Nona looked at Mum in the mirror. Her hair was beginning to grow, and her face was healing.

'What are you doing, Mum?'

'I'm thinking.'

'What are you thinking about?'

'I'm thinking about being good!'

Mum looked just like a little girl with her fuzz of hair, and Nona must have pulled a face, or even laughed, for Mum's expression crumpled and she said, 'There you are. That's what people always do if you say things like that. Nobody ever takes you seriously...'

'I didn't mean it,' Nona said quickly.

'I'm getting old,' Mum sighed at the mirror, no sign of the little girl now. 'My looks are ruined, don't tell me they're not. I'll have a scar for the rest of my life. Maybe I don't care. I'm tired of everything, Nona. My heart's wrung out with wishing I didn't make a mess of things.'

'But we love you, Mum. You're good enough for us.'

'I'm not. You know it. If I were good enough I wouldn't talk to you like this. You're only a child and I treat you like you're grown up. It isn't fair. I put too much on you.'

'It's all right, Mum.'

'It's not all right. You know that too. I want to change things, Nona, but I don't know how . . .'

Next day, to everyone's surprise because she *never* did things like that, Mum took them on a picnic. They climbed the worn, cliff path high up the headland, passing fields of grazing sheep and the first few lambs until they nearly reached the Head itself, which marked the end of their group of bays and the start of the next.

It was so warm that they wished they'd left their coats behind. They came to the Hundred Steps which led up to the top. A sign warned them of sheer drops down to the sea, and of landslides. Mum stopped them, reluctantly, from going any further.

'There's a place called Bird Rock over the top,' she said. 'It's covered with cormorants and oyster catchers—at least, it used to be—and you can see the grey Atlantic seals from it. I *did* want you to see them too—what a shame these steps are in such a state! Never mind, we'll have our sandwiches here . . .'

The sea was laid out beneath the sun like a piece of crumpled silk. Or so Nona saw it, who smuggled its memory into her wordbook when they got back home.

'I thought I'd try my hand at baking bread for tea,' Mum said enthusiastically.

'Don't overdo it, Mum,' muttered Nona, anxiously.

Hardly surprisingly, they all slept well that night, and next day the Larks came down and Mrs Lark helped Mum to get the washing done and Nona tried, unsuccessfully, to get over her stupid awkwardness with Beca and her disappointment that Owen hadn't come too. In the afternoon, Harry came in with more groceries. Bryn tricked him with his Welsh-dragon water pistol, but the only real discord was between him and Mum when, again, he wouldn't accept payment for the food.

When he'd gone, Mum sat quietly for a long time. Then she got up and said she was going to be a good mother from now on. This was going to be a fresh start.

But in the night, she was awake again. Nona heard her pacing down below. She dozed and woke again and the light was still on and she heard the creak of the chair as Mum got out of it, and the click of the light being switched off, but still no climbing up the stairs.

The next day was New Year's Eve, and the weather changed for it. It had started in the night, the wind getting up and the trees shaking. Maybe that was why Mum had been awake. By the time that the rest of them got up, it was raining hard and, even with all the lights on and the stove lit for the first time since what was now known as Mum's 'accident', the house was still bleak.

'It can't be worse out there,' said Nona, struggling into her anorak. 'It makes you feel so shut in, all that rain rattling on the roof. I know it's crazy, but I've got to get out of here.'

The stream had risen over the stone slab. Nona splashed across it, and between bushes that bobbed like tethered balloons. The wind roared. Not even on Christmas Eve had she heard it quite like this before. The grasses in the marsh shook like snakes. Nona scurried beneath a madman of a tree with its arms akimbo. There was only one place she wanted to be, down on the secret beach where the great shoulders of rock, the broad chest of the beach would protect her, where she'd huddle into some cleft in it, and watch nature's demons from a place of safety.

At the big beach, whole sheets of rain blew in from somewhere out on the misty sea. The tide was low enough

188

for her to have scrambled to the secret beach over small rocks, but she didn't dare. The bay seemed to have changed shape, with gigantic waves piling into it and its black granite edges blurred with seaspray and the rain. The roaring had become an outright war between waves and wind over which could make the biggest din.

Nona struggled behind the sea wall, her heart pounding in time with the stereophonic waves. She found the cliff path, began to climb up it. Stinging rain smashed into her face, and wind into her eyes. She had to turn her head away, turn her body sideways and navigate the path like a crab, for the wind was trying to snatch her very life's breath from her.

So intent was she on fighting it, that she didn't see Owen till she stumbled over him, hunched beneath a blackthorn bush just before a bend in the path. He was absolutely saturated by the storm.

'You'd better stop right where you are,' he grinned at her. 'One step round that bend and you'll be blown straight into the bay!'

Nona could well believe it. She crouched down with him, over a turbulent puddle that filled the path from side to side. Huge bubbles danced on its surface, and the rain burst them, every one.

'The stream's just the same,' Owen shouted, above the din. 'Have you seen where it comes out beside the pub? It's bubbling like a stew and it's gone all brown. Have you seen where it goes under the road, and all the tarmac's breaking?'

Nona nodded. She looked from the downpour on the frothing sea to the rain upon Owen's head.

'Don't you mind being drenched?' she said.

'I am, aren't I?' He rubbed his head and grinned. 'My coat's not waterproof any more and I'm absolutely frozen. Crazy, isn't it?'

'It's the same with me . . .' There had to be a leak, somewhere in her anorak; she felt her cold, sodden jumper against her skin. 'There's water running down my back.'

189

'Let's get a hot drink down at Ralph's!'

Billows of smoke blew every way out of the Mermaid Inn's chimney. Nona hauled herself onto her feet. With Owen at her side, she made her way down off the cliff. Ralph saw them coming. He was looking through the window, at the storm. He laughed at them when they stumbled in.

'You must be mad!' He shook his head. '*Everybody's* mad, down here...'

He spread out his arms. As if to prove his point, Griselda's tent was laid out all over the floor, and Griselda was wringing out her hair in front of the fire.

'Have a nice walk, did you?' she said, and she sneezed.

'It's time you stopped this camping lark,' Ralph admonished her. 'It's time you gave up with a good grace.'

'Gave up? Never!' Griselda said. But she didn't sound her usual, adamant self. She sniffed into a handkerchief, and sneezed again.

'I'd better make you some cocoa,' Ralph said, while the windows rattled and the wind blew smoke back down the chimney. 'I'll make you *all* some cocoa. What a New Year's Eve!'

When Nona got back home the burst stream had grown into a rushing pool which covered the 'bit'. This pool was fed by a new stream which poured off the rock-face behind the cottages and round the side of Miss Parry's. Glad of her wellingtons, Nona found the stone bridge and splashed over it and up the watery path to her front door.

'Thank goodness you're back,' Mum said, taking in the soaked sight of her. 'Get out of those clothes straight away.'

'I wish I could have gone too!' said Bryn.

'Do you think short hair would suit me?' Sharon said, turning before the mirror. 'Everybody nowadays has got short hair.'

'I've made some more bread,' said Mum. 'Mrs Lark's

recipe. It's lovely and warm, shall I cut you some...?'

After tea, when the curtains had been drawn and the fire made up for the evening and all of them, including Offa, were curled up in front of it, a commotion disturbed them, mixed up in the wind and rain and coming from next door.

'Whatever's that?' said Mum, and she drew back the curtains to see.

Miss Parry's outside light was on. It lit the flood-water on her path. It shone onto Miss Parry herself, sweeping frantically at her front door and crying, *'It's coming through the house! My carpet's ruined, it's coming up the stairs!'*

'Nona!' cried out Mum, far too quickly, as Nona saw it, to think what she was doing. 'Where are my boots?'

'Mum, you're not...' Nona began protesting. But, 'Find yours too!' Mum came back at her. 'You can help as well...'

Nona went out into the hall and stood in the dark, remembering the wicked glint in Miss Parry's eye when she fed them sticky cake and again, outside the front door on Hallowe'en night, when Cody had gone. She remembered the red painted letters on the boathouse wall, and she didn't do a thing.

'Nona...' Mum rushed in after her. 'What's the matter with you? Come on!'

'I'm glad her carpet's ruined,' Nona said in a low voice. 'I hope it floods her whole house! I hope it takes her with it! I hate her, I really do! How can you want to help her after the way she's treated us...?'

Mum pulled on her boots. 'Sharon, will you help...?' she called back into the living-room instead.

'Count me out!' called Sharon, furious as Nona.

'Poppy...? Bryn...?'

But Poppy and Bryn were nowhere to be seen. They'd taken themselves out of the way. Even King Offa had disappeared.

'We'll talk about this later,' Mum exclaimed. And without another word, she rushed off on her own.

By the time that she reached next door, the water had risen more, and Miss Parry's legs were trembling beneath the weight of her precious grandfather clock, as she tried to move it towards the stairs.

'Here! Let me help...' Mum sloshed into her parlour and grabbed the clock by its other end. Miss Parry said not so much as a 'thank you', just 'He's been in our family always, old Grandpa has. If you drop him you'll pay, you will...'

Between them they got the clock upstairs.

'Now my chairs,' Miss Parry said remorselessly, for it looked, momentarily, as if Mum might sit down and rest. 'You've got to help me with my chairs. Water's still rising...'

Mum helped her with the chairs. It took considerable manoeuvering, but they got them all up.

'Now my dresser,' Miss Parry said...

Nona sat up at her bedroom window in the dark. She hated herself because she should have helped, not for Miss Parry's sake but for Mum's, who was meant to be taking things easy.

Nona knew Mum would be expecting her to change her mind and go. She was the good girl, after all, who always put her feelings aside and did whatever was asked of her.

Not this time, though! she whispered to herself.

Two figures came from next door. They made their way together, the flashlight of a torch between them, through the flood-waters until they emerged on the bit of dry path in front of Nyth-y-dryw.

'She's bringing her in here!' Sharon burst into the room, Poppy and Bryn behind her.

'Get into bed,' said Nona. 'Pretend you're all asleep.'

When Mum and Miss Parry came in, there were no children downstairs, and the lights were out up above. Miss Parry squelched into an armchair before the fire, and wept as if she didn't care if she woke the lot of them. Her hair was a

192

bedraggled mess. She shivered with the cold. Her clothes clung to her.

'It'll be all right,' Mum tried to reassure her. 'It's stopped raining now and the water will go down. The furniture will dry out. It'll take a bit of clearing, but you'll get it nice again.'

Miss Parry hardly seemed to hear. She might have been mugged, her Billy dead, her very person violated, so loudly did she cry.

'You'll have to sleep here,' Mum said. 'That'll be the best thing. I'll get you some warm bedclothes, and a dressing-gown.'

'Perhaps I'd better.' Miss Parry sniffed, and wiped her eyes. 'I could have a bath as well.'

'I'll go and switch the water heater on.'

'While it's heating, you could get me a bit of tea. I haven't had my tea...'

When Miss Parry had been fed and she'd had her bath and gone up for the night, Mum crept into Nona's room. King Offa lay at the bottom of the bed. His green eyes glinted. Nona's eyes, peering out from under the covers, glinted too. She didn't look at Mum. Kept them fixed on the window and the light beyond it, of the Mermaid Inn.

'Move up, Nona. Make a bit of room for me...'

'Do what?'

'Miss Parry's staying the night. She's in my bed.'

Nona moved across and let Mum in. She didn't say a word. She didn't need to.

'I couldn't let her go back home,' Mum apologized. 'She's in an awful state, and so is her poor house. Whatever she's done to us, I couldn't leave her like that.'

She closed her eyes, and fell straight asleep. The wind dropped, and the light at the Mermaid Inn went out. At the end of the bed, King Offa closed his eyes too. Only Nona lay in the dark, still fuming.

26

Billy came down next day to take Miss Parry up to his house. He never so much as thanked Mum for what she'd done; his face was dark as though the flood had been her fault. They heard him cry out, even from next door, over the state of his sister's living-room floor. 'Territorial, that's what they are,' Ralph had once said. And now their territory had been invaded by half the mud and slime that had washed down from the village.

What a start to a new year! The rain continued, though not hard enough to bring down another flood. They returned to school. The only cheer on their struggle up and down the road was a bit of yellow gorse at the edge of the car park.

Within a week, Billy had got next door dried out and Miss Parry back in.

'Even he can't bear to live with her!' Sharon said glumly, for there had been—despite the weather—a holiday air while she'd been away, and none of them was ready to see her back again.

One day, between the storms, Mrs Lark caught Nona and Sharon coming home from school.

'I've been meaning to come down to you all week,' she said. 'How's your mother? Is she all right? Give this to her, will you?'

She handed Nona a plastic box, with a transparent lid. 'It

194

was wonderful, what she did,' she said.

Nona looked through the lid at a fancy chocolate cake with swirls on top of it. *'What she did?'* she asked, not knowing what Mrs Lark was on about.

'Yes,' said Mrs Lark, beaming. 'With Miss Parry. You know, New Year's Eve. Turning the other cheek...'

The cake was a *reward!* Even Sharon, at Nona's side, shuddered at the thought of Mum being encouraged in what she'd done. And Nona, in a sudden rage, wanted to flatten the box with her bare fists. She walked away without another word, threw the whole thing into the bushes as soon as they got down the road and out of sight. Sharon didn't complain, although she loved cake.

'I hate Miss Parry too,' she said.

But Nona's rage wasn't as simple as all that, and she didn't want to share it with anyone. Down in the car park, she told Sharon, sharply, to go on. She almost pushed her away. Then, with difficulty, she contained her anger all the way until the secret beach where, before the endlessly sympathetic sea, it burst out...

'I know it's bad of me. I know she's done a lot for us,' she began, dry-eyed and furious. 'I know we were footsoldiers together when Mum was ill but even so, I've had enough of that Mrs Lark! You don't have to like people just because they're nice. There's something about her. It's not just that she's Mum's friend now, and Mum never had a friend before. She's too good to be true, that's what it is, just like that Beca who wins races all the time, and always gets her homework right.

'What really gets me is the way Mum copies her. Home-made bread and fancy pies—all Mrs Lark's recipes, as if her own ones weren't good enough any more. She's even found a dress with white cuffs! She's even wearing aprons! She's even started darning Poppy and Bryn's socks!

'She goes from one extreme to another, Mum does. I used to have to do it all and now she says I'm not to do a thing (though of course I do) because she wants me to be a *little girl*. Well, it's a bit late for that now. I haven't been a little girl for years.

'Owen said, the other day, how old I seemed. Well, he's old too, in a funny sort of way, even though his parents can't see it. They treat him like a *baby*. He told me about his father and the boats. What an awful thing to do! I don't blame him for going down to Harry's behind their back so much. I don't blame him for wanting to run away.

'I gave him back his journal, the other day. I absolutely dreaded it, but he said it didn't matter, not now we're friends. He said it didn't even matter that I'd written in it, and there wasn't anything in it that he hadn't told me anyhow.

'Beca says at school that I fancy him, but it's not like that. Whatever he says about me being old, I'm just a little girl compared to him. He says a wren's nest's just the right size for me! Beca's cross because I never got back to being friends with her, that's what it is. The trouble is, she reminds me of her mother, with her golden plaits and all. And her perfect homework reminds me of the night Cody went away.

'He must be growing up now, Cody. A letter came from Susie yesterday and I wouldn't have read it, but I guessed she'd have news of him. She said he's getting big now. He goes to playgroup three times a week and he's out of nappies, which her mum says he never would have been if we still had him.

'I don't think I'll hear from Susie any more. She says she won't write again if I don't reply. Well, we've lost so much of Cody's growing. Even if we read about him in letters, it won't make it up. Even if we see him again, we'll still have lost all that.

'I miss him dreadfully—much more than Sharon, who used to make such a fuss of him! She's too busy trying to be all teenage now. All she cares about these days is whether to cut her hair or not. And of course, keeping King Offa all to herself...

'If only the weather would improve. I don't suppose a bit of wet means anything to you! It doesn't mean much to me either—it's the grey clouds that I can't stand; no colour in the common and nothing on the cliffs except shades of grey. You should see the common—flat as a pancake it is now, after all that rain.

'It's hard to believe you've never seen the common, or the village or the road or Nyth-y-dryw. The mountain was white with snow one day last week, and there was snow in the village, but it never settled down here. And it didn't last long. Just all melted straight away, and then the wind came back again.

'It's getting dark. Not so early as a week ago, so spring must just about be on its way. Thanks for listening. I do feel better when I've talked to you. I wish sometimes that I could sit and sit here, and I didn't have to go . . .'

By the time that Nona, calm again, reached the Mermaid Inn, it was nearly dark. As she came level with Griselda's tent, which looked as though it had been welded into the common and would never blow away again, she saw a light inside. She would have gone straight on, but she thought, mixed up in the wind, that she heard crying.

'Are you all right, Griselda?' she stood outside the tent and called, hoping that Griselda *was* all right and that she could continue on her way, her hard-acquired peace of mind intact.

The bulk of Griselda shifted inside. 'Ralph says we're stupid, stubborn and proud,' came, muffled, from within.

'Who are?' Nona said, uncomprehendingly.

'Harry and me.'

Nona still couldn't imagine Griselda presiding over Harry's caravan, with its stinking rabbit cutlets and week-long stews. And Harry looked so grey now that the winter—as he put it—had 'settled on his chest . . .'

'Would you go back to Harry, if it wasn't for his

girlfriends?' she found herself asking, surprised at her nerve.

'I wouldn't have him again for anything,' Griselda's voice came out, but so sadly that Nona wondered if she meant it. 'I couldn't trust him any more,' she said. 'I've had enough and it's not the girls. It's complicated and you wouldn't understand.'

'Why don't you go back home, then?' Nona said.

'*This* is my home . . .' Griselda sniffed. 'Where else would I go?'

'You'll feel better in the spring,' Nona said, helplessly. 'Everything feels better in the spring.'

'I've given up expecting there ever to be a spring!' came from inside the tent, all muffled again. 'It's only when you're young that you're mad enough to pin your hopes on blimming spring!'

27

The storms carried on right through January and then when Owen thought he couldn't bear any more of them, the snowdrops appeared and, on a lull of a Sunday, Nona's mum broke up the monotony of church by coming in shyly and sitting at the back with a long-faced Sharon, and Poppy.

February began, the wild weather back again. While the storms raged outside, Owen remained a chill wind at home. His determined ill-humours blew into every corner of the house, despite the cheer of his new-found friendship with Nona, and the models he was sneaking down to make at Harry's. He longed for half-term, when he could go down there more, longed for daffodils and spring weather so that he could, at last, run away. In the boredom of what felt like never-ending winter, he longed for something to happen that was really *different* ...

And then one night, the winter still battering outside, there was something in the air ...

Father's face was a picture of contained excitement. He stood before the mirror while Mother helped him into his coat. And it was like a conspiracy, they were both in it together, they were both excited, but they weren't telling.

'Are you going out?' Owen asked, stirred to interest, despite himself.

'I'm going to see Mrs Davies.'

'Can I come along for the ride?'

'Yes ...' Father sounded surprised. 'Of course you can.'

'I'll get my coat then.'

'His sulks are going,' Mother whispered, when he'd gone. 'He's coming round, I told you he would!'

'I'm not so sure,' said Father. 'There's something inside the boy. Something we can't *get at* any more. He still goes down to that fellow's, I'm sure of it. I can't help wishing we could move him right away...'

'*I'm ready, Father.*' Owen stood in the doorway, and they didn't know if he'd heard.

'Ah, yes, do yourself up. It's a nasty night.'

Nona was doing the dishes and her mum was drying them, when Owen and his father knocked upon the front door. Bryn, supposedly in bed, was thundering about upstairs. Sharon was weeping over a perfectly frightful hairdo. She rushed off after Nona had let them in, without a single word.

'Don't mind Sharon!' Nona said. 'I'll put on the kettle and make us some tea.'

'Not just now,' her mum said awkwardly. 'Mr Lark's come to talk to me. You wait with Owen in the living-room, and we'll have it later.'

Mr Lark settled himself at the kitchen table. Nona dried her hands and left the room without a word. She shut the door sharply. Her face was a picture.

'I don't know what they're up to,' Owen said, defensively.

'It's not important,' she said. 'Let's forget it, I don't care. Mum was going to help me with my homework, but you'll do just as well.'

She got her books out of her bag, spilling them all over the floor. But she did care. Owen could see that she felt left out.

'All right,' he said. 'I'm not much good at anything. But I'll do what I can...'

When they had finished, Nona said, 'I promised Griselda

I'd watch telly with her down at Ralph's. Do you want to come?'

Owen was about to say 'yes' when the kitchen door opened.

'I'm just going out,' Nona said, without even looking at her mum's white face.

'Your mother wants to tell you something,' Mr Lark said.

'It'll have to wait,' said Nona, coldly.

'It can't wait,' said Nona's mum.

'We'll go,' said Mr Lark. 'Come along, Owen.'

He propelled Owen through the door and out onto the path. Owen had a last glimpse of Mrs Davies with her head up, chin out, just the way Nona would have looked if she'd been expecting trouble . . .

When they'd gone, Mum called Sharon, Poppy and Bryn downstairs. They sat, as she bid them, around the fire, but Nona remained standing. Mum ran her hands through the stubble of her hair.

I'm getting baptised,' she said at last.

They stared at her, all four of them. 'What's *baptised*?' Poppy—for once not dreaming—asked suspiciously.

'It's a sort of wash,' Mum tried to explain to her. 'They put you in the water and you come up with a new life in front of you. It's a way of asking God to help you start again.'

'Oh,' said Poppy blankly.

'*Oh!*' said Bryn, who couldn't see the point of washing.

'How terrible!' bemoaned Sharon, whose understanding was clearer . . . 'My mother one of the Sion Baptists—what will they say at school?'

'When?' said Nona, with a tight little pain inside her chest.

'Up at Sion on Sunday morning,' Mum said, nervously.

'But you can't,' Nona protested. 'Not publicly, at any

201

rate—it's not like you.'

'It's not,' agreed Mum, and tried to reach for Nona who wouldn't let her near. 'But I've come to the end of *myself*, Nona, and as Mrs Lark said just the other day . . .'

MRS LARK, OH MRS LARK . . . ! Nona turned clumsily away, stumbling for the door as if she couldn't take any more.

'I hope you'll come, Nona,' Mum said. 'I want you all to come.'

Nona didn't answer. She went out into the rainy night without even bothering to shut the door.

The bad weather lasted for the rest of the week. On Saturday night, while Father and Owen prised up the chapel boards to reveal the cobwebbed baptismal pool beneath, the whole building shivered in the awful wind.

Owen shivered too. He couldn't stop wondering if Nona was all right. Mother went down the steps and cleaned away the dust. Father plugged the pool like a bath, and handed him the hose. Owen watched the water dribbling out of it.

Next morning, Father went to Sion early, to heat the water in the pool. The rest of them ate breakfast quickly. There was so much to do. The whole of Jerico would turn out for a show like this, even more than for Christmas. There were hymn tunes to go through and the upper room of the barn to prepare for the special lunch. There would be Nona's mum to dress in her baptismal robe. And there was the house to tidy, for Aunty and Uncle Lark were coming especially, and they'd stay for tea.

The chapel was already full when Owen arrived. The first pew had been cordoned off for Nona and her family. He slid into the one behind, where Beca sat, in best coat and hat, between Uncle and Aunty. Poppy, Bryn and Sharon came in after him, and took their seats. But there was no sign of Nona.

'Are you all right?' Beca asked, while Aunty whispered

to Uncle about the difference a choir would have made.

He was half way through replying that *of course* he was, when Nona's mum appeared. A ripple went through the congregation for she looked like an angel—or a ghost. She was dressed in a white robe, tied round her feet to keep it down when she went into the water. Her hair was a dark fuzz around her head, and her tiny face underneath it was strange and faraway. She sat without noticing anyone, not Poppy next to her, nor Mother smiling tenderly from the piano, nor Father striding up the aisle, nor the rest of the congregation whispering, as they did for brides, about how transformed she was.

During the first hymn, Nona arrived. Owen noticed her out of the corner of his eye. She came in holding Griselda's hand like a little girl, and there was no room at the back this time, and they had to sit in front of him. Her face, as she passed his pew, was white. She looked smaller than ever at Griselda's side. Griselda wore the biggest hat he'd ever seen, and a ton of spiky coral jewellery.

While the hymn was still being sung, Father came out of the pulpit and stood before the pool. He read about the veil in the holy place being torn. Then he prayed for 'Our Sister, Bronwen Davies, in whose Heart the Veil is torn.'

Owen's mind went back to their night at the cinema; again with Nona and Griselda right in front of him, Griselda dressed up to the nines and Nona shining, though differently then. For everything had been funny then, and this was grave.

When they got up for another hymn, Owen would have given anything to have had Harry by his side again, laughing Harry making everything all right, Harry for his protector, just as Nona had hers. He'd have given anything for Griselda to make him laugh, to trip over and fall into the pool just as she'd knocked the mead off the balcony.

But she did not. She sang loud enough to make Uncle and Aunty stare, but she sat down without an accident and

Father donned his waders and got into the water. Nona's mum went down as well. The congregation at the back stood on their pews and, upon the thin, pale, nervous declaration of her faith, Nona's mum was submerged like a drowning sack and then hauled up again, her white frock clinging, her new hair sticking to her head, her scar glaring in the whiteness of the rest of her. Mother rushed forward with a snowy bath towel and wrapped her in it before Emlyn, old Mr Pryce from up the headland or even Uncle could make out the shape of her...

In the upper room afterwards, an abundance of hot tea was produced with the aid of a huge water boiler. The tables were covered with cloths, and thick china places were laid out for the special lunch.

After the rest of them had climbed the steps and gone in, Owen lingered outside, waiting for Nona. She emerged from the chapel at last, with Griselda, holding her hat on in the wind and loudly explaining that she hadn't minded the service but she wouldn't stay for lunch because she really hated *white bread sandwiches, and fairy cakes with butter icing*. Nona let her go. Her high heels clacked down the path. Nona called after her, 'Thanks for coming...'

'It won't be such a bad lunch as all that,' Owen reassured, as Nona struggled up the steps. 'Mother's made a bacon and egg flan, and there's lots of salad and she's really good at egg custard pie.'

Nona stared at the door. She felt shut out again. 'They were kind when Mum was ill,' she said. 'But I hate them now. They've taken her away.'

'I hate them too,' admitted Owen.

'Are you *really* going to run away?'

'Of course I am...!'

Uncle Lark opened the door. '*There* you are...' His passionless eyes were almost animated by the events of the day. The skin on his neck wobbled as he spoke. 'Don't just stand there. Come in . . .'

They went in. Aunty was promising to teach Nona's mum to knit. Bryn was being fussed over by old ladies. Sharon was piling her plate high with cake. Poppy was sucking her thumb, with no interest in the food in front of her at all.

The trouble with the barn was that there were no windows, there was no view out. Poppy had nowhere to look. Owen knew how she felt. 'I hear your father has it in mind to move you,' Uncle Lark was saying, and Owen, staring through him, didn't hear.

At the end, when almost everyone had gone and Father was waiting to take the Davies family home, Owen witnessed a private moment between Nona and her mum. He'd been sent back to get them, for they'd been the last to leave, and they hadn't heard him come in.

'I want to give you something,' Nona's mum was saying, fumbling in her bag. 'It's been a special day for me, and I want it to be special for you. I want to give you *this*.'

Owen watched Nona unwrap the package. Even from a distance, he saw the ring as she got it out. He heard her guilty, awkward, 'Mum, it's . . . it's *lovely*.'

'Thank you for coming,' her mum said. 'I know how you feel. You don't have to say a word. I know how hard today has been for you. I'd have felt the same if I'd been in your shoes. It's just that I'm trying to put things right, the best way I can. Trying to *get hold* of something . . .'

Nona didn't answer, just turned over the ring.

'It was my engagement ring,' her mum said in a funny voice, as if she couldn't, even so long afterwards, bear the memory. 'Your dad gave it to me, but we were too young and my parents made a dreadful fuss. He would have married me, you know, but they wouldn't let him.'

28

Half-term week came at last, and the first day off school was Owen's birthday.

'This is for when you run away,' Nona said, down on the beach the day before. 'You mustn't open it until tomorrow morning.'

When the morning came, he found it was a penknife, with fold-away gadgets, including fork and spoon.

'And this is from us,' his father said, lifting a package across the breakfast table while his mother, not quite herself this morning, looked away.

The package—as if they, too, knew what he was up to—contained a suitcase, with straps and buckles and zips ... 'You'll be needing this,' his father explained. 'We've had a long talk with Uncle and Aunty, and all the arrangements have been made. It's very exciting, Owen. You're starting your new school after Easter.'

Owen was stunned. He couldn't believe it. And on his birthday too.

'But I don't want to go!' he protested. 'I can't *stand* Uncle and Aunty Lark. I don't *want* to live with them ...'

'You'll thank us for it, eventually,' his father said. 'Once certain influences have been put aside, you'll be glad we made you go.'

Certain influences? Owen, looking at his father, caught the fear and anxiety in his eyes. Of course ...!

'We know where you go,' Father said, as if it hurt him to

mention it. 'We know you've been deceiving us, but we don't want to make a fuss and spoil your day. You must open your cards. We'll talk about this later. Look, here's a present for you from Beca...'

Owen screwed up the cards without reading them, and ignored the present that Beca held out to him, looking for all the world as shocked as he was, because she hadn't known what they were planning either.

'Mother,' he said, in desperation, 'you won't let me go, will you?'

'It's for the best,' Mother whispered, getting up to clear the dishes away.

'FOR THE BEST!'

Owen erupted from the table, knocking his chair over on the way. He wouldn't stay in that callous place a moment more!

'I'm going out, don't you tell me I can't! I'd planned it anyway—I didn't want to spend my birthday with *you!* Don't expect me back for some stupid birthday tea! You can *stuff* your suitcase!'

He kicked the thing out of his way. Grabbed his coat from the hook beside the back door. Stormed out, slamming it behind him.

Nona was round at Harry's, watching him working on a fairground horse. On the shelf above her were the clay heads and model ships that Owen had made on his surreptitious visits.

'You're late. Are you all right?' she exclaimed, when Owen hauled back the door with more force than she'd seen him use before. 'You're wet. You've been on the beach, haven't you? Well you might have waited for us. Look, we've got the picnic ready and I told Mum I won't be back all day.'

Harry threw off his unravelling pullover and washed his hands. 'It's going to be a good day,' he promised. 'All those clouds are going to blow away. What's the long face for, boyo? It's your birthday!'

Owen shrugged.

'Where shall we go?' Nona asked.

Harry threw on his coat. '*Bird Rock.*'

They stopped half way up the Hundred Steps, to catch their breaths.

'No one comes up here,' said Harry. 'They all go round the headland in a boat, or take the track across old Pryce's farm. It's a shame. They don't know what they're missing!'

'My sister Beca would just *run* up here,' Owen panted.

'Don't believe you!' Harry laughed.

They clambered on. Only Harry had the nerve to look over the side. When they got on to the Head, the wind had blown the clouds away, just as he'd said it would. They sat upon tufty grass. Nona saw a small, brown snake, but it shrank away when she tried to dig it out. Owen angled his face to collect the sun. He felt better now. He told them about being sent away. They ate biscuits and sympathized. Harry looked far out to sea.

'I've got some bad news too,' said Nona. 'Listen to this. It came through our door, and I got it before Mum.'

She pulled out a piece of paper and read, 'IF THAT CAT OF YOURS DON'T STOP BOTHERING US WE'LL HAVE THE LAW ON YOU, BAPTISED OR NOT,' written in unkempt letters, with no signature underneath.

'But you thought your mum and her were all right now,' Owen exclaimed. 'You said, after that flood and all . . .'

'*Mum* thought that they were 'all right,' corrected Nona. 'Bryn's been playing with Cledwyn recently, and Mum thought everything was better. But I knew it wasn't. I've been waiting for it.

'What are you going to do?'

'I just hope we can hold her off till Easter,' Nona sighed. 'At least there's *something* to be got out of having to move somewhere new!'

'Come on,' said Harry, getting to his feet, 'or we'll never reach Bird Rock by lunch-time. Put your troubles behind you. This is meant to be a birthday!'

The sea had turned from cold mirror-glass to blue. Despite everything, Owen couldn't help but put his troubles behind him, for Uncle and Aunty's world was so far away. It had nothing to do with *this*.

Nona smiled too, and put the screwed-up letter back in her pocket. The wind blew her hair across her face as she followed Harry back on to the path. Owen looked down the black cliff to the distant, mumbling sea. As they came off the Head, he saw rocks coated with yellow lichen. The path was leading them towards a different, bleaker bay with no sandy inlets, and no way down. It cut a thin and giddy line along which they trod slowly and carefully. Down, then up again they went, underneath a hawthorn tree which arched right over the path, and onto a promontory which pointed up Wales, to the north.

'Here we are,' said Harry, flinging himself flat and peering over the edge. 'Bird Rock.'

Below them, a craggy molar of a rock stuck out of the ocean, white with years of excrement from the birds who'd nested on it.

'There are the cormorants,' said Harry, pointing to the black birds on the sea. 'Can you see them dipping? And over there, the seals...?' They watched the dipping cormorants and the black-and-white oyster catchers on the rock, and the Atlantic seals until, 'The birds are very nice,' said Harry, turning over and smiling secretly, 'but there's something else I brought you to see.'

'What?' they both said.

Harry got up again. 'Come and see my house!'

'*Your house?*'

Harry couldn't help but grin at them. 'Yes. Come on...'

He led them off the promontory, up above the path. They climbed beside a stream, until a bramble-covered earth mound blocked their way, and they could go no further.

'Here we are,' said Harry.

Nona stared. She didn't understand. But Owen had already seen the tattered wooden door behind the brambles.

'It was some old bird-man's place,' explained Harry. 'He dug it out to watch the Rock. I lived in it after he'd gone, before I had the caravan and sheds ... Come and look inside.'

He pulled back the brambles, struggled with the door and let them in. The place was dark like a cave. It smelt of the earth, smelt of secrets with its clay floor, and turf-and-wood roof.

With head stooped, Harry crossed the floor. 'Here's where I cooked,' he reminisced. He tore away more brambles, and light shone down a crumbling chimney upon an abandoned hearth.

'You'd never know this place was here!' exclaimed Owen, looking about him.

'You wouldn't, would you?' Harry sighed. 'I lived here with Griselda. They were happy days. But even she found it too hard in the end, and we gave in and bought the caravan...'

He smiled at his memories. It was the only time he'd mentioned Griselda and himself. 'It's late,' he said. 'Let's go out again, and have that lunch...'

They followed him out into the bright day. Voices came to them over the water, from a distant fishing boat.

'Voices carry so on the sea,' Harry said. 'Come on. Let's eat.'

He'd bought a battenburg cake, with pink and yellow squares, and at the end of the picnic he and Nona serenaded Owen with 'Happy Birthday', without caring who heard. Owen cut the cake with his new penknife, and they ate it. The sea twisted and winked and swished below them. Birds cried and wheeled and dipped. The distant fishermen's throbbing engine faded away.

'We should start back too,' said Harry, for the sun was

210

coming down the sky. 'We could cut across old Pryce's land. It would get us home quicker if we went that way.'

'What, and leave the sea!' they both protested.

'It's your day,' laughed Harry. 'Don't blame me if you get back late!'

They scrambled to their feet, and rabbits scattered every way. 'You should see Offa chasing rabbits,' Nona said. 'When he's in the mood he even goes for Billy Parry's dogs! I expect that's why they wrote that letter...'

Owen wished she hadn't said it, and he was sure that she did too, for her words cast a cloud over their sunny day. They packed away the picnic. Harry set off down the stream. They followed him in single file, back towards everything from which they'd wanted to run away.

'Mind this bit,' called Harry, where the path met with the stream. 'It's slippery.'

They followed him, carefully and silent, all the way back up the Head, to the top of the Hundred Steps. There the beach, the Mermaid Inn, Nyth-y-dryw and the road to Jerico spread out below them. Owen shivered. Uncle and Aunty were out there too, waiting to get him as the shadows had got the common. He stood absolutely still. Harry was half way down the steps, and Nona was at his side. He wanted to freeze the moment, keep it for ever, stop Harry reaching that bottom step, keep Nona by his side.

'What are you going to do?' said Nona.

'You *know* what I'm going to do!' He looked back the way they'd come, towards the bird-man's hidden burrow.

'You couldn't stay up there,' said Nona. 'It would be impossible. You heard what Harry said. Even Griselda couldn't stand it in the end.'

'I could stay till they gave up looking,' he replied. 'When the time was right I could move on somewhere else. You wouldn't tell on me, Nona, would you? You wouldn't tell them where I was, no matter how much they asked, or however upset they were?'

'I'll swear in blood, if you want me to!' promised Nona as though they were kids, like Bryn and Cledwyn, playing a game.

'I wish you could come too,' said Owen.

'So do I,' she said. 'But they need me at home. Mum's not better, just because she's darning our socks!'

'Come on, you two!' called Harry, who had reached the bottom step.

'We're on our way!' Owen answered him. Then, to Nona. 'You won't have long to change your mind. *I shall go soon.*'

29

When Nona got home, Billy's pick-up truck was next door, and King Offa was prowling around the house from one window-sill to another, as if he wanted to get at it.

'I'm going to let him out,' said Sharon, picking him up. 'I can't stand this any more.'

'Don't!' said Nona, sharply.

'Why ever not?'

Before Nona could tell her about the letter, Miss Parry's front door flew open noisily. King Offa sprang, yowling, out of Sharon's arms. He flung himself at the window, and neither of them could get near him. Ever afterwards, they said it was as though he knew what was coming next.

For Bryn came spilling out of Miss Parry's house. *'I didn't do it!'* he was yelling. *'Nona . . .! Mum . . .! Help me . . .!'*

Miss Parry had him by the hair of his head and one red ear. She dragged him down the front path and through her gate. She kicked him over the bridge with her meaty knees. He sobbed, and struggled to get free.

Nona left King Offa to Sharon's care. She rushed out of the house and down the path. 'Let go of my brother, you big fat cow!' she burst out, before she could stop herself. And just as she said it, Billy appeared.

'WHAT DID YOU SAY TO MY SISTER?!'

Nona hadn't meant to say it, at least not quite like that, and she certainly didn't know what to say now! Billy's eyes

213

were bulging and her voice dried up and her limbs wanted to melt away. 'Give Bryn to me,' she croaked, in what she hoped was a more conciliatory tone, 'please ...'

But the please didn't do the trick. Billy was rising to the occasion before her eyes, and so was Miss Parry, who pushed Bryn onto the ground beside the pick-up truck with such force that he grazed his knees.

'Do you know what this wicked child has done?' she spat, foam flying from the corners of her mouth. 'Do you, do you? He's *broken Grandpa!* And do you know how he did it? Do you? He bit the pendulum off! Bit it! *Bit it!*'

Bryn scrambled to Nona's side. His knees were bleeding. Nona put her arms around him tight. She saw Poppy at the window upstairs, Mum hurrying down the path, Sharon in the doorway, with King Offa in her arms.

'I didn't,' Bryn sobbed. 'I couldn't have—it's a great big thing! Cledwyn pulled it off! He thought it was funny! He laughed, and when she came in, he said that it was me ...'

'*My Cledwyn? A liar?!*'

Billy shook from head to foot. His face was purple and his eyes were coming out. His chest was about a mile wide, it seemed to have swollen so much, and his hands were like giant bunches of bananas. He jumped into the back of the pick-up truck and began rummaging around, hitting at the dogs every time they got in his way.

'We've had enough of you!' he spluttered, flecks of foam flying out of his mouth too. 'That little bastard's been leading Cledwyn astray and we've been nice, *nice* we have, tried to be *friendly* like, and we've nursed a viper to our bosom and it's come to this, THIS ...!'

One of his dogs bit him. He rolled his eyes and screamed. Nona thought he was going to have a fit, but suddenly he'd got his shotgun in his hand. '*Grandpa's broken, broken ...*' He began to cry. He was waving the thing around. For a frozen, dreadful moment, Nona knew that one of them was going to get it—and she didn't know who.

And in that moment, King Offa acted.

He leapt out of Sharon's arms, down the path and straight at Billy. A primeval cry surged from deep behind his sharp, white teeth. His red coat streamed with anger. It was the moment for which he'd been made so huge and fierce and wild. It was the frightful side of him that everyone guessed at, but nobody had actually seen.

Billy was beyond thinking. He raised his shotgun, aimed with devilish accuracy, and shot him dead. Then he staggered into his truck and drove, as if possessed, away.

They all stood, stunned, while Offa's blood spurted onto the path.

Nona didn't cry, even in the night, or next day when they buried Offa with full honours, as befitted a king. Mum said she was a tower of strength. Apparently, she'd done all sorts of things, like going down to Ralph's to call the police—who'd taken Billy's gun away—and putting Poppy and Bryn to bed and sitting with them. But she couldn't remember any of it.

'I was like that when your dad went away,' Mum said. 'I kept on smiling, but I couldn't remember a thing. I was in a state of shock. I knew it meant he didn't love me.'

Sharon, unlike Nona, wept even in her sleep, and Nona envied her for it. Her own heart had been locked inside a block of ice. Her only consolation was that while they buried Offa Miss Parry's curtains were drawn tight. No binoculars today, perhaps she was up at Billy's.

Sharon insisted on digging the hole. It took her an hour, with all the pauses to cry, but it was a big hole and she was surprisingly methodical about the way she made it. She piled up all the earth on a polythene bag so that, when King Offa was in the ground, its corners could be picked up and it could be tipped over him without a fuss.

When the hole was ready, Nona went for him, lying on the ground underneath a blanket. She lifted the blanket back.

King Offa's body was as hard as Harry's horsehair sofa. Even his tail would never sway again. His paws were cold. The bones beneath his stiffened skin were set. A black fly came out of his mouth. Indignantly, Nona brushed it away then, suspiciously, lifted back his lip. A cluster of cream-coloured eggs had been laid between King Offa's teeth, on his cold gums.

'Decay!' thought Nona, almost crying, not with sorrow but rage. 'It's started already! He's not even in the grave, and the worms have got him!'

Furiously, she reached for the edge of the blanket and wiped the eggs away. *Not yet! Not yet!* She scraped the body up and got it to the edge of Sharon's pit and called to the rest of them that it was time. Poppy came out in her new Sunday best. Bryn followed her. Mum wore an apron with the smell of lunch on it.

Nona heaved King Offa over the edge and he lay in the bottom of the pit, red fur upon red earth. Awkwardly, Sharon reached into her pocket and brought something out. It was a handful of her shorn and much lamented hair. She threw it into the pit. Bryn said, 'He ought to have some primroses' and grabbed the first, brave bunch of them that had opened out under the hedge, and threw them in too. Poppy sucked her thumb silently. Nona said, 'I'll cover him up.'

When they'd filled the pit and got down on their hands and knees and patted it smooth, Bryn went for his arrows, which he set all around it; guards of honour for the grave of a warrior. Poppy brought her collection of shells and decorated the top. Mum went in to finish lunch. Sharon sidled up to Nona, looking for all the world as if she wanted comfort.

But Nona didn't notice her. She stood very still, with pictures rushing back through her mind of all the things they'd done and said and seen down here. She got back as far as Cody and then her mind went blank, she thought of nothing.

They had spaghetti bolognese for lunch. Nona ate the pasta worms in silence and with difficulty, and when she'd finished Mum got up and cleared away the plates. She went to the cupboard and came out with a tin of pears and a bag of catfood from Emlyn. She threw the catfood in the bin, and began opening the pears. Half way through, she burst into tears. 'We can't eat these! They're *South African!*' she cried, and she cut her finger on the tin.

'It won't matter just this once,' Nona tried to console her, who hadn't known that politics meant anything to Mum. But it wouldn't do. Mum threw the pears in the bin as well. They ate bowls of custard on its own, and it wasn't the pears, or her bleeding finger, that Mum was crying about. Nona wanted to say, 'This is what you get for turning the other cheek to people like that!' She didn't feel sorry for Mum at all. Just hard towards her, bitter, as if it were all her fault.

She went upstairs without even offering to help clear up, and sat on her window-sill looking across the common. Mrs Lark's car appeared on the track and Nona saw it. She'd be coming with condolences. Nona couldn't bring herself to care. For nothing was the same. It was almost more, this loss of King Offa on top of everything else, than she could bear.

Mrs Lark pulled up against the boathouse wall. Nona watched her come up the path. 'She's probably brought us a cake!' she sneered, as Mum let her in.

'Nona!' Mum called, eventually. 'Come down here.'

Nona went down. Mrs Lark was crying. Nona was surprised, because she'd never taken any notice of King Offa before.

'Nona, have you seen Owen?' Mum said bleakly.

'Owen? Why?' Nona's face was a blank. She knew it was. She didn't have to struggle to hide a thing. It felt as though there was nothing left to hide.

'Owen's gone!' wept Mrs Lark. Her hair was out of place, her slippers wet and her raincoat muddy. 'I've been looking

217

everywhere. He left last night. His note said he wasn't coming back. Oh, Nona please, he talks to you. Did he have money? Do you know where he might have gone? You must know *something* . . .'

'I'm sorry,' said Nona, 'I'm afraid I don't.' And she didn't feel guilty, not a bit of it. She didn't feel a thing.

30

Owen's disappearance was big news in Jerico for the rest of half-term week. There were even police at school when it opened again on Monday morning, and it was the main topic of conversation in the playground.

'You can understand it, can't you?' said Aidan Hughes. 'It must be awful, everyone watching what you do because of who your dad is. They say he's gone to London. Well, good luck to him!'

'You were friends with him,' said Alice Pugh, to Nona. 'Didn't he tell you anything?'

'No,' said Nona, emphatically.

'You were Owen's friend,' said Griselda. They sat by Ralph's window, watching the night-time sea. 'He must have told you what he was going to do.'

'He never said a thing,' Nona replied, fed up with being asked. 'Why don't you talk to Harry? He was his friend too.'

'Where is Harry?' Griselda said. 'He hasn't been in all week.'

'Harry's sick,' called Ralph. 'He's laid up good and proper, didn't you know?'

'What sort of sick?' demanded Griselda.

'He's got a poorly stomach,' Ralph said. 'Not that it means anything to you! Aren't you going to get back to the fryers? We've got customers.'

Griselda got up, unwillingly. 'It's surprising more customers don't get *poorly stomachs*, when one thinks of what you offer them!' she said.

Nona left them to it. She went out through the Mermaid Inn's weather-tight door. When she got home only Mum was up, attempting to make a dress with Mrs Lark's sewing machine.

'Are you all right?' Mum said.

'Yes, I'm fine.'

Nona went up to bed. She didn't want to watch Mum sewing, and she was fed up with being asked if she was *all right*. She listened to the wind and wondered how Owen was getting on, and if he was warm enough. She wished he hadn't gone just when he had, just before King Offa had died, just when she needed him.

'I'll tell Mum I'm invited out to tea tomorrow,' she said, 'but I'll go up and see how he is instead.'

Owen awoke, wishing that he hadn't, for he was waking earlier every day. He didn't seem to be getting used to the ground at all. Rather, he seemed to be feeling it more; it was getting harder, he was sure of it. Unhappily, he tried to make himself more comfort-able, tried to lull himself back to sleep— gave up and watched the dawn break between cracks in the rough plank door.

Another long day stretched in front of him. Another cold day. Another hungry day. It was only Tuesday, *Tuesday!* Only a week since he'd run away, and already he'd licked the marmite pot clean and eaten all his tinned spam and biscuits—despite his lecture to himself on self-control! There were apples, of course, which he'd bake in the embers of tonight's fire. There was still a slab of chocolate and a final can of beer and two packets of dehydrated mashed potato. But that was all.

Owen went outside to examine the day. The wind had dropped and everything was misty and grey. He was glad for the change, even though it robbed him of his view. Last night's wind had blown down the chimney, blown out his fire, blown ash into his pan, ruining his attempts at spam stew.

'I'm starving,' he addressed the morning. 'I can't wait for tonight. I'll light the fire now and bake the apples. I'll finish off the beer!'

He went back into the burrow and scratched together the remains of last night's fire until thin smoke rose through the chimney. But then an engine throbbed out on the bay, and he had to smother it. He crept to the door, listened to the laughing fishermen as their boat emerged from the mist and weighed anchor, just off Bird Rock.

With another sort of hunger that he never would have expected of himself, Owen feasted upon the fishermen. He didn't know how long he listened to their chatter about mates, rugger, girlfriends, wives. He was so hungry for human company, and in any case, time seemed to have lost its meaning up here. What did it matter if it was morning or afternoon? It was hunger—of one sort or another—that marked out the boundaries now.

He must have fallen asleep, for when he awoke the dull sun had melted the fog, and the fishermen had gone. Owen sighed to have missed them, and now to be alone again. It was happening more and more, this sleeping at odd times and in the wrong places. He half-sat, half-lay against the burrow, just as he'd woken, frozen to the spot.

It had been so heady at first, realizing that he'd done what he'd always planned to do; that he was his own man, and free. But then had come the cold, the boring repetition of the food, the discovery that there wasn't as much of it as he had thought, the unexpected slowness of each day, where the biggest adventure was when he went down to collect more stores from his waning hoard at the secret beach. His mind went back to Saturday night when he'd finished nearly all the beer. He remembered waking in the night, outside on the bare ground where he'd collapsed. It had hit him, then, that he

221

didn't have a home any more. Panic had hit him, but even so he wouldn't go back. He wouldn't!

Determinedly, Owen went into the burrow for his sleeping-bag and the last bar of chocolate and his only book. It wouldn't be so bad if he wasn't on his own. It was the loneliness, more than anything, that got to him.

He slid into the sleeping-bag and broke up the chocolate, a piece for every chapter that he read. But he ate it all at once and, third time round, the book bored him anyhow. He fell asleep again, wondering if Harry and Griselda had felt the cold up here as much as him.

When he awoke, he knew that it was afternoon and he must have slept for hours. He was hungry again, *starving* and ashamed of himself for lying around all day instead of doing all the pioneer, 'Huck Finn' things he'd always thought he'd do. He got to his feet. A rabbit scampered out of his way and, 'I know what I'll do!' he thought. 'I'll catch a rabbit, and cook it for tea!'

With his new penknife in his pocket and only the vaguest idea of how rabbits were caught, he clambered up into Mr Pryce's top field. Rabbits no doubt heard him coming and hid, for, as he pounded down it and thrashed in and out among the trees, he saw not one of them.

He was climbing out onto a concrete lane and the day was fad-ing and he was still no closer to catching anything, when a tractor bore down on him. He darted back under the hedge and thought, 'If I get away with this and nobody sees me, I'll go back and make a fire and bake those apples. I'll give up on rabbits, really I will . . .'

His stomach complained at the thought of only apples for tea. But when the tractor had gone and he looked onto the quiet road, a dead rabbit lay in front of him, knocked clean onto its side as it tried to reach the hedge as well.

By the time Owen got back, the sky was heavy, not just with night but rain. Unexpected smoke was rising from his chimney. Nona came out to greet him.

'It's all right,' she called. 'It's only me.'

'Nona ... *Nona?*'

'Don't look like that,' she said. 'I'm not a ghost!'

He couldn't imagine a ghost in school uniform. He almost laughed out loud. He almost hugged her. 'What are you doing here?' he said, and then he saw her face and remembered something he'd thought about her once: *There's something wild and desperate in her. She'd do anything.*

'Are you all right?' he said.

She laughed, a hard little laugh. 'I just wanted to check up on you,' she said. 'Of course I'm all right, I don't know why people keep asking me. I told Mum I'd been invited out to tea. Look, I've brought you some milk.'

'Oh, Nona,' he said, pleased to see her, 'we'll have a feast tonight. Milk to drink and see what I've got!'

He produced the furry bundle of limp rabbit from underneath his jacket. Nona stared at it blankly. 'It's all right,' he felt the need to say. 'Look, there's hardly any blood.'

Nona looked. She didn't say a thing.

'It's *food*,' he said, defensively. 'There's nothing wrong with that, is there?'

She shrugged. Owen found himself slightly rattled. All he wanted was to get inside and skin and gut and cook the thing. 'If you were as hungry as I am, you wouldn't be so choosy,' he said. 'If you were as hungry as me, you'd probably eat *anything.*'

Nona looked at his dirty face, the shadows under his eyes, his untidy hair.

'You're probably right.'

She followed him inside. He laid out the rabbit, brightened up the fire. He felt for his penknife. 'You don't have to watch,' he said, nervous now that it had come to it.

'*I'm all right.*'

'I'll make a start then.' He picked up the rabbit, pinched

its fur the way he'd seen Harry do it and slit the skin. He slid his clumsy fingers in where the rabbit's body was still warm. Then he sliced down the skin and worked the body out—like a hand from a glove, as Harry put it.

Nona watched him all the time. She'd got that secret look in her eyes, and he wondered what she was thinking. He felt sick. But she didn't even flinch at the smell that rose to greet them both, the smell of bodies underneath their skin.

'Bring me the bucket of water.' He knew he couldn't finish with her watching him...

When she brought it over, the last bits were done and the heart, liver and spleen were in the fire. He rinsed the meat, and cut it into pieces which he put in the pan with dehydrated mashed potatoes, and an apple, to make a stew.

Nona turned over the rabbit's furry skin. 'Offa must have smelt like this.' She held it underneath her nose.

'What do you mean?' said Owen.

'Oh, I'll tell you some time, maybe tomorrow... I *can* stay with you, can't I, like you asked me to?'

'Of course you can,' he said. But he hadn't expected it. There was no spare sleeping-bag, not to say anything of the problem about food. He couldn't, somehow, see her eating rabbits every day...

To his surprise, she pocketed the skin. 'You didn't want it?'

'No.'

When the meat had been stewed and eaten and the bones spat out and thrown away, Nona poked the last of them and said, almost bitterly, 'Just skin and bones... We don't add up to much, do we?'

Her face was shut, the way it used to be. There wasn't anything of the little girl today. She was older than him—years further on.

'What haven't you told me?' he said. 'What's wrong?'

She shook her head. 'I'll tell you how your family are,'

she said instead. But she didn't. She was falling asleep...

She wouldn't take the sleeping-bag he offered her, just curled up in her coat and cardigan, with her school bag under her head, and shut her eyes. He built up the fire again, to keep her warm, and she drifted off. He couldn't sleep himself. He was trying to understand her, and she was beyond him.

Above his head, the rain beat down. In the fiery burrow they were safe and dry, at least for tonight. Outside, the distant, mumbling sea lullabied the whole coast. He fell asleep. He was none the wiser.

31

Nona awoke and the door had blown ajar in the night and the new day shone in upon the earth floor. Last night's rabbit bones lay around her in the dust. Owen snorted in his sleep. The die was cast, as Mrs Thomas was always saying. She, too, had run away.

'I'm going out to look at the morning!'

Owen grunted as she creaked to her feet, brushed down her coat, banged her stiff hands together.

'Empty out the bucket, bring back some fresh water...'

She took the bucket outside. The newness of the morning hit her like joy. She climbed up beside the stream and only at the top, with a heady view both down the fields, and out over the sea, did she stoop to clean the bucket and fill it with fresh water. Then she sat in the tufty, windswept grass, under the farmer's fence.

She wanted to think. A skylark sang above her head. The sun rose over the mountain behind Jerico, and the clouds were pink and scudding. All around her new bracken was unfurling, primroses opening out, brambles budding.

She pulled the rabbit's skin out of her pocket. It seemed such an inconsequential thing in the light of day. She turned it over, fur side down. Its surface was creamy as parchment. The red lines of the rabbit's veins ran all over it, looking for all the world like arterial roads on a map. She traced one of them. It ended at the edge of the skin. She lifted her finger to begin a new one, but the smell of insides on her hand was so strong that she threw the skin away, and washed her hands instead. She'd tell Owen about King Offa today. Tell him everything he wanted to know. She got up to go, and two men appeared...

She was in full view. Old Mr Pryce was one of them. The other was the policeman who'd taken Billy's gun. They were hurrying up the top field and they looked so purposeful; they were coming straight this way as if they *knew*.

Why they hadn't yet seen Nona she couldn't understand. She flung herself flat upon the ground. The policeman stopped to answer his two-way radio, and she seized the opportunity to slither down to the cover of some brambles. She'd got to get back to Owen, hadn't she? Got to warn him.

But before she could move on, they were at the fence. Farmer Pryce was saying this was the only place up here where a boy could hide.

'I hope I haven't brought you on a wild goose chase,' he said. 'I did see *something*, I know I did. Teatime yesterday, it was. In the hedge, see, when I drove by on my tractor...'

His fears were groundless. They went right past Nona on their way down, and there was absolutely nothing that she could do, apart from squeeze herself into the centre of the bush and hold her breath. Old Mr Pryce knew what he was looking for, all right. He led the policeman straight to the burrow. And Nona knew without even seeing it, that she'd left the door ajar.

'What's this, then?' the policeman said, and they stooped and entered...

After what seemed like a thousand years, Owen came out between them like a criminal, clutching his haversack and sleeping-bag and pans and even her school bag, as though they were apprehended loot. The policeman was heralding the good news to his radio. Mr Pryce was delighted to have got it right.

'You wait until your father gets you,' he said to Owen, 'and you the minister's son too!'

Owen didn't answer. He allowed himself to be led up beside the stream. Nona crouched inside her bramble bush. They stopped right beside her, to get their breath.

Nona didn't move. She wondered if this was how the rabbit had felt with the tractor almost on it, how King Offa had felt when Billy's shot whizzed through the air. They were going to find her too. She didn't stand a chance. They were going to look into the bush and here she'd be, scratched and in disarray, and in just about the worst trouble in her life.

She imagined Miss Parry with her binoculars, saying for everyone to hear that the wicked Davies girl had led the minister's nice son astray.

But it never came to that. Owen moved them on. He began to climb up the stream again and they sprang to either side of him. He clambered over the fence at the top and his eyes lingered briefly on the bramble bush, as if he knew that she was there. He was leading them away. But what could she do with what he offered her? She couldn't live up here alone. She'd have to go back, wouldn't she?

She crouched for a long time, too frightened to move. And when, at last, she scrambled down the bank with her scratched face and wild hair and torn coat, the burrow was full of ghosts—the last of the rabbit bones, the dregs of the fire. She thought of the bird-man living here before, and Harry with Griselda...

Where else could she go, but to Harry or Griselda? They were all she'd got. They'd tell her what to do.

She went the long, safe, secluded way—she took the cliff path, and she didn't see a soul. By the time she looked down upon the Mermaid Inn, the sun was high up in the sky. There was nobody in the car park. Owen must have long since been carted off. She stumbled, with scant regard for safety, down the Hundred Steps, past the track to the secret beach, over the stile. She skulked behind the sea wall, right the way along, because she didn't want Ralph to come out and ask why she wasn't at school. By the time she reached

Griselda's willows she was breathless.

And Griselda wasn't there.

Not only wasn't she there, but her tent had gone; her tent and everything in it. The tent that had been fixed so that no wind could blow it away; that could only be gone because Griselda had gone too . . .

Snowdrops grew beside the half-dismantled platform, and deeper in the common, white, garlic-scented ramsons were coming up. Wrens chattered in the rowan tree. Nona watched them. They were probably the ones Mum had fed on Christmas Day. Griselda had gone.

Nona followed the ramsons' trail deep into the common. 'It doesn't matter, it doesn't,' she said, remembering the red vein ending at the edge of the rabbit's skin, and her finger taking up a new road instead. 'Harry'll do just as well,' she said.

By the time she'd passed the side of Nyth-y-dryw, and made it to the dead tree, her shoes were all but ruined, and her legs soaked and scratched with brambles. Her feet were so blistered she could hardly walk on them. But she didn't mind. Griselda might pack up and go, but Harry would still be there.

'He'll understand,' she reassured herself. 'He'll make everything all right!'

Smoke rose from his chimney. She imagined herself upon his horsehair sofa, her feet soaking in a tub of water while he sorted out her life. She hobbled across the clearing and clambered up the steps. Then, just as she was about to knock upon the door, a voice inside burst into the anthem they sang up at school during every wretched inter-schools rugby match:

> *Not a life I ask of pleasure,*
> *Gold and gems are not for me,*
> *I desire a heart of goodness,*
> *Clean and honest, bright and free.*

> Heart of mercy, full of goodness,
> Fairer than the lily white,
> Such a clean and happy conscience
> Can sing loud by day and night ...

Nona would have gone straight away, but the caravan door flew wide open and Griselda stood on the threshold, the song dying on her breath and a heavy saucepan full of stodge drooping in her hand.

'Ralph was right,' she said and Nona saw Harry, on the sofa himself, with his feet up and blankets all around him and bits of curly hair sticking out of his chest. 'Harry's sick. It'll be those awful stews he boils up for weeks on end. Either them, or Ralph's dreadful sausages. I always knew he'd poison himself one day. I've said I'll stay and look after him. Hot milk and bread with salt on top—it's the cure for everything ...'

Harry groaned in protest, and Griselda laughed. She looked quite unlike her usual self. She'd abandoned glamour for huge army surplus trousers, braces, rolled up sleeves. It was as if she'd left the ranks of camp-followers and joined some sort of war. She wore no make-up. Her hair stuck out like the bristles of a brush. Her face was radiant. Nona would have known, without having passed the abandoned camping site, that she had come to stay. That forgiveness, *something*, had happened between the two of them. They were back together.

And it was the final straw. The thing that after the loss of Cody, changes in Mum, death of King Offa and now Owen's capture, she couldn't bear. The sight of happiness was just too much for her. She stood upon the step, excluded just as Uncle Brady had excluded her all those Sunday mornings when he'd shut the bedroom door. There was no place for her when people loved each other—or whatever it was they did. She jumped off the steps and on feet that she'd thought were finished, ran away.

'Hey! Nona! Hey, come back. What is it, what's wrong?'

They didn't know, did they, and she wasn't going to tell them. They were tucked up snug fighting Harry's sickness, and the outside world didn't matter for them. Well, let them get on with it! She was glad for their happiness, really she was. She wasn't crying because she minded. She didn't care a thing. Nothing mattered in the end.

She crashed through the common, right the way down until she came out by the pub. Her feet didn't hurt her any more. She found herself upon the sea wall, without shoes somehow, and then upon the cliff path again, and then down through the new bracken, on her way to the secret beach.

All the roads led to it eventually. All of them led where she was going now: to the very edge of all she'd ever known or understood—the *end of herself*, as Mum had put it—to the ever-waiting, always listening sea.

32

She'd come to *talk*. That much was for sure. But as she
stumbled onto the pebbles, Nona realized that some things
were beyond words. It wasn't that they were stuck inside,
like they'd been that awful night when she hadn't been able
to get them out. There were just things you couldn't tell,
unless you found another way of doing it.

Nona stood still upon the pebbles. She'd reached the
edge of the land and the sea waited—more than waited. It
seemed to call to her, 'Come on, come on. You don't have to
say a thing. There's another way...' It seemed to understand.

The tide was high, the beach was nearly full of it, and it
was very calm as it always was here, sheltered by the rocks.
Distantly, she heard waves pounding over other cliffs but
here the waves were whispering, whispering at the shore.

Nona removed her coat and cardigan, rolled them up
and stuffed them under the bottom step. A handful of sweet
papers fell out of her pocket, and her wordbook which she
pushed under too, for what use was there for words now?

She went to the water's edge, dipped a sore and weary
toe in the sea. She scooped up a handful of the stuff and let it
trickle away. She didn't take the toe out again. Just left it
there until it didn't feel sore—didn't feel anything—any
more and the sea had whispered past it with its 'yes...?
yes...?', over her foot, over her other foot, over her ankle,
back again, up again...

All the time she was looking beyond the small mouth of the secret beach to the slabs of cliff on the other side of the bay. The sun shone on those grey and rusty slabs, and on the gull in the sky, and on the water.

It was a picture-postcard setting. A perfect moment. Ripples and waves of sheer emotion broke over her, that where she'd once been afraid of the wild, big sea, her eyes and mind were full of it now—she was up to her calves, now up to her knees, and it was taking the pain from her, taking it all away.

'You used to frighten me,' she thought, 'I didn't *know* you. Oh, how glad I am, despite everything, that we came down here!' She took off her skirt, flung it back onto the pebbles. 'I want to wash all the horrid things away,' she would have said, if she'd had the words. 'I want to be clean. I want to *stop feeling things.*'

The gentle waves lap-lapped her school shirt and it clung to her, like Mum's baptismal gown in the dusty chapel pool. The sea was up to her waist now and although it took what was left of her breath away, it was so easy, starting swimming. She hardly even noticed that she was doing it. Suddenly, there she was with her head bobbing on the water and the sun shining on her face, and she felt like a grey Atlantic seal, turning over and over as she was carried out of the secret bay. She knew she should have felt cold, but she didn't. She kept putting her face into the water and watching shoals of tiny fish swim underneath.

Out in the bigger bay now, the water felt different. Clearer. Wholer. Stronger. Deeper, more *itself*—oh, she couldn't explain... She was happy because she couldn't see the bottom of it any more, could only see depth upon depth, a jellyfish with a frill, an occasional, drifting weed.

And the shoreline looked different too, from how she'd imagined it would be. The secret beach had gone, lost among all the others. Nona watched the sculpted cliffs that framed the edge of what had been her world, picked out with difficulty the Mermaid Inn and tiny figures running in front of it. She lay in the water and bobbed away from them and still she didn't feel coldness or think, in words, of what she was doing. The words were inside of her. Clear. Whole. Strong. Deep. She didn't have to spit them out. This drifting, soaking, bobbing was a new way of telling the sea.

She was nearly past the Head, drawing up Wales with the current, before she realized that she was drowning. She was looking at the line dividing sky and sea. It was so wide, and the numbness was wearing off and she felt the first cold and thought, 'so what?' for it didn't matter, even that. Nothing mattered.

Nothing mattered? Then why was something stirring her to swim, even though she didn't want to? Why was she moving her arms and legs as swimmers do, struggling for the great cliffs although it seemed that she was staying still, or drifting further out?

'Don't listen to your foolish heart,' whispered something—older than time and deep as another sea inside of her—in a voice that she couldn't help but hear. 'You want to live ...'

And it was true.

And then, in an instant, the living sea wasn't golden, wasn't calm and safe and smooth and friendly any more. It was a trap. It was full of monsters. It didn't want to hear or share. It wanted to consume. She'd got it wrong. She was nothing to it, nothing.

It was like waking from a dream, shaking off a powerful and strange delusion. Every part of her joined together to swim harder than she'd ever swum before. The Head was behind her now, and Bird Rock. If only she could get back. Climb on that rock and cling to it until someone found her.

'Respect the sea,' Ralph had once said. 'It won't respect you.' She hadn't known what he'd meant then.

'Give up, stop struggling!' the sea was telling her now.

'You belong down here, didn't you always know it?'

Oh, how she wanted to! Her body was ice, her limbs dead weights. She was so tired. She wanted to sleep. It was harder all the time to keep her head above the water. She couldn't feel her legs, tried to kick all the same and nothing happened.

'Give up ... Come down, down, down ... You're one of us, of us ...'

But she wasn't one of them! She didn't belong with the jellyfish and the mermaids and the rocks deep down below! She was a living girl, Mum's girl, and how was Mum, how were any of them, going to feel when they found her bloated, fish-picked body on the shore?

Nona struggled to swim again. The sea slapped her face and she couldn't, *couldn't* rise above it like the Atlantic seals. Couldn't think straight any more. She wished she'd had the sense to leave Mum, Owen, Harry, *somebody* a note, because they'd all think she'd done it because of them. They'd all blame themselves and never know that there'd been no-where else for her to go ...

She was out a long way now. The sea rose in great dark peaks that washed over her. She was bloating already, she was sure of it, the salt water taking off her skin. She thought of the white rabbit bones and wondered if the fish would eat her clean, and if her bones were white too. There was more to life than skin and bones. She knew that now. She knew the thing that fought inside of her didn't want her to die.

'It's too late for that. I've got you!' mocked the sea. It dropped another of its mountains on her head.

Too late? But what ...?

Beyond the wave, she saw a boat. She raised an arm as yet another peak fell on her. She went down and when she rose the boat was still there. She tried to cry, but it was too much effort to even open her mouth for it; too hard raising her arm. 'I'm here!!' she screamed inside herself. But another wave broke over her and 'It's too late,' she screamed again.

235

'This is the end of me!'

But she didn't go down. And when she came up again, there wasn't any boat and it had been madness, the mad instant of death, that had made her see one.

She went down again, a mass of hopeless limbs. She wasn't meant for happy endings. She was meant to die in the awful sea.

33

By the time the policeman allowed Father to see him from the house, Owen felt about five years old, Beca was nearly in tears on his behalf, and Mother's head hung as if she'd been the one who'd wasted all that official, public-funded time.

'You'd best go up and have a bath,' she told Owen, helplessly. 'You're in a filthy state, and you look half-starved. I'll make some lunch.'

When he came out of the bath, dressed in clean clothes and smelling soapy, Owen stood and sniffed the lunch, glad for this at least amongst all the fuss and trouble of the day. He was half way down the stairs when the telephone rang. Father came into the hall to answer it, and he heard his terse, *We'll be right down.'*

'What is it?' Mother called from the kitchen.

'They're picking a girl out of the sea,' Father said, struggling into his long, black coat. 'That was Ralph. He's got Harry Llewellyn with him saying it's Nona Davies!'

A screaming ambulance hurtled past the house and down the road in the direction of the beach. They all made for the car, lunch forgotten. Mother's cheeks were drawn in tight and thin, as if she knew already that Harry had got it right.

'Is she . . . ?' Owen tried to get out the word *alive*.

'I've told you all I know,' said Father.

The ambulance was parked and flashing in the car park, as close as it could get to the beach. The same old police car was back again. It was having a busy day! Emlyn Hughes stood outside the Mermaid Inn, with Ralph and Mr Pryce. Harry sat in the garden, in Griselda's arms.

Nona's mum stood alone on the wall. The way she held herself defied anyone to go to her, but Mother and Father went straight up, all the same. She never so much as looked at them. Just kept her eyes fixed upon the lifeboat which had shut off its engine now, and was edging into the shore.

Owen got on the wall as well, but further down. Beca held his hand and cried silently. They all watched the rubber-suited lifeboat men jump out of the boat and steady it. Watched them, black as undertakers, lift something off the floor. They carried this *something* onto dry land. It was a silver package. The ambulance men rushed down the beach for it. Once they'd got it on their stretcher, they rushed back up again. When they came close enough, Owen saw how the package shook. As they went past, he saw the face.

'Nona!'

Mrs Davies's hands went over her eyes. The policeman was quickly at her side and between Father and him, she was bundled into the ambulance too. Father got in as well, though Owen could see as they closed the doors that she still didn't know that he was there.

The ambulance screamed off, the police car after it. It was all over very quickly. Mother came down off the wall and said that they should go back home, but none of them moved. They all stared at the sea. Ralph shook his head at it, and Harry was grey. Beca looked like death herself, and Owen's appetite for lunch was well and truly gone. He'd remembered something Father had once said to him: 'Sea's like a hungry cat, waiting to pounce on you...'

After what should have been lunch, Mother went into school. She brought Poppy, Bryn and Sharon back with her and, just as they came, in Father came after them with his hat in his hands.

'She'll live,' he told them. 'Your mother's staying with her, of course. I said I'd collect her later. They've had her in a hot bath and she's warming up. She's going to be all right.'

'Oh, thank God for that!' cried Mother. 'Poppy, Bryn, Sharon ... she's going to be all right!'

'She'll have done it on purpose,' Sharon said, fixing her gaze on the kitchen wall, as if she didn't trust herself to look at them. 'She hates us, underneath all that goody-goody, helpful stuff. She's always wanted to get away.'

'Why, Sharon, what a thing to say!' exclaimed Mother, shocked. 'That's not like you!'

Sharon shrugged. Poppy began crying that she wanted King Offa back again, and Bryn's fragile grin crumpled into, 'I want my mum...!' And even then, Sharon kept her eyes upon that wall.

Mother let her be. She didn't offer cups of tea and cake, or say silly things. She went to Bryn and Poppy instead, and Beca went to them too, and they cuddled them until they'd finished crying, and then they wiped their tears away. Owen watched their kindness. He was proud of them.

'Nona will be well enough for you to see her soon,' Mother reassured them.

'You can count me out!' came from Sharon, by the wall ...

It was dark outside. Nona lay very still. There were bright lights in the corridor but in the ward there was only the one spotlight over her bed. The tea-trolleys with the bed drinks had all rattled away, and it was absolutely quiet at last.

She snuggled down beneath the turned-back, laundered sheet. Hers was the bed at the end, between the window and the door. She took in everything from the polished floor to the gleaming wash-hand basins and the plate glass view over the dark hospital garden. Beyond the garden was the old harbour road, and beyond that the sea. She was safe from it in here. She was warm. She was so weak that she couldn't move, and its saltiness was still in the corners of her mouth, but she was *alive*.

Mum, who had gone now, had prayed for her to be alive. 'Oh Jesus, please don't take her away,' she'd pleaded into the air above the bed, while Nona lay too weak to speak to her. Again and again she'd said it and then, as Nona nearly was asleep, she'd whispered, 'Why, why, why?'.

The doctors had asked Nona that as well, but she couldn't take their questions in. The big word RESCUE on the side of the lifeboat still had her in its sway, and the hands that had pulled her to safety, and the boat's wet bottom covered in black flexes, and herself wrapped in a silver blanket like a queen. She still hit the water with the front of the lifeboat as it bounced the waves. Her mind was still full of ambulances and flashing lights and *pain*.

'Nona, are you awake?' Mum had asked before she'd left, and all Nona could do was open her eyes in answer. 'Mr Lark's come for me,' Mum had said. 'I'll be back in the morning. The doctor says don't worry about talking if you're not ready to. Don't worry about a thing. You can tell us about it later.'

Nona managed a wry smile. She'd had her fill of *telling*, but Mum couldn't know that! Mum fumbled in her bag and drew something out which she dropped onto the quilt.

'Oh, and this arrived today . . .'

She went. Nona glimpsed Mr Lark holding open the door, and then they were gone and she folded her hand over what Mum had left her. The envelope was addressed to her. MISS NONA DAVIES, NYTH-Y-DRYW, CWMGWYNTOG COMMON, NEAR JERICO. She managed to open it. Mum had done so first, but she couldn't bring herself to mind. At least it wasn't Susie Lennox's awful handwriting. She drew the sheet of paper out. It was a letter, typed, with a fancy crest and special letter-heading . . .

This is to inform you, it said, *that your essay 'Henry V is alive today' has won the inter-schools eisteddfod and will be*

published at the end of the month in the Western Mail. Your
mature insight into Henry's ruthless and driven personality is
something that this panel of judges wishes particularly to con-
gratulate you for. We are writing to your school today. Very best
wishes.

Nona would have laughed, if she'd had the energy. But
she shut her eyes instead and suddenly, unexpectedly, sleep
took a hold of her as though she were a baby, and nothing
could excite her enough to keep it away.

Owen, in bed and wide awake, watched his door opening and would have given anything to have had the excuse
of sleep. For he'd been listening from his place on the stairs,
and he knew what was coming.

Father had been running about all evening, back and
forth to the hospital and then goodness knows where else.
He'd come in through the back door and, 'How did you get
on?' came anxiously from Mother.

'Not as bad as I expected,' Owen heard his father say.
'How's the boy?'

'You wouldn't believe how much he ate for tea,' Mother
said, and he could tell that she was crying, 'or how exhausted
he is. You must go up and talk to him. His light's only just
gone out, and I'm sure he's still awake.'

'All right,' said Father, and he sighed. 'I will.'

Owen scuttled upstairs, as fast as he could manage
without being heard. He supposed they had to go through
this. Even Nona's misadventure couldn't keep it away. Father
was going to have it out with him, every last bit of it.
There'd be all that stuff about 'you've no idea how you've
made your mother suffer,' and 'the example you've set your
sister,' and about his wicked selfishness and how it was all
Harry's fault, for leading him astray. There'd be no getting
out of it, would there? They'd probably take him off to Uncle
and Aunty's all the earlier, get him out of the way before he
hurt and embarrassed them any more.

241

'Am I disturbing you?' came from Father in the doorway. 'Are you asleep?'

He could have pretended that he was, but it was best to get it over with. 'No, I'm awake. Come in.'

Father didn't switch on the light, just crossed the room and sat down. He still had on his coat, but it was unbuttoned all the way down and he looked for all the world like anybody else's father and not, for once, the minister.

'I've been a fool,' he said, to Owen's astonishment. 'Your mother could see it, but I wouldn't listen to her. I should have recognized how very much you're my son. I never did what *my* father wanted me to do. He wanted me to play rugger for Wales, be a sportsman like him. But I had my calling and I wouldn't do it. I went my own way, just as you've got to do. You really don't want to go away to school, do you?'

'No,' said Owen. He couldn't believe his ears. 'Though I . . . I'd go to an *art* college, if you'd let me . . .'

'Harry thinks you'd do really well,' said Father.

It was Owen's night for surprises! *'Harry?'*

'I've just been down to see him.'

'You've done *what?'*

'Griselda was down there too,' said Father, smiling ruefully. 'She said I'm to stop telling you what to do, and listen to what *you've* got to say for a change.'

Owen could imagine her saying it. Despite everything, he almost smiled in the dark.

'So, I'm listening,' Father said.

He folded his hands, just like that, and waited. Owen couldn't believe it; Father waiting for him, Owen, to tell him what his hopes were, how he *felt*, to tell him anything he wanted.

'It . . . it's no good being frightened of the big world on my behalf,' he plunged in. 'There are ways of getting through, even if it is a fearful thing sometimes. It's like . . . oh, like Nona finding that boat. You've got to trust me,

Father, to find a way through too. But the trouble is, you never give me a chance. You crush my chances when they come along. Crush *me*.'

'I never meant to crush you, son,' said Father, staring at his hands, his smile all gone.

'Don't you know that I *hate* it when you call me 'son'?' Owen said, quite unable to stop now that he'd begun. 'It makes me feel like I'm *yours*. Like I'm not my own. Like I'm a member of a private club which has only got room in it for you and me, and doesn't care that Mother gets lonely and Beca never has the chance to show you what she can do. You never call me 'Owen'. Don't you know that?'

Father didn't answer. And suddenly Owen imagined him down in Harry's alien caravan, listening while Harry explained his son to him. And then he would have bitten his words back if he'd had the chance. For his father had done even that for him, at the end of what had already been a dreadful day. He should have bided his time, eked the words out bit by bit. But he had been asked for it, hadn't he?

'I'm sorry for running away,' he said. 'It was a terrible thing to do. And I'm glad the police found me. It was awful, thinking I didn't belong anywhere any more.'

'I'm sorry I crushed your boats,' Father said, holding out his hands. 'That was a terrible thing to do as well!'

Unexpectedly, Owen grinned. He couldn't help it. 'You didn't get them all!' He reached down beside the bed and triumphantly produced his favourite.

Father laughed out loud. It gave Owen such a shock that he nearly fell out of bed. 'Well, well, well!' said Father, and he took the boat and looked at it, that way and this. 'You'll have to put it with the others Harry showed me. They make a fine collection!'

A sense of goodwill washed right over Owen. He was glad, after all, that he'd said the things he had.

'You look exhausted,' Father said. 'Hardly surprising, what a day! We'll talk again tomorrow, with your mother

243

too. Can I show the boat to her?'

'Of course you can,' said Owen, snuggling down the bed, for Father was right, he *was* exhausted.

Father stood up. Owen hoped that any final words of wisdom he intended to impart would be over and done with quickly.

His father ruffled the top of his head. 'Goodnight ... Owen,' was all he said.

34

Harry brought Nona home in his rattling tin-can van, because she didn't want the ambulance with the whole village staring as she went by, and she had requested him instead. He was dressed up for the occasion, with a nice tie and an earring to match his garnet pin. Maybe he thought she needed cheering up, but he remained silent about it all the way until, 'There's something *about* the sea, I can understand what happened,' he said, as they came down the beach road. 'It's alive, like the eyes in faces. You know what I mean, *unfettered* ...'

Nona did indeed know, but she wouldn't talk about it and didn't have the courage to look its way. Until they reached the car park, she stared at her feet instead, or at Harry's garnet pin. When they turned outside the pub, she tried to miss the Mermaid sign as well, but the bill pasted over it couldn't help but catch her eye:

HOT FRESH SOUP.

'She's got what she wanted ...!' Harry pulled a face and tried to make Nona laugh. 'Ralph's letting her have a go, and *she* says when he tastes what she can do it'll be the end of sausages and chips.'

Nona obliged him with a rueful smile which lasted until Griselda's patch, bare now against all the growth around. Then the smile faded, for Nona couldn't imagine the common without Griselda's beleaguered tent, or looking from her bedroom window at night and not seeing that lonely light. In Harry's wing mirror she glimpsed bits of the platform scattered between the willows, and the stones of Griselda's fireplace sitting cold and bare.

They reached the cottages. Harry pulled up in front of the ruined boathouse wall, on Miss Parry's 'bit'. Nona looked nervously at Nyth-y-dryw, as if she expected changes here as well. But the only change was that the sun had made it round at last to the front windows and up the crumbling wall. It looked just the same as on that first, ridiculously hopeful day when Mum had drawn up in that furniture van, so sure that they'd be safe down here.

'Welcome home!' Mum, in jeans and best cardigan, came streaming down the path. 'Would you have believed it? It's the year's first sun, and it's come round especially for you! It's back inside again, right across the living-room floor!'

Before Nona could answer her, or Harry lift out her bag, or even Mum wrap welcoming arms around her, Miss Parry's front door clicked, and out she came. Mum's breath drew in. Harry stood absolutely still. Miss Parry came down her path and over the stream towards them. With a shock Nona realised something else *had* changed. *She* wasn't the same girl any more. 'If the sea can't destroy me, she certainly can't!' she thought. 'She's just Miss Parry, nothing more!'

Miss Parry came towards them. She didn't look her usual self at all. Her face was crumpled, her hair in a mess, her glaring eyes subdued. When she spoke her voice was funny; they could hardly hear what she said.

'I've got something for you,' she mumbled, and she wouldn't look any of them in the eye. 'Here. Take it.'

She held out a basket, inside of which something miaowed and scratched to escape. Her eyes roved from trees to common to stones beneath her feet. 'What my Billy did was wrong,' she muttered, as if it cost her dear. 'He's sorry, he is.'

Nona turned disdainfully away, but Mum stepped forward.

She didn't have any trouble looking Miss Parry in the eye. And she took the basket. 'Thank you,' she said. 'We'll be moving soon. It'll be nice having something to remember Cwmgwyntog Common by.'

Their hands met over the basket. 'Glad the little girl's safe and soundly home,' Miss Parry whispered. And she shuffled away.

'How can you stand touching her?' Nona asked, without lowering her voice.

'Well, it won't bring King Offa back,' Mum said, with a weary sigh. 'But it changes things inside, forgiving does. It makes a difference. Shall we go indoors?'

Harry reached into his van for Nona's suitcase. Mum thanked him and took it in. Nona lingered. There was something she hadn't asked him yet.

'Was it you who rang for the lifeboat?' she said.

He looked at her with his sea-green eyes. 'I made a mistake that first time you came to me for help, and I swore I'd never let you down again,' he said.

'You mean . . .?'

'We went round to Wren's Nest after you'd gone. Your mum told us you'd been out all night, and I thought of Bird Rock, straight away. We were on our way to it, just by the sea wall when we saw you in the water. I was still sick— what a day it was! We went back to the pub, and I rang for the lifeboat.'

'Thank you,' was all Nona could bring herself to say.

'Go along,' he said, bashful because he didn't like being thanked for things. 'Your mum's waiting. Don't forget to take that basket, will you?'

Inside, the living-room looked wonderful with sunlight on the floor and the carpet even scrubbed for the occasion.

'It'll be sad to go,' Mum said. 'But we always knew it would be a short stay.' She took the miaowing basket and opened it. A small, white kitten leapt out and made straight for Nona, who it scaled, draping itself across her neck so that

247

she couldn't help but laugh properly at last, and pull the thing round into her hands.

'Thank God you're alive!' Mum exclaimed, in a heavy, husky voice. 'Thank God for letting me have you back!'

'Oh, Mum . . .' Nona began to cry as she *knew* she would, but the words that came out weren't the ones that she'd expected; 'Thank God you're in your jeans and cardigan and don't look like Mrs Lark any more! Oh Mum, you were so *different*.'

It sounded stupid, trivial, inappropriate; it wasn't what she wanted to say. But Mum didn't laugh at her. She just took the kitten out of Nona's hands and held them tight.

'Mary Lark's a good woman,' she said, straight into Nona's eyes. 'But I don't need to be like her to be a better mum, or anything else I want to be. I realize that now. You've done more for me, these past few days, than you'll ever know . . .'

'I thought I'd lost you,' Nona cried.

'And I thought I'd lost *you!*' Mum shook Nona hard.

'I didn't realize what I was doing,' Nona said. 'I've never been so frightened in my life . . . !'

It was only when the gate uttered its old squeak and children's excited voices clattered up the path, that Nona pulled herself out of Mum's arms and wiped away her tears. The living-room door burst open and Bryn rushed in with a smile, at the sight of Nona, that looked as though it would last for ever. He was followed by Poppy who, far removed from the pale ghost she once had been, flung herself at Nona and held her as though she'd never let her go.

Sharon came in after the rest of them, and went straight upstairs. She didn't even look at the kitten, which Bryn was playing with now. Mum looked at Nona and Nona said, 'Should I go up?' and Mum said, 'I think you should.'

Sharon sat on her window-sill, glaring down the track. She'd thrown aside her bag and kicked off her shoes and when Nona came in, turned her back pointedly on the door.

'It's nice to be home again,' Nona said nervously.

Sharon didn't answer her.

'Mrs Thomas came to see me yesterday. Wasn't that kind of her? She brought a card with everybody's name on it.'

'Everybody's except mine!'

'I'm trying to say I'm sorry, Sharon...'

'Oh, yes? What for?'

Nona crossed the floor. She sat on the window-sill too, and tried to make Sharon look at her. But Sharon didn't move, didn't even turn her head, just stared off down the common. 'It's awful having you for a sister,' she said. 'I'm fed up with it. I really am. Even when you do a thing like this you're still the one Mum loves. I never get a chance. Mum always says, "Nona, will *you*...?" and she thinks you're the helpful one, not me.'

'But you're always moaning, Sharon!' Nona said. 'You know that's why Mum doesn't ask.'

'I moan because of *you!*' exploded Sharon. 'I'm fed up with being compared with *you*. I want Mum to say, "Oh *Sharon*, where would I be without you?" I'm fed up with being in your wretched shadow all the time. Fed up with being the *second best*, like when Mum was ill and I had to go to school, and *you* stayed home to look after her!'

Nona hadn't realized that Sharon felt that way. She stared out of the window at the view, which was slightly different from the one she knew. 'I'm sorry,' she said again. 'I just didn't think.'

'That's the trouble,' cried Sharon. 'You don't think when it comes to me! I *worried* that night you didn't come home. I was nearly *sick* when I heard they'd pulled you out of the sea. But as far as you're concerned, I'm just good for bossing about when there are jobs to do, and being better than, when Mum's around.'

'Oh Sharon!' Nona said.

'If anything had happened to you I'd have just *died*,' Sharon spat at her. 'And I don't know why, because I can't stand you!'

It was the hint of sun, at the end of a storm. For Nona smiled. She couldn't help herself. 'I can't stand you either,' she said. 'What a stupid pair we are!'

They sat in silence, looking down the common. Then Nona put her arm around Sharon's shoulder, and Sharon took her hand and gripped it tight.

'Let's stop squabbling,' Nona said.

Sharon looked for all the world like Offa when he'd fought one of his battles and come through unscathed enough to enjoy his tea.

'I'll be friends with you,' she offered in a triumph for her better nature, 'if you'll be friends with me.'

POSTSCRIPT

34, Withington Street,
London,
SW19

Sunday

Dear Owen,

Thank you for the birthday card. Did you make it, it's really nice. I can hardly believe it's a whole year ago now, that we came down to Cwmgwyntog Common. So much has changed. You're off to art college and I hope it's all you want it to be. And Beca won the national championship and she's your father's pride and joy. Well, it's about time he appreciated her. I didn't, and I'm sorry for that.

I think about Nyth-y-dryw all the time. I've had the letters from you, and Harry and Griselda's one (full of THE COMMON, but not much NEWS). Mum's heard from Ralph and your parents of course, and even Emlyn's been to see us and says he's coming again. So we haven't forgotten you all yet!

I wondered all summer long, who was staying in Nyth-y-dryw, and whether Miss Parry treated them all right. Thanks for the sand in the envelope and the tiny shells. Mum asked if I wanted to come down for my birthday. She said Ralph would put us up, but I still can't face it yet. It frightens me, that invisible strand that seems to start somewhere inside of me and leads along the track and over the wall and down the beach into the sea.

We've just been to a swimming-pool with a MACHINE

instead. Potted plants and shallow, warm lagoons and synthetic waves that come in too fast and make you realize how perfect is the sea's own timing.

Synthetic waves, and a real Cody—can you believe it, we've got him back!

Not all the time but for some weekends. Mum went and talked to Uncle Brady, who's got in with the mother of some girl I used to know. This girl's mum said Cody should spend time with us, instead of Uncle Brady always dumping him on her. So whenever we get him we do nice things, like go to the adventure playground and—Mum's got a job so we can afford it sometimes!—the wavy pool. I can face waves when there's concrete underneath my feet, instead of sand.

Today there were handicapped children in the pool. A boy in socks was carried into the water. He had putty-coloured legs. He just lay down in the shallow bit when the wave machine had been switched on, and let the waves wash over him. He didn't seem to realize the danger he was in. I thought, 'That was me.' An attendant waded in and pulled him out.

I do miss the most unexpected things. Like Mrs Thomas, and not listening to those radio plays any more. I've got a sort of boyfriend now, but I miss doing things with you. I even, despite everything and deep down inside, miss the sea ...

I've got a paper round, and I'm saving money fast. Sharon keeps trying to borrow it for clothes, but I'm after a better bike. I'll bring it down with me when I come back.

I will come back again, in the end. You know that, don't you?

Write again, won't you?

Nona

Also from Lion Publishing

MIDNIGHT BLUE

Pauline Fisk

Bonnie saw ropes hanging loose, poles falling away, tree-tops sinking beneath her. As they rose, the sun rose with them. Its warmth turned the dark skin of the fiery balloon midnight blue. They flew straight up. Above them, the sweet, clear music of the lonely pipe called to them. Then the smooth sky puckered into cloth-of-blue and drew aside. They passed straight through . . .

Winner of the Smarties Book Prize 1990

ISBN 0 7459 1925 1

THE MAGIC IN THE POOL OF MAKING

Beth Webb

'I risked *everything* to get you that water last night. You don't realize how little we've got. There's not a drop to be spared!' Johin shouted. 'You're a Sand boy, aren't you? Your people want to steal our water. And now I've saved your life!'

The River Planet is in danger. Its life source, the Lightwater River, is dying, poisoned through centuries of pollution and misuse. Manny, a starving and mysterious Sand boy, is the only person who knows how to put things right. Now, through a simple act of kindness, Johin is entwined in his dangerous quest.

As they cross the drought-stricken land, Johin realizes that the River offers life in more than one way. But clearing its source won't be enough. She and Manny also have to defeat the evil Brilliance . . .

ISBN 0 7459 2234 1

A WITCH IN TIME

William Raeper

Ralph's uncle was different somehow from other people's uncles. For a start, there were those striking eyes—grey and green and deep as the deepest lake—that seemed to see right into you. As Ralph explained to Maddy, with Uncle Alistair in charge anything might happen. And right next door, just over the wall, was a mysterious new neighbour, Mrs Morgan, whose sinister figure cast no shadow—no shadow at all.

Dark magic is in the air in this spine-chilling story. As the mystery unfolds, events move rapidly towards the heart-stopping climax. Maddy, Ralph and his uncle stand alone and apparently defenceless against Mrs Morgan's terrible powers—yet always watching, guarding, is the grandfather clock, with its measured tick and timeless promise.

ISBN 0 7459 2073 X

All Lion paperbacks are available from
your local bookshop, or can be ordered
direct from Lion Publishing. For a free
catalogue, showing the complete list of
titles available, please contact:

Customer Services Department
Lion Publishing plc
Peter's Way
Sandy Lane West
Oxford OX4 5HG

Tel: (01865) 747550
Fax: (01865) 715152